"I don't intend to let you draw your gun this time," Johnny said.

"It's too late," Hawke said.

"What do you mean?"

"I've already drawn my gun," Hawke said. "I'm holding it under the table, and it's pointed at your belly."

"You think I believe that? I know—"

Johnny's sentence was interrupted by the sound of a double click from under the table.

"You were saying?" Hawke said.

Johnny stood there for a moment, taking hard, angry breaths. He pointed his finger at Hawke.

"One of these days, I'm going to catch you without that gun," he said. Reluctantly, he started out of the café, turning at the door. "Do you hear me? We ain't finished!" he shouted.

Hannah, sitting by Hawke's side, spoke up quietly. "Would you have really shot Johnny?" she asked.

Hawke put his hands above the table. He was holding a fork in one hand and he flipped the tines with his thumb, duplicating the click he had made earlier.

"It would have been hard to shoot him with this," he said.

Books by Robert Vaughan

HAWKE

THE KING HILL WAR
THE LAW OF A FAST GUN
VENDETTA TRAIL
SHOWDOWN AT DEAD END CANYON
RIDE WITH THE DEVIL

HAWKE
THE KING HILL WAR

ROBERT VAUGHAN

HARPER

An Imprint of HarperCollinsPublishers

This book is a work of fiction. Names, characters, places, and incidents are products of the author's imagination or are used fictitiously and are not to be construed as real Any resemblance to actual events, locales, organizations, or persons, living or dead, is entirely coincidental.

HARPER

An Imprint of HarperCollins*Publishers*
10 East 53rd Street
New York, New York 10022–5299

Copyright © 2007 by Robert Vaughan
ISBN: 978-0-06-088849-7
ISBN-10: 0-06-088849-0

First Harper paperback printing: June 2007

HarperCollins® and Harper® are registered trademarks of HarperCollins Publishers.

Printed in the United States of America

Visit Harper paperbacks on the World Wide Web at
www.harpercollins.com

10 9 8 7 6 5 4 3 2 1

This book is for
Colonel Ernie Westpheling,
friend and fellow 7th Cavalryman.
Gary Owen, Sir.

HAWKE
THE KING
HILL WAR

Chapter 1

MASON HAWKE DID NOT THINK OF HIMSELF AS A piano player, but preferred to use the term pianist. That was because he was classically trained on the instrument, and at one time had a distinct honor bestowed upon him by the Queen of England. This honor was reported in the *London Daily Times*:

> From time to time, Citizens of countries which do not recognise the Queen as head of state may have honours conferred upon them. In every case these awards are "honorary" in nature, and confer no actual peerage within British society. However, those who, by service, deed, or accomplishment are granted such honours, are entitled to place initials behind their name, if not call themselves "Sir."
>
> In its benevolence, the United Kingdom does not

prevent foreigners from holding such titles. The government of the United States, however, being much more provincial, and irrationally frightened of what it does not understand, has laws restricting its citizens from accepting such honours.

The fact that they cannot accept the award does not preclude Her Royal Highness from recognizing the achievement of deserving individuals, and Mason Hawke, an American pianist, is just such a person. Recently knighted by Queen Victoria, Mr. Hawke is considered by many to be one of the top two or three pianists in the world.

Unfortunately, Mr. Hawke's European concert tour was interrupted when he returned to the United States to accept a commission in a regiment of the Confederate army. His departure will deprive many Europeans of the opportunity to hear this wonderful musician. However, Mr. Hawke is nothing if not a man of honour, and all men of good conscience will understand and respect his obligation to that honour.

Many men survived the war only to return home and struggle with grievous personal wounds. Though the wounds Hawke suffered to the psyche and the soul were not immediately visible, they were no less debilitating because they rendered him incapable of ever returning to the concert stage.

As a result of those wounds, Hawke was now a restless wanderer through the West, looking just beyond the horizon to the next town, and the next saloon where he could earn a few dollars playing piano.

The picture most often conjured in people's minds when they think of a saloon piano player is someone emaciated, bald, bespectacled, and with a half-chewed cigar stuck in his mouth. Hawke was the total antithesis. He was nearly six feet tall, clean-shaven, with a square jaw and penetrating blue eyes.

On this particular early spring day, Hawke was playing piano at the Saratoga Saloon in Dodge City, Kansas. As always, while he was working he dressed well, and today he wore a white ruffled shirt that was tucked down into fawn-colored trousers. A dark green jacket and gold cravat completed his ensemble.

As he finished the last few bars of "Buffalo Gals," several of the cowboys and all of the girls in the Saratoga Saloon in Dodge City gave a loud cheer.

"Whooeee! I tell you true, there ain't nobody in the world who can play a piano like Hawke," one of the cowboys said.

One of the girls approached the piano and smiled sweetly at him. "Mr. Hawke, would you play one of them songs?"

"What song would that be, Connie?" Hawke asked, though he knew what she wanted.

"You know, one of them real pretty songs you sometimes play. One of them highfalutin' songs," Connie said.

Like most of the other girls in the saloon, Connie was a soiled dove, a twenty-two-year-old who, suddenly finding herself on her own, had turned to the oldest profession to make a living.

Hawke smiled. "You mean something like this?" He began playing Fantasie in C Minor by Mozart. The golden tones of the music silenced everyone as they listened with rapt attention. It was for that very reason, however, that Hawke played classical music sparingly, for it did have the effect of bringing to a halt all business in the saloon, which was counterproductive to his continued employment. However most of the various owners of the many saloons in which he had played over the last sixteen years were tolerant, because they knew that his musical skills did bring in customers.

Connie Flagg was from the Ozarks of Missouri, and before coming here had never heard any music other than the Jew's harp, banjo, guitar, and jug-playing she had grown up with. She had never even seen a piano before, but became an instant fan of classical music the first time she heard Hawke play.

Hawke was three-quarters through the piece when the kitchen door opened and the cook, Elsie Maynard, stumbled into the room. Blood ran from her misshapen nose, and her left eye was black and swollen shut. There were bruises on her face and neck. Hawke saw her before anyone else and stopped playing, the last notes of the piece still resonating as he got up from the bench and started toward her.

"Elsie!" he said.

Connie, also seeing the cook, called out in shock, "Elsie, my God! What happened to you?"

"He didn't mean it," Elsie said. "I know he didn't mean it."

"Who didn't mean it?"

Connie grabbed a towel from one of the bar hooks, then hurried to Elsie's side. She began wiping the blood from her face as Elsie winced in pain.

"It was Angus, wasn't it?" Connie asked.

"Who is Angus?" Hawke asked.

"Angus is my husband," Elsie replied, her words accompanied by a whistling sound from her broken nose.

"He ain't your husband," Connie said. "Not for real, that is. You ain't never had no words spoke for you. You ain't even jumped over a broom together."

"He's all I got for a husband," Elsie said. "Look at me.

I ain't pretty like you 'n' the other girls. I got to take what I can get."

"Not nobody like him you ain't got to," Connie said.

Once the others in the saloon saw what was going on, they retuned to the bar or to their own tables and conversations.

"Ain't right for a man to beat a woman like that," one of them grumbled.

"Ain't right for a man to hit a woman a-'tall," another said.

"Yeah, well, if you ask me, Angus Oates ain't much of a man no how," still another said.

The disapproving observations faded into the background as Connie and Hawke continued to tend to Elsie.

"Honey, you need to get away from that no-'count," Connie said as she nursed the cook's wounds.

"Where would I go?" Elsie asked.

"You could go back to the Ozarks. That's where you come from, ain't it?" Connie asked. "You're a hill-country girl, just like me, only you're from Arkansas and I'm from Missouri."

"How'm I goin' to get there? I ain't even got enough money for a railroad ticket."

"Ain't you saved nothin'?" Connie asked. "I know you don't never spend none of your pay. You work in here from dawn to dark. What happens to your money?"

"Angus takes it all," Elsie said.

"Then that's all the more reason you should leave him. Cain't you see that he's just usin' you as his personal milk cow?"

"I would leave him if I could," Elsie said.

"Would you really leave him?" Hawke asked. "I mean, you aren't just saying that, are you? If you had the means to leave him, would you do it?"

Elsie nodded. "Yes, sir, in a heartbeat I would," she said.

Hawke reached for the inside pocket of his jacket to pull out a calf'skin wallet.

"Do you know how much it is for train fare back to Arkansas?" he asked.

"Yes, sir, I know. I done checked it a lot of times. It'd be eight dollars," Elsie said. "But from Little Rock I'd need to take another train on up to Boone County, and that'd be another four dollars."

"Here are thirty dollars," Hawke said. "That should be enough to get you home and buy your meals while you are traveling."

"Oh, Mr. Hawke, I can't accept this," Elsie said, but even as she demurred, she took the money.

"Come on," Connie said. "I'll help you pack, then get your luggage down to the depot."

"All right, but I got to tell you that Angus is still at the house," Elsie said.

"You want me to go with you?" Hawke asked.

Elsie shook her head. "No need to. By now he's more'n likely passed out drunk on the floor. He won't even know I'm there."

"I'm goin' with you anyway," Connie said.

"Connie," Hawke said. "Look through the window before you go in. If he's awake, come get me."

"All right," Connie replied.

Hawke watched as the two women left the saloon.

"That was a good thing you done, Hawke," Ben, the bartender said.

Ben was standing toward the end of the bar, polishing a glass. He had spent an inordinate amount of time on that simple task, allowing him to listen in on the conversation.

"Anyone would have done it," Hawke said.

"Maybe so, but it wasn't anyone, it was you," Ben replied.

Hawke returned to the piano and began playing again. He had been playing for about an hour when Connie returned.

"Did you have any trouble with Oates?" he asked.

"Ha!" Connie said. "It was just like Elsie said. That big dumb lummox was passed out drunk on the floor. He never even knowe'd we'uns was there."

"So she got off all right?"

"Yeah," Connie answered. "You should'a seen her, Mr. Hawke. She had a smile on her face as big as all outdoors when she clumb up on that train. This time tomorrow night she'll be back in the Ozarks, and that no-'count Angus Oates cain't never hurt her no more."

"Good," Hawke said as he went back to playing the piano.

"Connie, come over here, let us buy you a drink for what you done," one of the cowboys said.

"Only if you all buy a round for yourselves," Connie said, smiling at the cowboy as she got back to work.

It was about four hours later when Hawke looked up at the clock. The hands of the big "Regulator" indicated that it was ten-thirty, only half an hour before the saloon would close. It was one of the stranger aspects of this business, he thought, that the nearer it came to closing time, the greater the crowd. Right now, for example, there were more people in the saloon than there had been for the entire day, but even those who had not been present when Elsie came in badly beaten were aware of what had taken place, because conversations about the event continued throughout the evening.

On the top of his piano Hawke kept a bowl for tips. Tonight, he noticed, the patrons were much more generous than on any previous night. For a moment or two he wondered why. Then he realized that this was the customers' way of thanking him for what he had done for Elsie. That realization was borne out when one of the customers, who dropped a dollar into the bowl, said, "What you done for Elsie was a good thing."

"Thanks," Hawke said.

Not more than one block away from the Saratoga, Angus Oates opened his eyes. For just a moment he wondered where he was, then he became conscious that he was lying on the floor of the one-room shack he shared with Elsie. There was a sour smell all about him, and he realized that he was lying in a pool of his own vomit.

"Elsie?" he called in a slurring voice. "Elsie, you whore, where are you? Come here, help me get up."

When Elsie didn't show up, he rolled over. "Elsie?" he called again.

Angus pulled himself up from the floor, then reached for a bottle that was on the table.

The bottle was empty.

He went over to the chest of drawers where he knew that Elsie kept money rolled up in a pair of stockings, or she had the last time he had checked. But there were no stockings in the drawer when he opened it. There was nothing at all in the drawer, nor was there anything in any of the other drawers.

"What the hell?" he said to himself. "Where at's all her clothes?"

Angus stepped out onto the porch and began urinating. There was an outhouse behind the little shack, but since the shack itself was in the alley, and since it was dark, he didn't bother to use it. He had just finished when he saw two men appear out of the darkness. The Long Branch stayed open one hour longer than the Saratoga, and he knew that people who were leaving one saloon to go to another often took a shortcut through the alley.

"Hey!" Angus called to them.

"You speaking to us, mister?" one of the two men replied.

"Was you two boys down to the Saratoga tonight?"

"As a matter of fact, we were."

"Did you see my wife down there?"

"Your wife?"

"Elsie. She's the cook. Did you see her down there?"

"Ah, so you're the one, are you?"

"I'm the one what?"

"You're the one who beat her up."

"She's my wife, I reckon I can do whatever I want with her," Angus said. "So, she is down there, is she?"

"Not anymore she isn't."

"What do you mean, not no more?"

"She's gone. She left town. Where was it they said she was going, Lou?"

"Arkansas, I think," the other said. "She took the train this evening. The piano player bought her ticket. Isn't that right, Paul? Wasn't it the piano player?"

"Yes," Paul answered. "And I say good for him. Mister, anyone who treats a woman like you did ought to be horse whipped."

"I told you," Angus growled. "It ain't none of your business what I do to my own wife."

"Yes, well, you won't be doing it any longer, will you?" Paul said. "Come on, Lou, let's walk down by the pig lot. The company is better there."

"It'll sure as hell smell better there," Lou replied, and, laughing, both men walked away.

Angus stood on the front porch for a moment longer,

watching as the two men faded into the darkness. He was trying to make his whiskey-befuddled brain understand what they had said.

"The piano player," he grumbled aloud. "That's what they said. The piano player give her money to leave. Well, Mr. Piano Player, me 'n' you's about to have us some words."

The first indication Hawke had of Angus's sudden intrusion into the saloon was when a bullet from Angus's gun smashed into the bowl holding his tip money. Glass flew and paper money and coins spilled from the shattered bowl, falling with a clatter to the floor.

Even before the second bullet plowed into the sound board of the piano, Hawke was off the bench and running toward the bar.

"You son of a bitch!" Angus shouted. "What right do you have interferin' between me 'n' my wife?"

Angus fired two more shots at Hawke as he dashed across the saloon toward the bar. One bullet hit the stove pipe, sending out a puff of soot to mix with the growing cloud of gun smoke. Another bullet crashed into the face of the big Regulator clock.

Hawke was not the only one running. With shouts and screams of alarm, everyone else in the saloon, men and women alike, were trying to get out of the way of the mad gunman's bullets.

Angus's fifth shot was fired just as Hawke leaped toward the bar. This shot hit a full whiskey glass that one of the patrons had abandoned in his own wild dash. The sixth shot, fired as Hawke rolled across the bar and onto the floor behind, hit the mirror, leaving several shards, which had the effect of multiplying all that was going on.

Hawke lay on the floor for a moment, breathing a sigh of relief that the sixth shot had been fired.

"I've got you now, you son of a bitch," a low, raspy voice said.

Rising up, Hawke saw Angus Oates standing at the end of the bar. Angus's left arm was hanging down by his side, his left hand curled around a smoking pistol. But it was his right hand that worried Hawke, for Oates had pulled a second pistol from the waistband of his pants.

"Oh, my God, he has a second gun!" the bartender said. It wasn't until then that Hawke realized Ben was on the floor behind him.

"If you know any prayers, you better say 'em," Angus said, pulling back the hammer on the Colt .44.

Looking to his left, Hawke saw the shotgun that Ben always kept behind the bar. Grabbing it, he rolled back to his right just as the hammer fell on Angus's .44. Angus's bullet tore into the floor, sending a little shower of splinters into Hawke's face.

Bringing the shotgun to bear, Hawke pulled both triggers. The roar of the two shells discharging at the same time was much louder than the pistol shots had been. The twin loads of ten-gauge double-aught buckshot opened up the gunman's chest, driving him back through the window to crash out onto the porch in front of the saloon.

Hawke lay the gun down, stood up, and walked over to the window to look out at the body. One of Angus's feet was on the windowsill, the other folded up beneath him. His chest looked as if someone had taken an axe to it. What was left of his heart and lungs were visible, as well as the white of his shattered rib cage.

"I'll bet that feller don't never try that no more," Ben said from behind Hawke.

By now the others in the saloon, realizing that the danger had passed, were also coming over to have a look.

Several of them patted Hawke on the back, and nearly all congratulated him.

"What the hell happened here?" a gruff voice asked.

Looking toward the door, Hawke saw the sheriff coming in.

"It sounded like a war was going on."

"Ask Oates," one of the men said. "He's the one come in a-blazin' away."

The sheriff walked over to the shattered window to look out at the body. Angus's arms were thrown out to either side and both hands were clutching pistols. His mouth and one eye were open.

"Doesn't look to me like Oates is going to do much talking," the sheriff said.

"He come in here shootin' all over the place," Ben said.

"And before he done that, he beat up Elsie," another said, and soon everyone was speaking at once, so that the effect was no more than a babble of voices.

"Hold on, hold on," the sheriff said, holding up his hands to call for quiet. "Don't all of you talk at once. What I want to know is, who was it shot the fella that's layin' out on the porch? It was obviously a shotgun, and I'm guessing it's the one you keep under the bar. Did you do it, Ben?"

"I shot him," Hawke said.

"You shot him? How did you get the shotgun?"

"It wasn't easy," Hawke said.

One of the patrons laughed. "Hawke, here, is the one that Oates come gunnin' for. You should'a seen ol' Hawke leap over the bar. Beat anything I ever seen."

"Oates needed killin', Sheriff," Ben said.

"That's the truth," another added.

"All of you, keep quiet," the sheriff said. "I want to hear the story from Mr. Hawke."

"Do you mind if I listen in, Sheriff?" a small, bald-headed man asked. He was holding a pencil and pad. "I want to do the story for the newspaper."

"I don't mind," the sheriff said. "So long as you don't get in the way of my investigation."

Ben put a drink in Hawke's hand.

"Thanks," Hawke said.

"You don't have to thank me," Ben said. "Ever'one in the saloon's wantin' to buy you one."

"All right, Mr. Hawke, suppose you tell me what happened here," the sheriff said.

Hawke took a sip of his drink. "The story has been told," he said. "Oates came gunning for me, I was unarmed, so I borrowed Ben's shotgun. That's all there is to it."

Chapter 2

IAN MACGREGOR ROLLED A CIGARETTE AS HE leaned against a cottonwood tree and looked out over the gently waving grassy plain that rolled out before him. Low swells of prairielike ground sloped down toward the south. Dark evergreen trees, few and far between, stood out prominently, and here and there on the prairie he saw clusters of red and gray rocks. Farther to the north, up the gradual slope, rose the Soldier Mountains, a ten-thousand-foot-high snowcapped range that loomed dark purple, its ten-mile-long wall stretching to the east and west, towering over the richly grassed Camas Valley.

To the west, the prairie rose in some ancient upheaval of the earth, ending in grooved walls, castellated cliffs, and gray escarpments. And in the middle of this vast panorama was a sea of wool, a flock of twenty-five hundred sheep, grazing on what was, officially, open land.

Before Ian could light his own cigarette, a match flared and Emerson Booker held the flame first under Ian's cigarette, then his own. He took a puff, then spit out a loose bit of tobacco before he spoke.

Ian Macgregor was a sheep rancher, and he and the other sheep ranchers—Emerson Booker, Clem Douglass, Mark Patterson, Chris Dumey, Allen Cummings, Ed Wright, George Butrum, and Mitch Arnold—had combined their flocks for safety. They brought them onto the open range in a direct challenge to the cattlemen who had given them specific orders not to do so.

"You think anyone is going to show up to challenge us?"

"It's more than likely someone will," Ian answered. "Joshua Creed will see to that."

"This is open range, but Creed has the cattlemen thinking it's their own private grazing land," Emerson said.

"Is everyone ready in case Creed and his crowd show up?" Ian asked the group.

"We're all ready for him, Ian. It was a good idea you had for us to band together for this."

"There's no one of us who can hold off the cattlemen, but all of us together . . ." Ian let the sentence hang for a second. Then he continued. "Well, truth to tell, even if we are all together we can't beat them in an all out war. But maybe if they see us all sticking together it will make them stop and think a bit before they do anything."

At 100,000 acres, Joshua Creed's Crown Ranch was not only the largest cattle spread in Alturas County, but one of the largest in Idaho. Lonnie, his son, had the same dark hair and eyes, but beyond that, was more like his mother; a narrow nose, high cheekbones, and a full mouth. There were times when Joshua thought his son might be too handsome, almost to the point of looking effeminate. But that was only on first glance. There was something else about Lonnie, a manner and perpetual sneer, that more than offset his fair features.

Lonnie was sitting on the top rail of the corral, watching the cowboys saddle their horses. His hat was pushed back on his head and he was chewing on a small string of rawhide that dangled from his mouth. Even in this, there was a degree of arrogance to his demeanor that was almost palpable.

"Lonnie, we're purt' near ready to go," said Asa Crawford, a cowboy who worked on the ranch.

"Is my horse saddled?" Lonnie asked.

"We saddled him up first off," Asa said.

"Good. Let's get this done."

Lonnie put the little string of rawhide in his pocket and jumped down from the fence.

"You sure your pa is all right with this?" Asa asked as he walked with Lonnie toward the saddled horses.

Lonnie looked at Asa, and even in the darkness his eyes flashed with anger at being challenged.

"When are you goin' to learn, Asa, that as far as you are concerned—as far as any of the cowboys who work on this ranch are concerned—whatever I say is the same as my father sayin' it."

"Don't go gettin' sore about it, Lonnie," Asa said. "I didn't mean nothin' by it. It's just that . . . well, I've been cowboyin' for a long time, and I've been in more than a few range disputes. But I ain't never killed another man's livestock before. I mean, they're just dumb critters that don't really have no stake in whatever might have us riled."

"They are sheep, Asa. Do you understand that? Sheep are about the lowest type of critter there is, and that bunch of sheep herders is runnin' them on our land."

"Well, it ain't actual your land, Lonnie. I mean, from what I know, it's open range for all the cattle."

"That's just it, Asa. *Cattle*," Lonnie said, emphasizing the word. "Not sheep. Any cattle rancher is free to use that land. But ever'body knows that the sheep crop the grass so low there's nothin' left. And what's more, the grass don't grow back after sheep have grazed. You want all of Camas Prairie to turn into desert?"

"No," Asa said. "I don't want nothin' like that."

"Well, the only way we're goin' to keep that from happenin' is to run the sheep off the grazin' land. And if you can't understand that, why then, maybe you should get yourself a job in town cleaning out stables at the livery, or sweeping the floor in the general store."

Asa shook his head. "I ain't never done nothin' but cowboy, Lonnie. You know that. Hell, I was cowboyin' for your pa when you was just a kid."

"Then you, of all the people who ride for the Crown, should know what we are about tonight."

"I reckon I do," Lonnie said.

Most of the other cowboys were already mounted when Lonnie and Asa reached the horses. The two of them mounted as well, then Lonnie looked out over his riders.

"All right, boys, let's ride."

In the big house, Joshua Creed stood at the window watching as the riders left at a brisk trot. He was holding a glass of bourbon, and he lifted it to his lips as they passed under the gate that spelled out CROWN RANCH. Along with the name of the ranch, a large, iron crown was mounted above the gate.

Ian was talking to a couple of the other sheep ranchers when his Basque foreman, Tomas Gainza, came over to join them.

"There are riders coming our way, Señor Ian," Tomas said.

Ian sighed. "Yeah," he replied. "I expected it. I was hoping they wouldn't, but I was expecting it. Which way are they coming from?"

"They are coming from the west, from Señor Creed's ranch, just the way you said."

"All right, boys," Clem Douglass shouted to the others. "Get your guns ready."

By now nearly everyone could see and hear the approaching riders.

"Damn, look at that!" Douglass said. "There are at least twenty of them."

"Twenty," Ian repeated and sighed. "I hadn't really expected this. I didn't think there would be more than five or six."

"Ian, I don't think we can fight twenty men," Mark Patterson said.

"Maybe we won't have to fight," Ian said. "Maybe if they know we're here, watching them, they'll leave. I'm going to talk to them."

"Ian, no!" Douglass warned. "They aren't ridin' in here like they're wantin' to talk."

"Keep me covered," Ian said as he mounted his horse.

"Señor Booker, I don't like the looks of this," Tomas said. "I don't think Señor Ian should go out there."

"His mind is made up," Emerson Booker replied. "I don't think anything we can say will stop him."

"Lonnie, one of 'em's ridin' out here," Asa called out, pointing to the lone rider who was approaching, holding up his hand to stop them. "It's Ian Macgregor. Looks like he's wantin' to talk."

"What are you doing out here, Macgregor?" Creed

shouted when they were close enough to hear each other.

"Tending the flock," Ian answered, reining his horse.

"You have no right to be here. Get these stinking sheep off Crown Ranch land."

"Lonnie, you and I both know this is open range," Ian replied.

"This is open range for cattle," Lonnie said. "Cattle, not sheep. This is your last chance. Get 'em off this range."

"There's grass enough here for all of us," Ian replied.

"Start killing the sheep boys!" Lonnie shouted.

At his order, the riders with Lonnie began shooting into the sheep.

"No!" Ian yelled, and spurred his horse toward them.

"I warned you!" Lonnie said as Ian approached, and a moment later, shot his horse. The animal went down, trapping Ian under it.

Whooping and yelling, the cowboys rode at a gallop into the massed sheep while shooting into the woolly mass. Scores of sheep fell, while the rest, bleating in pain, terror, and confusion, began to run.

Among the sheep herders, Clem Douglass said, "Emerson! Should we shoot?"

"No!" Emerson replied, shaking his head. "We can't take a chance on shooting, not with Ian out there."

So the sheep men stood by, watching helplessly as the cowboys continued their senseless slaughter. The shooting didn't stop until the panicked flock was more than a mile away and still running across the prairie.

"You bring them stinkin' sheep back onto this pasture again," Lonnie shouted, "and it won't be just sheep that we shoot!" Then waving his hat and shouting to the others, he and his cowboys galloped away.

As the drumming of galloping horses receded in the distance, the dozen sheep herders stood in stunned silence over what they had just witnessed, listening to the bleats of the dying sheep. The night air was redolent with the smell of gun smoke, dust, blood, and sheep excrement.

"How come Señor Ian hasn't come back?" Tomas asked, his voice showing his concern.

"He must be hurt," Emerson said. "Ian!" he called. "Ian, are you out there?"

"I'm here, boys," Ian called back, his voice strained.

"Are you all right?"

"My horse fell on me," Ian answered. "I think both of my legs are broken."

"Come on, boys," Emerson said. "We've got to get Ian back home."

Sixteen-year-old Hannah Macgregor saw a wedge of light shining under her bedroom door. Thinking it strange to see a light this late at night, she got out of bed and padded, barefoot, into the parlor. Her mother was sitting in a rocking chair by a low-burning lantern, the same lantern that had projected the light under her door.

"Mama?"

Cynthia looked up when her daughter called. "Oh, darling, I'm sorry," she said. "Did I wake you?"

"No, I—" Hannah started, then changed in mid-sentence. "Mama, what are you doing up so late? Where's Daddy? Is something wrong?"

"I'm . . . I'm very worried about your father," Cynthia said.

"What is it? What's wrong with him?" Hannah started toward her parents' bedroom.

"He isn't in there," Cynthia called out.

"He isn't? Where is he?"

"He and some of the other sheep ranchers are keeping watch over the flock out on the open range tonight."

"The open range? Isn't that the land the cattle ranchers say is theirs?"

Cynthia nodded. "They say it's theirs, but it isn't. It's open range, and that means it belongs to anyone who wants to use it."

"You think there's going to be trouble, don't you, Mama?"

Cynthia nodded, without replying.

"Why?" Hannah asked, approaching her mother. "I mean, why do the cattlemen hate us so?"

"Oh, honey, they don't hate us."

"I know that not all of them do," Hannah said. "Jesse Carlisle doesn't hate us. In fact, he's very nice."

"Yes, he is a nice young man, but . . ."

"But what?"

"Hannah, don't get too taken with him. I mean, you're still young, there will be plenty of other boys for you. There is no need for you to make a mistake so early in your life."

"You are just saying that because his father is a cattle rancher and Papa is a sheep man," Hannah said.

Cynthia sighed. "I suppose I am."

"That's not fair, Mama. I like Jesse, a lot. And I know that he likes me."

"I know it isn't fair, honey, but it's life. And sometimes a person just has to make an accommodation with life."

"What would you know about it, Mama," Hannah asked. "You've got Papa. If I can't have Jesse, I don't have anyone."

Cynthia chuckled, then put her arms around Hannah and pulled her daughter to her. "You are a very pretty girl, Hannah," she said. "Trust me. You will have someone when the time is right."

"It's just that—" Hannah started to say, but was interrupted by the clattering of hoofbeats in front of the house.

"Mrs. Macgregor! Mrs. Macgregor, it's Emerson Booker! Are you awake, ma'am?"

Carrying the lantern, Cynthia hurried to the front door and opened it. She saw several mounted men out front, nearly all of whom she recognized. Then her heart leaped to her throat.

She didn't see Ian.

"Ian!" she gasped. "Where is Ian?"

"I'm here, Cynthia," her husband said, his voice coming from the darkness.

"Where?"

"He's behind my horse," Emerson said.

"Behind your horse?"

"We had to make a travois to bring him back. He is injured, Mrs. Macgregor."

"Injured? Oh, my God! Ian!" Cynthia called, hurrying outside.

"Don't get all worried about it, Cynthia," Ian said when his wife stood over him, looking down. "I just broke a couple of legs, is all."

"A *couple* of legs? My God, Ian, all you have is a couple of legs."

Cynthia's comment struck Ian as funny, and he began laughing. The other men laughed with him, and seeing that Ian was in good spirits, Cynthia laughed as well.

"Mr. Booker, would you and a couple of men bring him inside, please?" she asked.

"Of course," Booker said. "And by tomorrow morning I'll have the doctor out here to see to his injuries."

"Thank you," Cynthia said.

Three days after Ian's injury, Emerson Booker showed up at the house carrying a chair that had been fitted with wheels.

"What in tarnation is that?" Ian asked.

"It's called a wheelchair," Emerson said. "I ordered it from Denver."

"A wheelchair?"

"Yes. What you do is sit in it and use your hands to roll the wheels. Watch, I'll demonstrate."

Emerson sat in the chair and rolled himself forward and backward. Then, stopping one wheel while rolling the other, he showed Ian how to change directions.

"What do you think?" he asked, getting up from the chair with a broad smile on his face.

"That's great," Ian said dryly. "How do I get it on a horse?"

"Ian," Cynthia scolded. "That's no way to act after Mr. Booker made a special trip into town just to get that for you."

"I know, I know," Ian said. "And I'm grateful to you, Emerson. It will be a blessing to be able to get around the house. But I don't mind tellin' you, I'm worried about this business with the cattlemen."

"It's been pretty quiet since the night you were hurt," Emerson said. "Of course, the first thing we did after we rounded up all our sheep was bring them back onto our own land. And, since we aren't running the sheep on the open range, the cattlemen have been leaving us alone."

"How many sheep did we lose?"

"About a hundred," Emerson said. "And we divided up the losses, just as you suggested. That way, none of us were too badly hurt."

"You're a good man, Emerson."

Booker sighed. "No, I'm just an ex-schoolteacher trying to make it as a sheep rancher. You are the one everyone looks up to. You are the natural leader."

"I'm not much good as a leader now," Ian said. "Not

with this, I'm not." He thumped on one of the plaster casts on his legs. "Emerson, you and I both know that the small parcels we own won't support the sheep. We have to be able to graze on the open range."

"I know," Emerson agreed.

"Without the open range, we could wind up losing everything. All of us."

Emerson nodded but said nothing. Then, looking at Cynthia, he smiled. "I picked up your mail just as you asked. There were three issues of the *Boise Tri-Statesman*, so you'll have some newspapers to read."

"Thank you, Mr. Booker."

"And for you, little lady," Emerson said to Hannah. "Mr. Bloomfield at the mercantile said you had been looking for this." He handed Hannah a brown paper package.

Hannah tore the paper and looked inside, then smiled broadly.

"Oh, Mama, it's the calico you ordered!" she said. "You can help me make my dress now."

"Oh, honey, I don't know if I'm going to have time," Cynthia said. "With your father hurt, I'm afraid I'm going to be pretty busy."

"I'm sure you can find time to help her with her dress," Ian said. "I know how she's been lookin' forward to that."

Cynthia smiled. "You're right," she replied. "I'll find the time."

"Thank you, Mama. I just have to have it before the Fourth of July. And thank you, Mr. Booker, for bringing the calico."

"You're very welcome," Emerson said. "Have you read the book I left you?"

"Yes, I have. I'm enjoying it, but I must confess that sometimes Shakespeare is a little difficult to understand."

"Don't try to understand Shakespeare by the language

we use today," Emerson said. "Just listen to the rhythm and alliteration of the words. Once you are comfortable with that, the meaning will be more clear."

"Spoken like a schoolteacher," Ian said with a chuckle.

"I guess I did sound like I was back in the classroom, didn't I? Well, once a teacher, always a teacher, I suppose."

It wasn't until late that evening, after both Hannah and Ian were in bed, that Cynthia took a little time to herself to read the newspaper. She gasped out loud when she started to read one of the articles.

It is a rare treat to drop in at the Saratoga upon Mr. Mason Hawke and listen to the beautiful music he plays for the saloon customers. Mr. Hawke is a lover of good music, and by his skillful selection of tunes and brilliant performance at the piano, he draws crowds of attentive listeners.

But Mr. Hawke is more than a skilled piano player. He also enjoys the reputation of being a man of courage, resolve, and steady nerve, coupled with a sense of justice. These attributes were recently tested when Hawke came to the aid of an unfortunate woman who was the victim of frequent beatings, administered by her common-law husband. Hawke provided the woman with enough money to buy a railway ticket to a safe place, away from the drunken lout who had so abused her.

The common-law husband, one Angus Oates, upon learning the identity of his wife's benefactor, presented himself at the Saratoga, not to listen to the beautiful music, but to disrupt the concert with his malevolent behavior. It is said by witnesses that Oates already had his gun in play before he called out Mason Hawke.

Only by an athletic leap over the bar did Hawke avoid being killed. There, fortuitously for Hawke, he happened upon the loaded double-barrel shotgun that the bartender kept behind the bar, and, making use of the deadly instrument, dispatched the late Mr. Oates to his Maker, where, no doubt, final judgment was made upon this evil man.

Cynthia's head was spinning as she read the story. This had to be the Mason Hawke she knew, the Mason Hawke who was the brother to Gordon Hawke, the man to whom she had once been engaged.

She sat in the chair holding the paper for a long moment. Had anyone glanced her way they would have been convinced that she was still reading the newspaper, but she wasn't. She was formulating a plan.

As the details of the plan came into focus, Cynthia put down the newspaper and went over to the cupboard where she kept paper, a bottle of ink, and a fountain pen. Taking the paper and writing instruments to the kitchen table, she sat down and composed a letter.

Hawke had just finished playing the piano and was lighting a cheroot when Ben came over to him, carrying a letter.

"I was just down to the post office," Ben said, "and this came for you."

Hawke looked up in surprise, then shook his head. "A letter for me? There must some mistake. I don't get mail."

"Well, you got this one," Ben said, handing him the letter.

The return address was Mrs. Ian Macgregor.

"Well, I remember an Ian Macgregor," he said as he read the envelope. "He was the sergeant major of my regiment. But I didn't know he was married."

His curiosity aroused, Hawke opened the letter.

Dear Mason,

I know this letter must have come as a great surprise to you, and you may be wondering who Mrs. Ian Macgregor is. You knew me as Cynthia Rathbone.

I am sorry that I was not there to welcome you when you returned from the war. But first Gordon was killed, then shortly after that my sister died. And when it seemed as if my brother was going to make it, he was killed in the final month of the war. Of course, you know all of that, you were with both Gordon and Edward when they were killed.

I don't know what I would have done if it had not been for Ian Macgregor, and I thank you for letting him bring Edward's body home to me. Ian helped me pick up the pieces of my life, and we were married shortly after he came back.

Now, Ian, my daughter Hannah and I live in Idaho near the small town of King Hill. We are raising sheep in what was once all cattle country.

As you can imagine, sheep herders in cattle company is causing some friction. But I believe that, were it not for a man named Joshua Creed, who owns Crown Ranch, the biggest cattle ranch in the county, we would be able to live together in peace.

However, it seems to be Mr. Creed's personal goal to bring about a range war between the cattlemen and the sheep herders, and in a recent confrontation with some of the cattlemen, Ian was badly hurt. He is recovering from two broken legs and, during the recovery, is unable to run the ranch. We have some wonderful Basque people to tend the sheep, but I am sure that the cattlemen, goaded on by Mr. Creed, will take advantage of Ian's injury. You see, Ian has acted as sort of a leader of the sheep herders, and without him, I fear the others will succumb, one at a time. If that happens, none of us will be able to save our ranches.

Mason, like many from the South, Ian and I lost everything we had in that terrible war. This small ranch is all that we have. If we lose it, I have no idea where we will go or what we will do.

I read an article about you in our local paper. I have taken a chance on mailing this letter to you in care of the Saratoga in the hope that it finds you. If this letter does find you, and if, indeed, you are the same Mason Hawke that I knew, the brother of the man I loved and the fiancé of my own sister, then I pray that you will see fit to answer this plea for help from one who, but for the war, would have been your sister-in-law.

Sincerely,
Cynthia Rathbone Macgregor

Although Hawke finished reading, he held the letter for a long moment, just staring at the pages. How odd were the twists and turns of life. Had it not been for the war, Cynthia would have been his double sister-in-law, for she was going to marry his brother, and Hawke was going to marry her sister.

Seeing Hawke sitting there holding the letter but obviously in deep thought, Ben came over to talk to him.

"Anything important?" he asked.

"Yes, I think so," Hawke replied. "Ben, I think I'm going to have to tender my resignation."

"Say what?"

"I'm going to give up my job here. I have a train to catch."

"Damn, I hate to hear that, Hawke. I don't believe I've ever heard a piano player as good as you are. But, you did tell us when you took the job that you wouldn't be staying very long. Where are you going, if I may ask?"

"Idaho."

Chapter 3

WHILE ON THE PRAIRIE, THE TRAIN WAS A BEHE-
moth, overpowering the small plants and shrubs that bor-
dered the track. But once it entered Veta Pass it became
nothing more than a poor attempt by man to challenge the
grandeur of nature. The Sangre de Cristo range ran down
from the north, a towering spine that dwarfed the small
train, which, by that perspective, was little more than a
worm making its feeble way through the mountains.

Darkness was falling, and a broad bar of black was over-
taking the sky, except in the west, where a strip of pale blue
was gradually retreating. As part of the process, the setting
sun played upon clouds of vivid color and shape.

Then, as light surrendered to shadow, the color began
to fade, tone and tint leaving the sky a dark purple. Finally,
as if making one last, desperate attempt to assert itself, the
sun sent a single golden shaft shooting straight up, only to

be quickly blotted out by the encroaching darkness, and the day was done.

"Did you enjoy your meal, sir?"

Hawke, who was sitting at a table in the dining car, had been looking through the window at the light show of the dying day. When the waiter spoke, he turned toward him.

"Yes, thank you," he said. "It was quite delicious."

"I'm glad you enjoyed it. What time will you want your breakfast table ready?"

"Eight o'clock, I think."

"Very good, sir."

As the dishes were cleared away from the table, Hawke left the dining car and returned to his seat in the Pullman car. Some of the beds had already been made and he had to walk a narrow aisle between hanging green, sackcloth curtains to reach the back end of the car.

Sitting next to the window, Hawke turned up the gimbal-mounted lantern so there was enough light for him to read the letter from Cynthia again. When he finished it, he looked outside at the little patches of projected light that slid along the ballast as the train hurried through the night, recalling the first time he'd met Cynthia. It had also been the first time he met Tamara. . . .

The more prominent families of Georgia knew each other, if not by actual contact, then at least by reputation. To be a member of the privileged few in one community meant ex-officio entitlement to membership in all.

Jefferson Tinsdale Hawke was a former member of the Congress of the United States who resigned his seat when Georgia seceded from the Union. He was also owner of one of the largest and most productive plantations in Georgia. Because of that, the Hawke family had full entrée into the top tier of society, not only in Georgia, but all over the South.

One week after Mason Hawke returned from Europe, where he had been engaged in a grand concert tour playing piano before adoring crowds from London to Berlin, Charles Brubaker, one of the wealthier farmers of the county, hosted a huge barbecue for the regiment. Half a steer and ten hogs were spitted and being turned, slowly, over glowing coals, and the aroma of roasting meat competed with the fragrance of flowers and the ladies' perfumes. The ladies were all dressed in butterfly-bright dresses, and sporting jewelry that flashed and sparkled at bare throats, in their hair, and on broaches.

Most of the men, Mason Hawke included, were wearing the gray and gold uniforms of the newly activated Georgia 15th, which, because the regiment was commanded by Colonel Jefferson Tinsdale Hawke, was often referred to as "Hawke's Regiment." In the button holes of many of the men's tunics were snippets of hair—black, brown, blonde, or red—snipped from the lady of their choice.

Hawke was a newly commissioned second lieutenant, and his brother, Gordon, a captain, in the regiment.

"Why did Dad make me a lieutenant?" Hawke asked his brother. "What do I know about the military? I'm a pianist. I should be a private."

"Does being a pianist make you more qualified to be a private than to be an officer?" Gordon asked in response.

Hawke shook his head. "Being a pianist doesn't qualify me for anything, except being a pianist."

Gordon chuckled. "There you go, then, little brother," he said. "Since you aren't qualified for either position, you may as well be a lieutenant. Trust me, you'll like it much better. Now, come, I want you to meet someone."

Hawke smiled. "What do you mean, meet her? It's Cynthia Rathbone, isn't it? We've known the Rathbone's all our life."

"Well, yes, but Cynthia isn't the only one I want you to meet."

"What do you mean, not just Cynthia?" Hawke laughed. "Good heavens, Gordon, don't tell me you have two women."

"Not exactly," Gordon said. "But Cynthia has a sister."

"Of course she has a sister, I remember her. What is she, about fourteen or so?"

"She's nineteen," Gordon said. "And she's a knockout."

Hawke shook his head. "I don't know what you are getting me into, but I'll go along with you . . . for now."

"There they are, standing by the hall tree," Gordon said, pointing to a couple of young women.

Although not twins, the two young women looked very much alike. Both had brown hair that hung in dark curls, and eyes that were so dark as to be almost black. They were each holding a fan, and they used them to hide their smiles and the words they exchanged as the Hawke brothers approached.

"Ladies, may I present my brother, Mason?" Gordon asked. "Mason, this is my fiancée, Cynthia, and her sister, Tamara."

Hawke surprised everyone by clicking his heels together and bowing slightly, as he had seen it done in Europe. Then, as he had also seen it done, he kissed the hands of first Cynthia and then Tamara.

Shortly after meeting the two ladies, there was some unscheduled excitement. Someone saw a mouse on the dance floor, and it caused quite a panic among all the women. Many of them ran from the frightened rodent, screaming hysterically. Somebody knocked over the punch bowl, another crashed through the window.

It turned out that the mouse wasn't on the floor by accident. It had been intentionally released by Brubaker's fourteen year-old daughter, Angel, who was displeased because she had not been allowed to come to the barbecue.

Hawke had thought of that night many times since then. That was the day the old Mason Hawke, the gentleman of music and art, of culture and decorum, of hope and faith, died. And somewhere, in the din and crash of battle, the new, soulless, and very deadly Mason Hawke was born.

Eighteen months after that party, Hawke's father, Colonel Jefferson Tinsdale Hawke, was killed at "the "bridge" during the Battle of Fredericksburg. Eighteen months after the colonel was killed, Major Gordon Hawke was killed.

Hawke had become engaged to Tamara before the regiment left. But the marriage was never to be. Tamara died shortly before the end of the war. There probably would have been no wedding anyway. Hawke had lost his soul long before that.

"May I make the gentleman's bed, sir?"

"What?" Hawke asked, jerked out of his reverie.

The porter, leaning slightly over the seat, touched the bill of his cap. "May I make your bed for you, sir?" he asked again.

"Oh. Yes," Hawke said. "Yes, thank you." He got up and stood in the aisle as the porter pulled the seats together to make the bunk. Since no one else was sharing the seat, there was no need to pull the top bunk out from the wall.

Chapter 4

AS THE TRAIN SAT IN THE STATION, HAWKE STARED through the window at the little one-street town. The sign hanging on the weathered depot identified the town as SQUAW CREEK, IDAHO TERRITORY. There were no more than six or seven people on the platform, and whether they were waiting to board the train, or to meet someone, or to just watch it pass through, Hawke had no idea.

A couple of riders passed close to the train, their horses badly lathered, as if they had been run hard. Hawke was certain they would head for the livery so the horses could be rubbed down, but instead the riders dismounted in front of the saloon.

Muley Thomas and Quint Weathers had ridden their horses hard, and when they dismounted in front of the Red Star Saloon, both animals were covered with sweat lather and breathing heavily.

"If we had enough money, we could get on that train and ride it to wherever it's a-'goin'," Quint said, pointing to the standing train.

"And if a frog had wings, he wouldn't bump his ass ever' time he jumps," Muley replied.

"What's that mean?" Quint asked.

"It means we don't have enough money for a train ticket, and there ain't no sense worryin' 'bout somethin' that can't happen."

A gray-bearded old man was sitting in a chair on the front porch of the saloon, whittling on a stick. He looked up as the two riders dismounted, and seeing the condition of the horses, he frowned in obvious disapproval.

"You boys must'a rode them horses pretty hard," he said. "You got no right to just walk away from 'em like that. You should rub 'em down."

"You rub 'em down, mister, if you are so worried about them," Muley said.

"Ain't my horses."

"That's right," Muley said. "They ain't your horses."

With a grunt of contempt, the old man went back to whittling.

"You really think someone is chasin' us?" Quint asked as the two stepped into the saloon.

"I don't know," Muley said. "Tucker said he heard the Regulator was after us, and I thought I seen somethin' back there on the trail. Could be I was just spooked, though. Maybe I didn't see nothin' a-tall."

"What are we goin' to do about them horses?" Quint asked.

"What? Are you talkin' like the old man now? You think we should rub 'em down or somethin'?"

"No, I'm not talkin' about that. I'm talkin' about the fact that they ain't our horses."

"The hell they ain't. We roped 'em and broke 'em ourselves. Ain't nobody ever rode either one of 'em 'cept me 'n' you," Muley said.

"Well, that's true. But we was workin' for the Double Y. And that means that all the horses we rounded up and broke belong to Mr. Yancey."

"He's give horses to ever'one that's ever rode for 'im," Muley said. "What makes you think he wouldn't of give these to us?"

"'Cause we didn't tell 'im we was quittin'," Quint said. "We just rode off."

"Yeah, well, there ain't no way I'm goin' to ride for that pissant of a brother he's got ramroddin' the outfit now."

"Still, we should'a said somethin' to him about it," Quint said. "The way we done it, it makes it look like we stole them horses."

The bartender came down to where the two cowboys were standing at the bar.

"What can I get you gents?"

"Beer," Quint said.

"The same," Muley said.

"You boys just passin' through?" the bartender asked as he sat the two beers in front of them.

"Mister, where we're goin' ain't none of your concern," Muley said.

The friendly smile left the bartender's face. "I reckon you're right about that," he said as he walked away.

"You didn't have no call to talk to him like that, Muley. He was just bein' pleasant, is all. He's a bartender, that's his job."

"Yeah, well, like I said, I'm spooked. If Yancey really did get the Regulator after us, then the farther away we can get, the better off we are. And it'd be better for us if nobody knows where we're goin'."

"You been spooked ever since Tucker tol' you that," Quint said. "Who is he, anyway? I never even heard of anyone called the Regulator."

"Well I've damn sure heard of him," Muley said. "Some say he is the fastest gun ever lived. His name is Clay Morgan, and he used to be a U.S. Marshal till he got fired."

Quint chuckled. "Well, if he got fired as a U.S. Marshal, then he must not be all that good. What'd he get fired for? Not bein' able to bring his man in?"

"No. He brung his men in, all right. But what he done was, he brung 'em all in dead. They say he kilt ten or twelve men when he was a marshal. And they say he's kilt more as a Regulator than he ever did when he was a marshal."

"He's a bounty hunter now?" Quint asked.

"Well, he calls hisself a private detective, you know, like Pinkerton and the railroad detectives?" Muley said. "But from what I've heard, he's mostly just a hired gun."

Quint shook his head. "Then we ain't got nothin' to worry about. Mr. Yancey wouldn't never do nothin' like that. He wouldn't hire a gun just to run down a couple of cowboys who quit on him. Even if we did take the horses."

"Titus Yancey wouldn't, but his brother Jack would," Muley said. "He'd do it in a heartbeat, and you know it."

They heard the train whistle blow, then the puffing of steam as it began pulling out of the station.

"The train's leavin'," Quint said.

"So it is."

"I wish we was on it. Especially if this fella you're talkin' about really is after us."

"Yeah, well, we ain't," Muley said. "So the best thing we can do is just keep ridin'."

"That's them," a voice said from just inside the front door.

Turning toward the door, Muley and Quint saw the old

man who had been whittling on the front porch. The man was pointing to them.

"They was the ones who was ridin' them horses. And they left them poor critters just standin' there, more dead than alive," the old man said. "And like I tol' you, Sheriff, there ain't no call for anyone to treat horses like them boys did."

"I'm not a sheriff. I'm a Regulator."

"Oh, God, Quint, it's him," Muley said in a quiet, frightened voice. "It's Clay Morgan."

The man Muley identified as Morgan was big, well over six feet tall. He had steel-gray eyes and a scar that started just below his left eye then ran down his cheekbone like a purple flash of lightning before hooking into a full handlebar moustache. He was wearing a badge on his vest.

"Would you two boys be Muley Thomas and Quint Weathers?" he asked.

Muley nodded. "Yes, sir, Mr. Morgan. I'm Muley, this here is Quint," he said. "May I inquire as to why you are askin'?"

"I think you know why I'm asking, Mr. Thomas," Morgan replied. "I expect you two horse thieves had better come with me."

"No, sir, we ain't a-goin' nowhere with you," Muley said. He pointed to the badge on Morgan's vest. "You're wearin' that badge, but you ain't no real sheriff. You just said so yourself. That means you got no right to take us anywhere."

"Oh, but I do," Morgan replied. "Mr. Yancey swore out a warrant against you both for horse stealing, and he hired me to bring you back."

"Which Yancey would that be?" Muley asked.

"Mr. Jack Yancey," Morgan replied.

Muley sighed. "It would be him," he said. "'Cause I

know that Titus Yancey would never do a thing like that. Look, why don't you just take the horses back to Jack and we'll call it quits?"

Morgan shook his head. "Too late for that. You boys are goin' back to hang."

"What?" Quint gasped. "Did you say we was goin' back to hang?"

"That's what they do to horse thieves, isn't it?" Morgan replied.

"No, sir. I ain't goin' back to hang," Muley said.

"Didn't figure you'd go back peaceable," Morgan said. He moved his hand down to his pistol. "It's your call, boys. You can go back to hang or you can take your chances with me."

"What are we goin' to do, Muley?" Quint asked in a frightened voice.

"You want to go back to hang?" Muley asked.

"No."

"Then there's only one thing we can do."

"You mean . . . you mean draw against him?"

"There's two of us, Quint. Only one of him," Muley said. "I figure we got no choice but to try."

Morgan smiled, though it was a smile without humor. "Your friend is right, Quint. There's two of you, and only one of me. You can either try me or you can hang. Which is it?"

"Let's do it!" Muley shouted, making a desperate grab for his gun.

Clay Morgan had his gun out before either Muley or Quint touched theirs. His two shots were fired so close together that those who heard the confrontation but didn't see it thought only one shot was fired.

Morgan stood there for just a moment, holding the smoking pistol as he looked down at the bodies of the two men he had just killed. Then, slipping his pistol back into his holster, he stepped up to the bar. The beers Muley and Quint had ordered were still there, both mugs more than half full.

"Are these their beers?" Morgan asked easily.

The bartender, his eyes wide in wonder over what he had just seen, nodded once.

"They already paid for?" Morgan asked.

"Yes, sir."

"Well, then, there's no sense in letting them go to waste, is there?" Morgan asked.

"No, sir, I don't s'pose there is," the bartender said.

Morgan drank both beers, then wiped his mouth with the back of his hand. Turning his back to the bar, he looked out over the saloon, where some of the shocked patrons had walked over to look down, in morbid curiosity, at the two men who were lying on the floor.

Morgan pulled a pencil and a piece of paper from his shirt pocket and started to write.

"I'm going to need some of you folks to sign this paper telling what happened here," he said.

"Mr. Morgan, you don't have to worry none about the sheriff," the bartender said. "Ever'body here seen that them two boys went for their guns before you did."

"I'm not worried about the sheriff, barkeep," Morgan said. "This paper is just to show to Yancey so I can justify my pay."

Chapter 5

"TOMAS SAID YOU WANTED TO SEE ME, MRS. Macgregor?" Emerson Booker asked.

"Yes," Cynthia said. Looking over her shoulder to see that Ian was still in the bedroom, she stepped out onto the front porch and closed the door behind her. "Let's talk out here. I don't want Ian to know about this."

Emerson frowned and shook his head. "Oh, I don't know," he said. "I wouldn't want to keep any secrets from Ian."

"Well, don't worry, we aren't going to be able to keep this a secret very long. As soon as you bring him here, Ian is going to know about it."

"Bring who here?"

"Mason Hawke," Cynthia said. "I wrote him and asked him to come help us."

"Help you with what? Help you run the ranch? Look,

Mrs. Macgregor, you didn't need to do that. If Tomas can't keep up with the work, I'd be glad to send over someone to help out. I'm sure any one of us would."

Cynthia shook her head. "No, it isn't that. Tomas and the other hands are doing a fine job with the ranch. I'm talking about the other thing."

"The other thing?"

"The trouble Mr. Creed is causing. I want Mr. Hawke to help us fight the cattlemen."

"I see what you mean about not telling Ian," Emerson said after a moment's pause. "Ian is a very proud man. I'm sure he would be a little put off by thinking you called in a stranger to fight his battle for him."

"Mason Hawke isn't a stranger," Cynthia said quickly. "I have known him since I was a little girl. Why, his family and my family were friends back in Georgia, before the war."

"I see. And you think this man, Mason Hawke, can help us fight the cattlemen?"

"I know he can," Cynthia said. "He is an exceptionally capable man."

"All right, I'll bring him here for you. Where will I find him?"

"According to the letter he sent me, his train will be arriving in King Hill, today."

"How will I recognize him?"

"He's quite good looking and—"

Emerson laughed and held up his hand. "Mrs. Macgregor, I'm not sure I would know what 'good looking' means, for a man. You are going to have to do better than that."

"Well, he's tall and slender, dark hair, blue eyes, and he dresses well."

"Dresses well?"

Cynthia chuckled. "Yes. He always has been somewhat of a dandy about dressing. Just pick out the best dressed man you see and it'll be Mason Hawke. Oh. He also plays the piano, beautifully."

"He plays the piano," Emerson said. "Yes, I'm sure that playing the piano will come in very handy in our fight with the cattlemen."

"Don't judge him before you see him, Mr. Booker. I told you, he is an exceptionally capable man."

"I'm sorry, Mrs. Macgregor," Emerson said. "Of course you are right, I had no call to say such a thing. I'll defer to your judgment. I'll bring your man to you."

"Thank you."

Still on the train, Hawke had his elbow on the window ledge and his chin cupped in his hand as he gazed at the panorama unfolding before him. In the distance he could see the mountains, dark blue at their base and rising to majestic heights where little spindriftlike tendrils of snow trailed away from the brightly gleaming snow-covered peaks; white, against the bright blue sky. The prairie below the mountains was ablaze with a colorful profusion of wildflowers; yellow yarrow, red Indian paintbrush, light blue mountain phlox, and purple trillium.

Close by, a jackrabbit rose to the challenge of the train and began running alongside the track, actually outpacing the steam engine for a short distance until it grew tired. Then the rabbit stopped and watched in disbelief as the slower but inexhaustible locomotive continued its same, unrelenting pace.

To the south of the track was the Snake River; to the north, a building came into view, low lying and built of sod, so that at first glance it appeared to be nothing more than a clump of nature, hardly discernable as a man-made structure. Another building followed that one, this time made of wood, and with a barn and corral. After that, as the train slowed down, the number of buildings increased and Hawke realized that they were coming into a town.

"King Hill. This stop is King Hill," the conductor called out, walking up the aisle.

As the train rattled, creaked, and clanged to a stop, Hawke stood up and stretched. He had been on it for the better part of three days and was looking forward to getting off.

After making arrangements to have his grip stay at the depot until he called for it, he walked up Pitchfork Road until he reached the Cattleman's Saloon. Stepping through the bat-wing doors, he moved to one side, then slid back against the wall while he perused the saloon, looking closely at every patron. He had never been in this particular part of the country before and didn't expect to have any personal enemies here, but he had no intention of being any less vigilant because of that.

This particular saloon was new to him, but only because of its geographic location. In fact, with all the saloons he had encountered over the last sixteen years of his life, they had by now become part and parcel of his heritage. There was a familiarity to the wide-plank boards that made up the floor, an acquaintance with the long bar with brass foot rail, the mirror-reflected bottles proudly displayed behind the bar, and, especially, the piano that sat at the rear of the saloon.

It was early afternoon, the saloon was so quiet that a couple of the bar girls had found time to sit at a table and talk to each other. A couple of men were at another table, while two more were standing at the bar. What energy there was came from a third table where six men were talking and laughing. One among them, a young man, was loud and overbearing, while the other five were submissive to him. Hawke had seen his like before, obnoxious and sure of themselves, and he knew that they often needed to reinforce their own sense of self-worth by such behavior. If he was going to have any trouble in this saloon, he realized instinctively that it would come from this young man.

Hawke stepped up to the bar and ordered a beer.

"Just get off the train, did you?" the bartender asked as he set the beer in front of Hawke.

Hawke chuckled. "Yes, I did. Why? Is it that obvious?"

"Well, I knew I hadn't seen you before," he said. "And I know the train just arrived, so it was a pretty safe bet. You going to stay for a while, are you?"

"Yes, but I'm not sure how long I'll be here. I'm looking for the Macgregor place," Hawke said. "Do you know it?"

"Yes, I know it."

"Can you give me directions to it? I understand that it's near here."

"Hey, you! Fancy Dan!" the young man who was holding court at the table called. "If you're lookin' for the Macgregor place, it's easy enough to find. All you have to do is follow the smell of sheep shit."

The others with him laughed.

"Well, I'm glad to see that King Hill has one," Hawke said, drifting toward the table.

"Has one?" the young man replied, his face screwed up in confusion. "Has one what?"

"A resident ass," Hawke said, stopping a few feet away.

"What?" the young man sputtered. "Mister, do you know who I am?"

"I thought we had already determined that you were the resident ass," Hawke said.

"My name is Creed, mister. Lonnie Creed. Does that name mean anything to you?"

"Would you be Creed of Crown Ranch?"

Lonnie pulled the little string of rawhide from his pocket and stuck one end of it in his mouth. An arrogant smile spread across his face. "Yeah," he said, chewing on the rawhide. "You have heard of me, haven't you?"

"I've heard of you."

"Then you know what an important man I am around these parts," Lonnie said.

"Oh, yeah," Hawke said. "I've heard how important you think you are."

"Then you know better than to get on my bad side," Lonnie said, not recognizing the sarcasm in Hawke's reply. "Tell me. What do you call that little piece of lace around your neck?"

"It's called a cravat," Hawke said. "But it isn't lace."

Lonnie smiled. "It isn't lace yet, but it will be lace when I get through with it," he said, pulling his knife and reaching for the cravat.

Moving so quickly that Lonnie had no time to react, Hawke grabbed his arm and twisted it, turning Lonnie around. Hawke then took his knife from him and put the point of it to Lonnie's neck.

"Ahhh!" Lonnie called out in surprise and fear.

"Why don't I just turn your neck to lace instead?" Hawke asked.

"No, please!" Lonnie shouted in terror. "Somebody do something!"

The cowboys at the table were on their feet now, and a few of them started toward Hawke, who stuck the tip of the blade into Lonnie's neck, just enough to bring blood.

"Come ahead," he said quietly. "He'll be flopping on the floor like a gutted fish before you get here."

"No!" Lonnie shouted. "No, don't do anything!"

The cowboys stopped moving.

"I expect you boys better go on home now," a new voice said.

Looking toward the sound of the voice, Hawke saw a man wearing a badge.

"Mister, you want to let Lonnie go?"

Hawke hesitated a second, then pushed Lonnie away. Lonnie put his hand to his throat, then brought it down to look at the blood in his palm.

"Do something, Sheriff," Lonnie said. "This son of a bitch cut me."

"You've been cut worse shaving," the sheriff said. Then, to Hawke, he said, "I'm Sheriff Tilghman. And you are?"

"Hawke. Mason Hawke."

"You want to get rid of the knife, Mr. Hawke?"

Hawke held the knife by its point for a second, testing its balance, then threw it across the room, sticking it in the side of the stairs that led up to the second floor, where it was too high for anyone to reach from the floor.

"Now, what was all this about?" the sheriff asked.

"You seen it yourself, Sheriff," Lonnie said. "This fancy dressed fella tried to cut my throat."

"I saw that," the sheriff said. "But I also recognized the knife. The knife is yours, isn't it, Lonnie?"

"Well, yeah."

"How did he happen to get your knife?" the sheriff asked.

"He took it from me," Lonnie admitted.

"Well now, that's quite a trick, isn't it? He took it from you? How did that happen?"

"I was just havin' a little fun with him is all. I didn't mean nothin' by it. He took it all wrong."

"Yeah, it looked to me like you was havin' just a whole lot of fun," the sheriff said. "I think you should get on back out to the Crown now."

"Sheriff, I—"

"Get on with you," the sheriff said. "Unless you want to spend the night in jail."

"My father wouldn't like that."

"Your father wouldn't be in jail, you would," the sheriff said. "Now, it's your call, Lonnie. Which will it be?"

Lonnie glared at the sheriff for a long moment, then looked at the others. "Come on, boys, let's go," he said.

The five cowboys who were with Lonnie followed him out the front door.

The sheriff waited until all were gone, then turned to Hawke, who had gone back to the bar and his beer.

"Mr. Hawke, I take it you just got off the train?" he asked.

"Yes."

"You passin' through?"

"No. I plan to stay for a while."

"Well, I don't mind tellin' you that you made an enemy today. And when you have Lonnie Creed as an enemy, you'll have his pa and the whole Crown Ranch."

"It was bound to happen anyway, Matt," the bartender said. "This fella has already asked how to get to the Macgregor ranch."

"Mr. Hawke, you don't strike me as a shepherd," the sheriff said.

"No. I'm a pianist."

"A what?"

Hawke pointed to the piano. "A pianist," he said. He started toward the piano.

"Well, what business do you have with the Macgregors?" the sheriff asked.

"I'm a friend of the family," Hawke said. He sat at the piano and began playing, the music sweet and clear.

"I'll be damned," the sheriff said. "He is a piano player."

Hawke finished the song, then turned around to see someone standing just behind him.

"You would be Mason Hawke, I take it?" the man asked.

"I am."

"I thought so. Mrs. Macgregor said you played the piano well."

"Who are you?" Hawke asked.

The man stuck his hand out for a handshake. "The name is Emerson Booker. I'm a friend of the Macgregors, and I'm here to take you out to their spread."

Hawke looked over at the sheriff, who, leaning against the bar, had stuck around long enough to listen to the music.

"Will you be needing me for anything, Sheriff?"

"No, Mr. Hawke. I won't be needing you."

Hawke nodded. "Then I'll be going. Thank you for your timely intervention."

"Good day to you, Mr. Hawke."

The sheriff watched Hawke and Emerson leave the saloon, then asked the bartender, "Dan, did you see what happened between Lonnie and Hawke?"

"Yeah, Matt, I seen it. It was the damnedest thing you ever saw. Lonnie come at the fancy dressed fella with a knife, and he took it away from him as easy as takin' candy from a baby. Who woulda thought some piano player could handle Lonnie Creed like that?"

"He isn't just any piano player," the sheriff said. "He's Mason Hawke."

"Yeah, that's what he said, but the name don't mean nothin' to me. Should it?"

"If he stays here for any length of time, you'll know who he is," the sheriff said. "You can mark my words on that."

Chapter 6

"I UNDERSTAND THAT YOU AND MRS. MACGREGOR are old friends," Emerson said as he drove the buckboard from town toward the Macgregor ranch.

"Yes, back in Georgia, before the war, our families had adjacent farms," Hawke said.

"Have you met Ian?"

Hawke nodded. "I've known him for a long time as well. I didn't know he and Cynthia were married, though, until I got the letter."

"I'm a little concerned as to how he is going to take to having you show up like this," Emerson said. "I mean, him not knowing anything about it."

Hawke glanced over at Emerson. "Wait a minute, what are you talking about? Are you telling me that the sergeant major doesn't even know I'm coming?"

"Sergeant major?"

"During the war, Ian was the sergeant major of our regiment," Hawke said.

Emerson chuckled. "He never talks about the war, so I didn't know that," he said, then nodded. "But now that you mention it, I could see Ian as a sergeant major. He certainly has that kind of leadership quality."

"And you say he doesn't know I'm coming?"

"No. I think Mrs. Macgregor thought he would be too proud to ask for help, so she took it on herself to write to you."

"I expect she's right," Hawke said. "The Ian Macgregor I remember is a proud man and not someone who asks for help very easily."

"Yes, sir, that's Ian Macgregor, all right," Emerson said.

As the buckboard proceeded along the long, straight, road, Hawke sat warming in the sun, recalling the last time he had seen Ian Macgregor.

It was in late April 1865, and the Georgia 15th had boarded a train for its run south over the bucking strap-iron and rotted cross ties of the railroad. Since both Colonel Jefferson Hawke, the original commander, and Major Gordon Hawke, the next commander, had been killed, the regiment was no longer referred to as Hawke's Regiment except by some of the older soldiers who had been with it from the beginning.

The Georgia 15th was now part of the army of Richard Taylor, a Confederate general who also happened to be the son of Zachary Taylor, hero of the Mexican War, and former President of the United States.

The regiment that boarded the train was less than thirty percent of its mustering-in strength when it had gathered so proudly at the home of Charles Brubaker for a predeployment barbecue. Of the thirty-five officers who had taken to the field with the regiment, all had been killed except for Edward Rathbone and Mason Hawke. Captains both, the men had started the war as second lieutenants.

Major James Coleman was now in command of the regiment, having been put in that position by General Taylor.

Though Coleman was officially in command, everyone in the regiment, Coleman included, deferred to Sergeant Major Ian Macgregor, who had held that same rank since the beginning of the war. Macgregor had been offered a commission but declined, stating that he believed he could best serve the regiment by staying in his current position.

When the explosion took the engine off the tracks, the first three cars of the train telescoped in on themselves, causing a tremendous number of casualties, killing Major Coleman and five other regimental officers.

Hawke was riding in one of the rear cars, and his only indication that something had happened was in the fact that the train came to an almost immediate stop, throwing men into the floor. Even as some of the men were swearing about the incompetence of the engineer, Hawke realized what had happened, and he started urging the men to get off the cars.

The train had been hit by a bomb that was placed on the track by Federal soldiers. These same soldiers were waiting in ambush, and they opened fire as soon as the men of the regiment began pouring off the train.

Hawke, Rathbone, and Sergeant Major Macgregor rallied the regiment.

"Take cover in the train wreckage!" Hawke shouted, and the men scrambled to do so.

The Yankees had one artillery piece, a 12-pounder, which fired an explosive round every couple of minutes. Fortunately, the position of the gun was such that the Federals could not get the proper angle to drop the shells in on Hawke's men. Though the incoming rounds were loud, they weren't threatening, or even frightening, to men who had already been through four long, bloody years of war.

"Why don't they attack?" Rathbone asked. "Don't they realize how easily they could overrun us?"

"I think they are new troops," Hawke replied. "They got lucky when they blew up the train, but they don't have the experience to follow it up."

They heard the swooshing sound of another shell coming in, and were easily able to follow its path by the sputtering, smoking fuse that traced its arc through the sky. It hit about forty yards away, booming loudly, but sending the shrapnel out in an ineffective cone.

"Mason, I'm going to take that gun out!" Rathbone said.

"Eddie, no, why bother?" Hawke asked. "They aren't even coming close. It's not worth the risk."

"Yes, it is worth the risk," Eddie replied. "Think about it, Mason. You said it yourself, they are green troops. If they lose that gun, I think they will also lose their confidence. They may just pull up stakes and leave."

Hawke didn't argue with him anymore. The two were equal in rank, and Hawke had no authority to stop him. He also knew that Rathbone was right. If the Yankees lost the gun, they might perceive they had also lost the advantage and leave.

A few minutes later Rathbone had three volunteers prepared to go with him. He gave the signal to Hawke that he was ready.

"All right, men, keep Captain Rathbone covered!" Hawke shouted to the others.

Muskets roared and gun smoke billowed up from the Confederate soldiers in the wrecked train, answered by the

Union soldiers who had taken up their own positions in the tree line across the open field. Eddie Rathbone and three volunteers started across the field, disappearing quickly into the clouds of billowing smoke.

For the next thirty minutes the gunfire continued at such a pace that Hawke was afraid they would soon run out of ammunition. Then he noticed that the artillery fire had stopped.

"The cannon has stopped!" Ian said, putting to words what Hawke had only thought. "Captain Rathbone must've gotten through."

"Yes," Hawke agreed. "Let's just pray that he and his men get back all right. Keep firing men, keep firing," he called.

"Cap'n, we're runnin' low on powder and bullets," one of the men said. "Don't you think we should ease up a bit?"

"No," Hawke said. "Keep firing."

Although Hawke didn't explain his reasoning, he was keeping up a brisk rate of fire as much to feed the cloud of gun smoke as to inflict any damage upon the enemy.

Then, out of the cloud of gun smoke that obscured the field, they saw the volunteers returning. Only this time, one of the men was being carried. Even from his vantage point, Hawke could tell that the wounded man was Captain Rathbone.

"Sergeant Major," Hawke said.

"Yes, sir?"

"Set fire to the grass. As soon as the smoke has built up, order the men to pull back. Captain Rathbone bought us some time . . . let's take advantage of it."

"Yes, sir," Ian replied.

Within moments the smoke from a dozen grass fires mixed with the gun smoke to completely blot out the field.

Then, outnumbered and outgunned, Hawke withdrew his men, thus avoiding the necessity of surrender.

Some five miles away from the point of the ambush, Hawke called a halt to the retreat. Looking around, he counted eighty-seven men. Just eighty-seven from a regiment that had once been six hundred strong.

"Captain Hawke," Ian said, a bloody bandage around his right arm and another around his head.

"Yes, Sergeant Major?"

"I thought I ought to tell you, sir. Captain Rathbone just died."

"Damn," Hawke said with an expulsion of breath. He and Eddie Rathbone had fished and hunted together as children.

"What do you want to do now?" Ian asked.

"Nothing," Hawke said.

"Nothing, sir?" Ian asked, surprised by the response.

"That's right, Sergeant Major. I want to do absolutely nothing. Major Coleman told me, yesterday, that General Lee had already surrendered and General Taylor was just trying to reposition us to get better terms. As far as I'm concerned, we'll make our own terms, right here, right now. I've only got one last order for you. That is, if you are willing to carry it out."

"Give me the order, sir, I'll carry it out," Ian said.

Hawke opened his knapsack and took out a piece of paper and a pencil, then began writing.

"You are hereby discharged from the army," Hawke said, handing the paper to Ian. "If anyone is actually still looking for deserters, this should clear the way for you. I want you to take Captain Rathbone's body back to what is left of his family."

Ian nodded. "Yes, sir," he said. "I'd be proud to do that. But I'll be coming back. I wouldn't feel right abandoning the regiment."

"There's no regiment to abandon, Sergeant Major. I'm going to release them all and tell them to go home and try and put their lives together again."

"What about you, Captain? What are you going to do?"

"I have no idea what I'm going to do, Ian," he said. "I have no life to put together."

Chapter 7

CYNTHIA WAS COOKING SUPPER WHEN IAN
rolled himself into the kitchen.

"Something smells awfully good," he said, sniffing.

"I'm baking a hen," she replied. "And I'm making dressing and dumplings."

"Whoa, a hen? Dressing and dumplings? That's a lot of food for three of us, isn't it?"

"There will be five."

"Five?"

"Mr. Booker will be here with Mason Hawke by suppertime."

"Captain Hawke is coming here? How about that? I haven't seen him since the war. It'll be good seeing him again. How did you find out he was here?"

"I sent him a letter, Ian. He is here because I asked him to come," Cynthia said as she put a pan of biscuits in the oven.

"You asked him to come? Why?"

"I thought he might be able to help us."

"Help us do what? Tomas and the others are doing a good job of running the ranch right now."

"I asked him to help us fight the cattlemen," Cynthia said.

Ian was quiet for a long moment before he spoke. "Cynthia, don't you think you should have asked me about this?" he said.

"Would you have agreed to it?"

"Definitely not," Ian said emphatically.

"That's why I didn't ask you."

"Cynthia, I can't believe that you would just do something like that without first talking to me about it."

"I'm sorry, Ian, perhaps I should have. But at any rate it's too late to talk about it now," she said. "I see them coming up the lane now."

Shaking his head in quiet anger, Ian turned his chair around and rolled out of the kitchen.

"Ian," Cynthia called to him. "Please, understand that I did this for you."

"I'll try to understand, Cynthia," Ian said. "I'll try."

"Would you go on the porch and meet them? I want Mason to know that he is welcome."

"Ah, good," Emerson said as he drove the team into the front yard. "I see that Ian is out on the front porch. She must've told him about you."

"I'm glad," Hawke said. "I hope he took it all right."

"He must have," Emerson replied with a chuckle. "He's not holding a shotgun."

Hawke laughed with him.

"Hello, Emerson," Ian greeted.

"Ian," Emerson replied.

"And, Captain Hawke. It is good to see you again after all these years."

"You too, Sergeant Major," Hawke said.

Ian laughed. "I suppose we can drop the 'Sergeant Major' and 'Captain' now, can't we?"

"Lord, I hope so. I'd hate to think I was going back into the army."

"Me too," Ian replied with a chuckle. "Well, climb down, the two of you, and come on in. The wife has fixed us a big supper and I've been smellin' it all afternoon. It's got me so hungry I could eat a horse."

"Best invitation I've had all day," Emerson said, climbing down from the buckboard and tying off the team.

"Cynthia," Ian called when they went into the house. "Come into the parlor and greet our guests."

Cynthia came at Ian's bidding, and when she reached the parlor she stopped. For a long moment she said nothing. She just stared at Hawke. He looked so much like she remembered Gordon that it took her breath away.

"Well, are you just going to stand there and gawk, or are you going to speak to him?" Ian asked.

"Hello, Mason," Cynthia said. "I can call you Mason, can't I?"

"Of course you can," Hawke replied.

Hawke hadn't noticed her staring at him, because he had been staring back. Cynthia and Tamara had always looked alike, and it didn't take much imagination for him to think that he could be looking at Tamara now, had Tamara lived.

"It is so good to see you again after all these years," Cynthia said. "And so wonderful of you to answer my plea for help."

"Hawke, I want it well understood that sending for you was all Cynthia's idea," Ian said, "I knew nothing about it, and would have never presumed to get you mixed up in all this."

"Ian, my good friend," Hawke said. "You saved my backside more times than I can remember during the war. And Cynthia has been a friend since we were both children. Do you think, for one minute, I would hesitate if I thought I could help you in any way?"

"I know," Ian said. "You are a good man, and of course you would do anything you could to help us if you knew we were in trouble. But it is important to me that you know I didn't want to get you involved in this. I also want you to know that it could get very dangerous."

"All the more reason I should be here," Hawke replied. "Now . . . are we going to eat some of this delicious food I smell? Or are we just going to stand here and talk all day?"

Everyone laughed, and Cynthia issued the invitation for them to go to the dining room.

Entering that room, Hawke saw a very pretty young girl setting the table.

"You must be Hannah," he said.

"Yes, sir," Hannah replied demurely.

"Well, now, what a beautiful young lady you are. Ian, Cynthia, you must be very proud of her."

Ian and Cynthia exchanged a quick glance, then Ian nodded. "She is a wonderful daughter. I can't tell you how much I love her, or how proud I am of her."

Hannah went over to the wheelchair and wrapped her arms around his neck. "I love you too, Papa," she said.

"I can see why you are so proud of her," Hawke said.

"Oh, by the way, Mrs. Macgregor," Emerson put in, "you are right about Mr. Hawke being a pianist. I had the pleasure of hearing him play when I picked him up in town."

"Mama told me that you were very good," Hannah said. "We have a piano in the parlor."

Hawke nodded. "Yes, I saw it when I came in."

"I took lessons for a while, but I'm not very good."

"It takes a while to learn," Hawke said.

"Would you play something for us?"

"Hannah, I'm sure Mr. Hawke is tired from his long journey," Ian admonished her. "Don't be pestering him to play the piano."

"It's no problem, Ian," Hawke said. "I'd love to play the piano for Hannah. That is, if it isn't an imposition."

"Imposition? Of course not," Ian said. "I would love to hear you play."

The dinner over, everyone went into the parlor where Hawke saw an upright piano, similar to many of the same kind of instruments he had played in saloons across the West for the last sixteen years. The only difference was, this piano was in much better condition than many of the pianos he had been forced to play.

Hawke sat down, then played Consolation Number Three, a composition of Franz Liszt, his old music teacher.

The music filled the parlor with the repeating bass theme and the soaring melody. When he finished, he saw tears in Hannah's eyes.

"Darlin', what is it?" Ian asked. "Is something wrong?"

"Wrong? Papa, what could be wrong?" Hannah asked. "I have just heard the music of angels."

"Matthew Tilghman," Joshua Creed said as the sheriff rode up to his front porch and dismounted. "Come on in, you are here just in time for supper."

"Thank you, Mr. Creed, but this isn't exactly a social call," the sheriff replied.

"Yes, I heard about the little fracas in town today between Lonnie and some eastern dude. And I don't blame you for breaking it up. But Lonnie's young ... hell, we were all young once. You know what it's like when you're all full of piss and vinegar. He was just having a little fun with the tenderfoot, that's all."

"Is that what he told you? That he was just having a little fun with a tenderfoot?"

"Well, yes. That, and the fact that you came in to break it up. And, like I said, I don't blame you for that. I don't blame you one bit."

"Mr. Creed, if I hadn't broken it up when I did, Lonnie might well be dead now."

"What?" Creed said, surprised. "What do you mean Lonnie might be dead now? What are you talking about?"

"Is Lonnie here?"

"Yes, he's inside."

"Call him out," Tilghman said. "Call him out and ask him, in front of me, to tell you exactly what happened in town today."

Creed stared at Sheriff Tilghman for a long moment, then called back over his shoulder.

"Lonnie! Lonnie, are you in there?"

"Yeah, Pa, I'm here," a voice sounded from inside the house.

"Get out here," Creed said.

A moment later Lonnie appeared on the porch, where he saw the sheriff but seemed unconcerned over his presence. "What do you want, Pa?"

"Tell me what happened in town today," Creed said.

"Well, nothing really," his son replied. "Like I told you, I was just having a little fun with some Fancy Dan is all."

Sheriff Tilghman produced Lonnie's knife. He threw it, and stuck it in the floor of the porch. The handle quivered for a second or two.

"What the ... ?" Creed said, then looking more closely

at the knife, registered recognition. "Wait a minute, Lonnie, isn't that your knife?"

"Yeah," Lonnie said. "It's mine."

"What did you do, Sheriff? Take his knife away from him? Well, good for you. He's too damn handy with that knife as it is."

"I didn't take it away from him," Tilghman said. "The dude did."

"What?" He looked at Lonnie. "You let someone take your knife from you?"

"I was just playin' around, Pa," Lonnie said again. "Hell, I never thought Fancy Dan was going to take it so serious, so I wasn't paying that much attention. One minute I was just teasing him, all in fun, like, and the next moment he had my knife. I'm not even sure how he got it."

"Well, now, that's a little different than the story you told me when you got back home," Creed said. "The sheriff didn't break up your fun, he saved your life, didn't he?"

"Ah, I don't think Fancy Dan would have actually used it. He was about to wet his pants, he was so scared. I doubt he's ever even seen a dead man."

"Oh, he's seen dead men before," Sheriff Tilghman said. "And a lot of them he has seen are dead because of him. You'd do well to stay away from him."

"Really?" the elder Creed said. "Tell me, Sheriff, just who is this man Lonnie ran into today?"

"His name is Mason Hawke," the sheriff said.

"Mason Hawke? I don't believe I've ever heard of him."

"Well, I have," Tilghman said. "And trust me when I tell you this, he is as dangerous as any man alive."

"Are you kidding?" Lonnie asked with a little laugh. "Why, he dresses like a . . . a Nancy Boy."

"Like I said, Lonnie, you'd do well to stay away from him," the sheriff said. He remounted.

"Sheriff," Creed called.

"Yes?"

"Do you have any idea why he's here?"

"I've got an idea, yes," Tilghman said. "But it would only be speculation."

"What would that be?"

"Oh, I wouldn't want to speculate. But he did say he is a friend of the Macgregors," Tilghman said. "So I'll let you figure out for yourself why he might be here."

"Thanks," Creed said.

Creed and his son stood on the porch, watching as Sheriff Tilghman passed under the Crown Gate.

"Lonnie?" Creed said.

"Yes, sir?"

"Don't you ever embarrass me like that again."

"Pa, it's like I said—" Lonnie started, but before he could finish, Joshua Creed reached out, unexpectedly, and back-handed him, hard. Lonnie went reeling across the porch, preventing himself from falling only by grabbing one of the supporting posts.

"If you ever pull a knife or a gun on a man again, kill him," Creed said.

Lonnie used the back of his hand to wipe the blood away from his lip as he watched his father go back into the house.

Chapter 8

THERE WASN'T ROOM FOR HIM IN THE BUNKHOUSE, so Hawke slept in the tack room of the barn, throwing out his bedroll on some soft hay. On the third night it rained, and though he didn't get wet, he did notice that rain was coming through the roof. He mentioned it the next morning.

"Yes," Ian said. "I have a pile of shingles ready and I was going to get around to fixing the roof myself before I broke my legs. Tomas offered to do it, but I didn't want him to waste his time. Without me, he and the other two boys are kept busy watching the sheep. Sheep aren't like cows, you know . . . they have to be watched over twenty-four hours a day."

"I'll fix the roof for you," Hawke said.

Ian held up his hand. "Hawke, you don't have to do that. I'm about to decide that maybe Cynthia was right in sending for you, but not so you could roof my barn."

Hawke laughed. "It won't be the first time I've ever worked on a roof," he said. "My brother and I roofed the entire barn once. You've got nails?"

"I do."

"I'll get started on it right away."

"All right, then, if you are going to do that, I'll help," Ian said.

"Now, how are you going to help with your legs broken?"

"Most of the time when you're putting on shingles, you are sitting down, aren't you?" Ian replied.

"Well, yes, but you are sitting on the roof."

"Then all I have to do is get on the roof."

"And just how are you going to do that?"

"You're going to use the hay hoist to get me up there," Ian replied.

Hawke smiled. "I'll be damn," he said. "Yes, that might work after all. That's a good idea."

It took Hawke half an hour to attach another stanchion to the barn, just under the roof. Adding a pulley to the stanchion, he then looped the hay-lift rope over it and, attaching a hay bale, tried it out.

"All right," Hawke said as he tied the end of the rope around Ian's waist. "I can hoist you up to the roof, but the problem is going to be when you get there. Somehow, you're going to have to pull yourself onto the roof."

"I can do it," Ian insisted.

"Mama," Hannah said, looking out the open front door at the activity. "What are Mr. Hawke and Papa doing?"

"Mr. Hawke is going to fix the roof of the barn," Cynthia said.

"Then, why is he raising Papa up on the hay hoist?"

"What?" Cynthia said in surprise. "What are you talking about?"

Cynthia dusted the flour from her hands and hurried to the door to look outside. She saw Hawke on the ground, pulling on the rope, hand over hand, lifting Ian slowly but surely toward the top of the barn.

"Ian, what in heaven's name are you doing?" she called out.

"I'm doing what I should have done two months ago," Ian answered. "I'm fixing the roof."

"You've got no business up there. Mason, bring him back down."

"No!" Ian called. "Hawke, you keep pulling me up! Cynthia, this is something I have to do. Do you understand? This is something I have to do. I can't just sit around on my backside day after day, doing nothing."

Cynthia and Hannah watched anxiously as Ian was hoisted to the top of the barn. Then, as Hawke held onto the rope below, Ian managed to pull himself onto the roof. With a little wave of success, he called down to Hawke.

"I'm here!"

Hawke began sending up bundles of shingles, then climbed up the ladder to join him.

The two men had been working for a little more than an hour when Hannah came up the ladder, carrying a basket.

"Honey, what are you doing up here?" Ian asked.

"I brought you both some cookies," she said.

"Well, I'd say that's worth a break anytime," Hawke said, smiling, and took the basket from her.

"Mr. Hawke, Mama says that you knew Papa during the war," Hannah said.

"That's right," he answered.

"I'll bet he was a good soldier."

"He was the best and bravest soldier I ever knew," Hawke said.

Hannah beamed proudly. "I knew he would be," she said.

* * *

The sign in front of the building read: FELIX GILMORE, AT-TORNEY AT LAW. Gilmore stood as Joshua Creed came into his office.

"Mr. Creed," he said.

"I understand you have some information for me," Joshua Creed replied.

"I do indeed, sir," Gilmore said. "Have a seat and I'll show it to you."

Gilmore put a sign on his front door that read IN CON-FERENCE, then locked it and pulled the shade down before coming back to sit at his desk.

"You wanted to know about Mason Hawke," he said.

"Yes. What did you find out?"

"Quite a bit, actually," Gilmore said. "He is a piano player who has worked in saloons all over the West and—"

Creed laughed in loud guffaws. "A *piano* player?" he said. "Is that what you said? That Mason Hawke is a piano player?"

"Yes, and evidently he is quite good. According to the information I've been able to ascertain, he was a concert pianist before the war, playing before audiences, not only in the United States, but over in Europe as well."

"A piano player," Creed said, still chuckling.

"Evidently, when the war broke out he returned home to join his father's regiment."

"Let me guess. He played piano in the ballrooms of Washington."

"No, sir. In the first place, he fought for the South, not the North. And he fought quite well, frequently mentioned in the dispatches. In fact, it was during the war that he met Ian Macgregor. They are two of the very few members of their regiment who survived the entire war."

"Well, I appreciate all that, Gilmore," Creed said. "I was wondering what he was doing out here with Macgregor. Now I know he must've come to play piano for a birthday party," he added, laughing again.

Gilmore shook his head. "I wouldn't dismiss him that easily."

"Why not? What else would a piano player do?"

"It turns out that our Mr. Hawke is considerably more than a piano player. In fact, he is establishing quite a reputation as a pistoleer."

"What is a pistoleer?"

"Some people refer to such men as gunfighters," Gilmore said. "And from all the evidence I've been able to gather, Mason Hawke is an exceptionally skilled and deadly gunfighter."

Creed squinted his eyes at Gilmore. "How deadly?"

"I've not been able to determine the exact number," he said. "But I think a guess of twenty would not be too far off."

"Are you telling me he has killed twenty men?"

"I would say that is a conservative estimate, yes."

"If he has killed that many men, why isn't he in jail?"

"According to my sources, every man he has killed, he has faced. And, apparently, he has been on the right side of the law on every occasion. He has simply bested them all."

"I see," Creed said, less ebullient now. "Well, in your research, have you been able to determine why he is here?"

"I don't have any definitive evidence, but I would suggest that he is here to help his friend, Macgregor, in the confrontation between the sheep men and the cattlemen," Gilmore said.

"In other words, Macgregor has hired himself a gunfighter," Creed said.

"Exactly."

Creed drummed his fingers on the desk for a moment. "Well, now, a gunfighter. If that doesn't make Rosie sing."

"Mr. Creed, I can't warn you strongly enough," Gilmore said. "If, in your dispute with the sheep men, you engage in any physical confrontation, you will be doing so at your own risk. Like I told you, this man Mason Hawke is quite deadly."

"You aren't telling me to walk away from this, are you?" Creed said. He pointed back toward the prairie. "Those damn sheep are destroying the grass, don't you understand that? The open range has always been there for all of us to use. But when the sheep use it, they kill it."

"I can take care of that for you, but it's going to cost you," Gilmore suggested.

"I don't expect to use a lawyer for free," Creed said.

Gilmore shook his head. "I'm not talking about my fee. I'm talking about what we will have to pay Hodge Eckert."

"Eckert? From the government land office?"

"Yes."

"What has he got to do with it?"

"The open range is government land. Eckert is in charge of it. For a fee, we could convince him to get a court injunction that would prevent the sheep from using it."

"For a fee?" Creed said. Then he smiled. "You mean for a bribe, don't you?"

"No, not a bribe. If you pay a bribe, I could be charged with setting it up, and you could be charged with paying it. But if it is a fee, and the fee turns out to be illegal, only Eckert could be charged with wrongdoing."

Creed's smile grew broader. "I like the way you do things, Gilmore. Do you think the court will give us an injunction?"

"Yes. Since Eckert represents the government, that gives the government an interest in the case. At least until there is a hearing on the matter."

"Yeah? Can you guarantee that the hearing will rule in our favor?" Creed asked.

"No, of course I can't guarantee it," Gilmore said. "But it doesn't matter, because the injunction will be in effect until the hearing is actually held. And, with a little manipulation, we can put the hearing off indefinitely, thus giving the injunction the authority of law."

"How do you put off the hearing?"

Gilmore stroked his cheek. "Oh, if you have a skilled and motivated lawyer, there are many ways to accomplish this."

"Uh-huh," Creed said. "And you know where I might get this skilled and motivated lawyer?"

"Skilled I am, Mr. Creed," Gilmore said. "It is the motivation that you must deal with."

"Would five hundred dollars motivate you?" Creed asked.

Gilmore smiled broadly. "I think it would motivate me quite well," he promised.

"What about Eckert?"

"Oh, I doubt that his fee will be more than one hundred dollars."

"All right, come to the bank with me and I'll draw out the money," Creed said. "But I'm counting on you to get that injunction."

"You will have it within the week," Gilmore said confidently.

Some 130 miles away from King Hill, in the town of Eagle Rock, Clay Morgan was sitting at a table in a saloon, his back to the wall, playing a game of Solitaire. He didn't even look up when Sheriff Majors entered. Morgan had been in town for a week now, and though the sheriff had come into the saloon several times during that week, Majors had not appeared to take notice of him. Morgan knew that was because he was afraid. And that was good. As long as men were afraid of him, he would always have the edge.

He started to go back to his card game, then noticed something that caught his attention, something different.

Sheriff Majors was carrying a shotgun. There was also another man with him. And like Majors, the other man was wearing a start on his vest.

"Clay Morgan?" Sheriff Majors said.

Morgan felt all of his senses heighten. It was a familiar feeling, one that he always felt just before he killed.

He felt giddy, almost excited.

"You know who I am, Sheriff," Morgan said. "I've been sitting here at the same table for a week now, and you've seen me every day. Why the sudden interest?"

"This is Deputy Colmes from over at Squaw Creek."

"Squaw Creek? I was just there a few days ago," Morgan said. "Nice town you have there."

"Muley Thomas and Quint Weathers," Deputy Colmes said. "Do those names mean anything to you?"

"Yes."

"You killed them," the deputy said.

Morgan nodded. "As a matter of fact, I did."

"Good Lord, he's not even denying it," Majors said.

"They were a couple of horse thieves. I was serving a warrant."

"Turns out there was no court warrant on those boys," Deputy Colmes said.

"Oh? Ask Jack Yancey about that."

"Yancey is in jail. He's about to be tried for the murder

of his brother," Colmes said. "And for paying you to kill Muley Thomas and Quint Weathers."

Morgan went back to his card game. "Well, there you go," he said. "It looks like you got your man."

"All he did was pay you to do the job," Colmes said. "But when you come right down to it, you are the one who killed those two boys."

"Like I said, I had a warrant," Morgan said. "And whether it was real or not isn't my problem."

"Oh, but it is your problem," Colmes said. "I'm taking you back."

Morgan got up from the table then and stepped out to one side. He let his hand hang loosely by the pistol he had strapped at his side.

"No," Morgan said. "I don't think I want to go back."

Because he had been there for about a week now, the other patrons of the saloon had come to an uneasy acceptance of Morgan's presence. They had even come around to enjoying, in some macabre way, the fact that they were drinking with a man as notorious as Clay Morgan, realizing that this was something they would be able to tell their grandchildren years from now.

But it was now clear that Clay Morgan's peaceful stay in the little town of Eagle Rock was about to come to an end. Realizing that in all likelihood shooting was about to break out, the patrons of the saloon began moving out of the way.

"You don't have much choice, Morgan," Sheriff Majors said, emphasizing his comment with a little thrust of his shotgun.

"I see. You plannin' on helping him, are you?" Morgan asked.

"There's no helpin' to it," Sheriff Majors replied. "You're going to unbuckle your gun belt, then stick your hands out so we can put your wrists in cuffs."

Morgan said nothing in response, and the silence became palpable.

Sheriff Majors pointed the shotgun at Morgan and pulled back both hammers. They made a loud, double click in the room.

"I said, unbuckle your gun belt," Majors repeated.

Morgan shook his head. "I'm not going to make it easy for you, Sheriff."

The three men stared at each other for one long moment. Not only the three principals, but not one other person moved or talked, creating an eerie tableau, a scene that could have been reproduced in *Harper's Weekly*. The silence was broken only by the measured tick tock of the clock that hung on the wall by the piano.

Then, suddenly, Morgan drew his pistol, drawing and firing so fast that those who were watching were barely able to make the transition between seeing the pistol in his holster and the pistol being fired in his hand.

As soon as he saw Morgan start his draw, Sheriff Majors pulled the trigger on both barrels of his shotgun, but it was too late. By the time he reacted to what he was seeing, it was over. The double-aught charges from his shotgun tore large, jagged holes in the floor of the saloon, even as the heavy bullet from Morgan's gun was slamming into his heart.

Deputy Colmes was the most surprised man in the room. He had not even bothered to draw his pistol, believing that, since Majors had the drop on Morgan with a double-barreled shotgun, the situation was well in hand. He realized, too late, that he was wrong, because even as his pistol was clearing leather, Morgan's second shot crashed into his forehead. Colmes went down, dead before his body hit the floor.

"I reckon you fellas all saw this," Morgan said, his voice

as deadly calm as if he had done nothing more that spill his drink. He pointed to the two bodies. "They drew on me first."

"Of course they did. They was lawmen," someone said. "They was here to arrest you."

"Arrest me, or kill me?" Morgan said. "Did any of you see a warrant?"

"I didn't see no warrant," one of the saloon patrons said.

"Me neither. If you ask me, it was self-defense," one of the others said.

"Are you crazy, Michael? It can't be self-defense if they wasn't doin' no more than tryin' to arrest him."

"It was self-defense," Michael said again, staring pointedly at his challenger.

It suddenly dawned on the challenger what Michael was saying.

"Oh, uh, yes," he said. "Yes, now that I think about it, it *was* self-defense."

The others in the saloon, catching on quickly to Michael's lead, began agreeing that it surely was self-defense.

"I thought you boys would wind up seeing it my way," Morgan said. Returning to his table, he very casually finished his beer, then walked out the door, totally unconcerned that anyone would dare challenge him, even from behind.

Chapter 9

BACK AT THE MACGREGOR PLACE, THE ROOF HAD
been completed and Hawke was on the ground, getting
ready to lower Ian.

"All right," Ian called down. "I've got myself tied in.
Lower away."

Untying the rope, Hawke started letting it down hand
over hand. But Ian was barely below the edge of the roof
when the rope stopped.

"What is it?" Ian said. "Why aren't you lowering me?"

"Something's wrong," Hawke told him. "The rope has
gotten hung up. Can you get back on the roof?"

Ian reached for the edge of the roof but was unable to
grab hold.

"No," he called down.

Hawke jerked on the rope a few times but nothing happened.

"I see what it is," Ian called down.

"What?"

"The rope is off the pulley up here. Maybe you can flip it and get it back on."

Hawke flipped the rope several times, but without success.

"I can do it," Hannah said.

It wasn't until then that Hawke realized that both Hannah and her mother were standing just behind him, looking up anxiously.

"What?" Hawke asked.

"I can fix the rope," Hannah said. "I can climb up there and put it back on the pulley."

"No, Hannah, you can't," Cynthia said.

"Yes, I can," Hannah insisted, and ran to the ladder.

"Hannah, no!" Cynthia called, but even as she called out, her daughter was scrambling up the ladder.

"Darlin', you can't reach that from the ladder," Ian said. "Listen to your mama and go on back down."

"I can do it, Papa," Hannah insisted. She climbed onto the roof, then, lying on her stomach, inched out to the edge and strained for the rope. It was just beyond her reach.

"I told you, you can't get it," Ian said. "Now, go on back down before you fall."

Hannah stretched a little farther, then felt herself sliding off the roof.

"Hannah, no!" Ian shouted.

Hannah grabbed the stanchion and hung from it for a long moment.

"I can get it now," she said, and holding on with one hand, reached up and managed to loop the rope over the pulley.

"Ian, I'm going to let you down quickly," Hawke

shouted. "Then I'm coming up for Hannah. . . . Hannah, hold on!"

Hawke let Ian down very fast, slowing only as he reached the ground. Ian wound up lying on there, unable to get up.

"I'm going to have to leave you there for a moment," Hawke said. "Hannah, hang on, I'm coming!" he shouted.

"I can't hold on much longer!" Hannah called down, her voice quivering now, in exhaustion and fear.

Hawke climbed the ladder two rungs at a time. Then, following the same path as Hannah, he lay on his stomach and worked his way down to the edge of the roof, just above the stanchion.

"Hurry, Mr. Hawke," Hannah said, her voice showing the strain.

Hawke reached down to her, then wrapped his hand around her wrist.

"I've got you," he said. "Let go of the stanchion."

"I . . . I can't let go," she said. "I can't make my hands work."

"All right, I'll do all the work," Hawke said.

He began pulling her up, but because he could only get one hand on her, and because he was at an angle where he had no leverage, he was lifting dead weight.

Down on the ground, Cynthia had run over to stand beside Ian, and now they both looked up anxiously as slowly, laboriously, Hawke pulled Hannah back onto the roof. Finally he had her up high enough where she could help herself, and she scrambled the rest of the way up onto the roof.

"Oh, you saved my life!" she said, hugging him tightly.

Hawke chuckled. "I wouldn't say that," he said. "I probably just saved you from breaking a leg."

"Ha!" Ian shouted up from the ground. "Wouldn't that be great now, with two of us having broken legs?"

"Come on in the house, you three," Cynthia said with a sigh of relief. "I'll make some lemonade for you."

"Lemonade?" Ian said. "Well, now, that'll be good enough for Hannah, but Hawke and I might want something a bit stronger."

Cynthia chuckled. "I'll see what I can do," she promised.

Joshua Creed had planned to just glance through the newspaper then put it down, but an article on page three caught his attention.

There are few who would deny that the one they call "the Regulator," a man by the name of Clay Morgan, is skilled with a pistol. But the demonstration in Cade's Saloon in Eagle Rock on the fourth, instant, no doubt establishes Morgan as superior to such men as Wild Bill Hickock, Clay Allison, Temple Houston, and all others who have earned a reputation by the skill with which they handle a gun. It is said by credible witnesses that the noted gunman, when confronted by two lawmen, was able to draw his pistol quicker than thought, dispatching his two adversaries, Sheriff Major and Deputy Colmes.

According to those who were present at the time of the fateful confrontation, the two lawmen entered the saloon for the express purpose of placing Clay Morgan under arrest. Sheriff Morgan was holding a double-barrel shotgun, with both hammers cocked. It would require only a twitch of his finger to detonate the charges.

Morgan requested that a warrant be produced for his arrest, and when the sheriff admitted that he did not have one, Morgan refused arrest. Intent upon completing his arrest, even though he had no warrant, Sheriff Major attempted to pull the trigger on his shotgun. However, Clay Morgan, anticipating his adversary, drew his pistol and killed, not only Sheriff Major, but Deputy Colmes as well.

As it developed, the sheriff had no warrant for Clay Morgan's arrest, because, indeed, no warrant existed. The supposed crime that brought the sheriff and the deputy on their fatal mission to the saloon were the killings of Muley Thomas and Quint Weathers in the week previous. Unbeknownst to the two lawmen, further investigation of that killing had ruled it as justifiable homicide.

Clay Morgan, who owns and operates a private detective agency in Boise City, has been cleared of all charges, and is free to continue pursuing his business.

Laying the newspaper aside, Morgan walked over to his liquor cabinet, took out a bottle of bourbon and poured himself a drink. He smiled as the amber liquid burned its way down his throat. This might be just the answer he was looking for.

Leaving the train at Thurman City, Joshua Creed boarded the riverboat *Horatio* for the thirty mile run up the Boise River.

"What time will we reach Boise City?" he asked as he stepped aboard the small stern-wheeler.

The purser looked at his watch. "If we don't hit a sandbar or an underwater snag, we should be there by three o'clock this afternoon," he replied.

"What happens if we hit a sandbar or a snag?" Creed asked.

"Why, the boat blows up and we all die," the purser answered with a high-pitched laugh.

"And how soon before the next boat comes back?"

"Mister, this *is* the next boat," he said. "We'll make the run back tomorrow, leaving at nine o'clock. If you miss that one, you'll have to wait two more days."

"I'll make tomorrow's boat," Creed said.

Creed climbed the stairway up to the hurricane deck. Because it was a warm day, he chose to sit outside and found a place on a bench near the railing.

The pilot signaled for the engine to be put into reverse, and down on the boiler deck, the engineers responded. Steam boomed out of the steam relief pipe like the firing of a cannon. The wheel began spinning backward as the boat pulled away from the dock, then it turned, with the wheel going downriver and the bow pointing upriver. The engine lever was slipped to full forward and the wheel began spinning in the other direction until it caught hold, overcame the force of current, and started pushing the boat upstream.

The riverboat hit no sandbar or underwater snag, and as the purser had told him, they did indeed arrive in Boise City in three hours time. Now, Joshua Creed looked up at the sign hanging in front of the building that read: CLAY MORGAN DETECTIVE AGENCY. He pushed the door open and went inside. A young man was sitting at a desk, making entries into a ledger. Creed paused for a moment, a little taken back over the youth of the detective.

"May I help you?" the young man asked.

"Are you Clay Morgan?"

The young man smiled. "No, I'm just one of his assistants. Mr. Morgan is here though, would you like to speak to him?"

"Yes."

"May I tell him what it is about?"

"I would like to hire him," Creed said.

"And your name, sir?"

"Creed. Joshua Creed."

"Very good, Mr. Creed. Wait here for one moment."

The young man went through a door and disappeared into the back of the building. As Creed waited, he looked around the office and saw scores of wanted posters on the wall. At first he thought they were all active posters, and then he saw that there were inscriptions on each one of them.

KILLED IN IDAHO CITY
KILLED IN LARAMIE
KILLED IN CHEYENE
KILLED IN DENVER
KILLED IN FLAGSTAFF

Nearly every poster he saw had the same resolution. The wanted man had been killed.

"Mr. Creed?"

"Yes."

"Mr. Morgan will see you now. Please go in."

"Thanks."

Clay Morgan was standing when Creed went into his office, and because he was, Creed could see that he was a big man. Morgan rubbed his finger across the purple scar on his face, then pointed at a chair.

"Have a seat, Mr. Creed," he said. "I understand you want to hire me?"

"Yes."

"What kind of job do you have in mind?"

"I represent a consortium of cattle ranchers down in Alturas County," Creed said. "Recently, several sheep herders have moved into the Camas Prairie. They are turning their sheep loose on the open range and that is destroying the grass for cattle."

"What do you expect me to do?" Morgan asked.

"I want you to run them off."

"And how would I do that?"

"I don't know . . . whatever it takes, I suppose," Creed said. "Mr. Morgan, I may have been misinformed about you. And if so, I'm wasting your time and mine."

"What, exactly, were you told about me?" Morgan asked.

"I was told that you were very . . . efficient," Creed said, struggling for the word. He pointed to the outer room. "On the wall back there, you have posters of dozens, perhaps scores, of men who were wanted. And on nearly all of them you indicated that they were killed. Is that true? Were they killed?"

"Yes."

"Then you aren't afraid to take . . . extreme . . . measures," Creed said. He shook his head. "I don't know, I thought you were just the man I was looking for. Perhaps I'm wrong."

"Mr. Creed," Morgan replied, "I will take extreme measures when such measures are warranted. But I must have some legal justification. In the case of every man out there, I was covered by the law."

Creed smiled. "Oh, well if that's all you need, you've got it," he said.

"I have what?"

"Legal justification," Creed said. Reaching into his inside pocket, he pulled out a folded piece of paper.

"What is that?" Morgan asked.

"It is a court order, demanding that the sheep herders stay out of the open range area."

Morgan looked at the document for a moment, then smiled and nodded.

"Yes," he said. "Yes, this I can work with."

"Then you will work for us?"

"If the price is right," Morgan replied.

"I'm sure we can come together on the price," Creed said.

Chapter 10

WHILE WAITING FOR THE MEETING TO START, the visiting ranchers had gathered into conversational groupings to exchange pleasantries and information. When Creed said that the meeting was ready to start, the little groups broke up and everyone started looking for a place to sit.

When everyone was settled and quiet, Creed announced: "I called all of you together because we have a big problem on our hands. As I'm sure you know, the sheep herders pushed their sheep into the range last month. My son, Lonnie, and a few others rode out to see them and managed to . . . persuade . . . them to leave. I reckon you all know Lonnie." He pointed to the tall, slim young man leaning against the wall, chewing on a piece of rawhide. Lonnie barely nodded in recognition of his father's introduction.

A few of the ranchers, who had already heard the story as to how Lonnie persuaded the sheep herders, laughed.

"Joshua, I agree with you," Rome Carlisle said. Although Creed's ranch was the largest, Carlisle's wasn't far behind. "But the question I have is, what legal right do we have to keep them off the open range?"

"Rome, is that you talking or is it your son?" Jared Wilson asked.

Carlisle squinted at the man who had asked the question. "Just what are you talking about, Wilson?" he demanded.

"Everybody knows that Jesse is sweet on the little Macgregor girl," Wilson said. "Seems to me like someone should show that boy where his home range is."

"You leave my son out of this, Wilson," Carlisle said. "If a pretty girl has turned his head, well, he's only seventeen years old. It's no big thing, and it is certainly none of your business."

"Seems to me like it's all of our business if it colors how you feel about runnin' the sheep herders off."

"Don't get the wrong impression just because I want to know whether or not we've got the law on our side," Carlisle said. "I want them out of here, same as all of you do. But I don't want to wind up losing my ranch in some lawsuit, and I damn sure don't want to go to jail."

"Rome is right," Creed said.

"What? What do you mean, Rome is right?" Wilson asked. "Hell, Creed, I thought you were the one putting all this together."

Creed smiled broadly. "I am the one putting it together," he said. "But Rome is right saying he wants it to be legal." He held up a document. "What I have here is a court injunction, a legal order filed by Hodge Eckert on behalf of the United States government telling the sheep herders that they cannot use the open range."

"Good man, Josh!" Dalton Fenton said. "How did you get that?"

"I hired Lawyer Gilmore to present our case to the judge, and he issued the order."

"Well," Carlisle said. "That ought to be the end of it, then."

"Yes, well, you would think so, wouldn't you?" Creed replied. "But it's not going to be so easy. I don't believe the sheep herders are going to turn and run. In fact I think it is just the opposite. They are going to fight us."

"Well, how much of a fight can they actually make of it?" Dalt Fenton asked. "We average, what . . . at least ten cowboys apiece working for us? And there are twelve of us here. We have over one hundred men. What do they have? Twenty? Thirty, tops? And they are all Basque shepherds who won't put up much of a fight."

"Fenton is right," one of the other cowboys said. "Let them put up a fight. We've got a court order, that means we have the law on our side."

"It may not be as easy as all that," Creed said. "They've hired themselves some help."

"What are you talking about?" Carlisle asked.

"They've hired a man by the name of Mason Hawke. He's a gunfighter."

"Well, he can't be much of a gunfighter," Fenton said. "I've never heard of him."

"Sheriff Tilghman has," Creed said. "If you want to know more about him, just ask Tilghman."

"Where is he now? What does he look like?" Carlisle asked.

"He's staying with the Macgregors," Creed said. "And from what I've heard, he doesn't look very tough. But I suppose that's one of the things that makes him so dangerous. He is a piano player, and he dresses rather like a fop."

"Wait a minute, Pa," Lonnie said, speaking up. "You aren't talking about Fancy Dan, are you?"

"I am."

Lonnie laughed. "Don't worry about him. I'll handle him for you."

"Would that be the same Fancy Dan who took away your knife?" Jared Wilson asked, chuckling.

"He didn't take away my knife," Lonnie replied in quick anger.

"That ain't the way I heard it," Wilson replied.

"I was just havin' some fun with him," Lonnie said. "I was just playin' around . . . I didn't know he was goin' to take it so serious. He would've never taken the knife if it had been for real."

"If you say so, Lonnie," Wilson said.

Lonnie pointed at the cattleman. "Maybe you'd like to take my knife away from me," he said in a low, menacing voice.

The smile froze on Wilson's face, and he looked around at the other cattlemen to see if anyone would come to his aide. Not one returned his glance.

"Well, Mr. Wilson," Lonnie said, "shall we put it to the test?"

"Look here, Lonnie, I didn't mean nothin'," Wilson said. "I was just tellin' what I heard, is all. Whoever told me must've got it wrong."

"They did get it wrong," Lonnie said.

"Calm down, Lonnie," Creed said to his son. "Right now the important thing is to figure out what we are going to do about Mason Hawke."

"What do you have in mind, Josh?" Fenton asked.

"I'm glad you asked that," Creed replied. "Because I've already taken steps to handle the situation. I've hired Clay Morgan."

"Clay Morgan? Do you mean the man they call the Regulator?" Rome Carlisle asked.

"That's exactly who I mean."

"Oh, Joshua, I don't know," Carlisle said. "That's a little drastic, isn't it?"

"I don't think so," Creed replied. "I've always believed in fighting fire with fire. They hired a gunfighter, we've hired a gunfighter."

"What do you mean, we've hired him?" Carlisle asked. "Are you saying you've already done that?"

"Yes."

"How much is this costing us?"

"Fifteen hundred dollars."

"Fifteen hundred dollars?" Wilson said. He whistled. "Isn't that a little steep?"

"Not as steep as having all our cattle starve to death because of what the sheep have done to the grass," Creed said.

"I don't know. Fifteen hundred dollars is a lot of money."

"I'll pay one thousand myself," Creed said. "All you men will have to come up with is five hundred dollars."

"Well, hell, five hundred?" Fenton said, brightening. "Yeah, we can do that. I know we can."

"And another six hundred for the court injunction," Creed added.

Over at the Carlisle Ranch, half a dozen cowboys were busy branding calves. Johnny Carlisle, the owner's oldest son, was sitting on the upper rail of the corral, watching the operation. When one of the calves got loose, Jesse, his younger brother, leaped into the saddle and started after the calf at a gallop, twirling a lariat overhead.

"Run 'im down, Jesse, run 'im down!" one of the cowboys called.

Although he was only seventeen years old, Jesse was already known as the best rider on the ranch, and he showed it now, guiding the cow pony with varying pressure from his knees, moving with the horse as gracefully as if they shared the same blood and musculature.

Jesse threw the loop and it fell easily over the calf's head. Then, again only with pressure from his knees, he brought his pony to a dead stop, jerking the calf down when he reached the end of the rope.

The cowboys all applauded when Jesse came trotting back to the corral, the docile calf following alongside.

"Whooeee," Ralph Day said. "I tell you true, there ain't nobody in the whole territory of Idaho that can ride a horse like your little brother can."

"Yeah, he's pretty good with a horse, all right," Johnny said. He spit out a stream of tobacco, then wiped the residue off his chin. "But he ain't got the sense of a blind Chinaman when it comes to picking out his women."

"You're talking about that sheep herder's daughter?" Ralph asked.

"Yeah."

"Well, I cain't really say as I blame him much," Ralph said. "She's a looker, that girl."

"Yeah, well, if she was the Queen of Sheba herself, he ain't got no business messin' with her," Johnny said.

Jesse jumped down from his pony as a couple of the other cowboys threw the calf then held a branding iron to it. The flesh singed and smoked, the calf bawled, and then, with the Rocking C brand shining brightly, it got up and hurried off.

"Hey, Jesse," Ralph called. "It's Saturday. Several different ones of us is goin' into town after a mite. You want to go with us?"

"Yeah, I'll go," Jesse said.

"What are you goin' for?" Johnny teased. "You know Pa won't let you go to the saloon."

"The saloon isn't the only thing in town," Jesse said. "There's the Farmers and Ranchers Supply, there's a couple of nice restaurants, there's plenty of things to do in town."

"Wait till you're eighteen and Pa lets you go to the saloon," Johnny said. "Then you won't care a whit 'bout goin' to any of them other places."

"When are we goin'?"

"Real soon," Johnny said.

"Then I better get cleaned up."

Ralph laughed. "Cleaned up? Hah! How'd you become such a dandy? Ol' Johnny here don't care if he looks like a hog in a waller when he goes into town."

"Yeah, well, this is Saturday," Johnny said, "which means all the sheep herders will be comin' into town, and ol' Jesse there has him a sheep herder's daughter to get cleaned up for. Funny thing, she probably stinks so much of sheep shit, I don't know why he bothers."

"She doesn't stink," Jesse said.

"She doesn't stink," Johnny mocked.

"I don't like it when you talk like that, Johnny."

"You don't like it huh? Well, little brother, seein' as I got about four inches and thirty-five pounds on you, what are you goin' to do about it?"

"Nothing," Jesse admitted. "I was hoping to appeal to your good side, that's all."

Ralph laughed. "Good side? What makes you think Johnny has a good side?"

Playfully, Johnny hit Ralph on the shoulder. Then he looked back at Jesse.

"Little brother, one day it's going to get down to nut-cuttin' time," he said. "And when that happens, you're going to have to choose sides between your family and the sheep herders. I hope you do the right thing."

Chapter 11

BECAUSE THE FAMILIES LIVED SO FAR APART, SATurdays became great social events. The men would come into town and take care of their business at the blacksmith shop, or the hardware store, or whatever other store they needed, then gather at the saloon, called the Cattlemen's, but the management was neutral enough that the sheep herders didn't feel uneasy. This was especially true on Saturdays, when there were nearly as many sheep ranchers and their Basque hands as there were cattle ranchers and cowboys.

The women used these opportunities to take care of their shopping, then to visit, often gathering at Vi's Pies, a pie house run by the widow, Violetta McGraw. There, the women would talk about babies, exchange recipes, and discuss the latest dress patterns.

Tomas hitched up the wagon and Ian drove it, taking

himself, Cynthia, Hannah, and Hawke into town. His wheelchair was in back of the wagon.

Cynthia and Hannah were excited about going into town and they talked during the ride in about what they were going to buy.

"Mama, do you think Mr. Beasley will have any peanuts?" Hannah asked.

Cynthia laughed. "I should have never taught you how to make peanut brittle," she said. "If you had your way, you would make it just about every day."

"But you said you had it all the time you were growing up."

"I grew up in Georgia. We always had peanuts and molasses. Out here, everything has to come by train and it is much more expensive."

"But if he has some, will you buy them?"

"I don't know, honey, there are things we need more than peanuts."

"Buy some peanuts," Ian said. "I like peanut brittle myself."

Cynthia laughed. "I hate it when the two of you team up on me."

"The three of us," Hannah said.

"Three of you?"

"I know Mr. Hawke likes peanut brittle. So he probably wants some too."

"How do you know he likes it?"

"You said you knew him when you were a young girl," Hannah said. "That means he grew up in Georgia too. And if he grew up in Georgia, he likes peanut brittle."

"Well, I do like it," Hawke said, laughing. "But you aren't going to get me drawn into this."

Ian came into town, then stopped the wagon in front of the Farmers and Ranchers Supply Company. A sign out front read:

SUPPLIES FOR ALL MANKIND.
NO ORDER TOO LARGE TO FILL
NO ORDER TOO SMALL TO APPRECIATE

Ian pulled his watch out of his pocket and looked at it. "It's three o'clock," he said. "Will three hours be long enough for you ladies to get all of your gabbing done?"

"Hah!" Cynthia said. "Like you and the other men won't be gabbing away down at the saloon."

"Whatever gabbing we do can be done in three hours," Ian said. "What about you?"

"Three hours will be plenty of time," Cynthia answered.

"All right, then Hawke and I will meet you at the City Pig restaurant at six o'clock and we'll have supper before we start home."

"Oh, we get to eat out," Hannah said. "How wonderful!"

Stepping down onto the boardwalk, Cynthia and Hannah watched the wagon drive away before they went inside. In the store, a large sign advertised:

WE WILL HAVE BUNTING FOR THE FOURTH OF JULY

Jesse Carlisle was riding into King Hill with his brother and three other men from the Carlisle Ranch. Just as they came into town, Jesse saw Hannah Macgregor and her mother stepping down from the wagon in front of the Farmers and Ranchers Supply Company.

"You fellas go on," Jesse said. "I've got some business to attend to."

"Will you fellas listen to my little brother?" Johnny said. "He's got some . . . business . . . to attend to." Johnny set the word business apart, dragging it out mockingly. "We know what your business is." Johnny laughed. "You ever seen an old hound sniffin' around a bitch dog? That's the way you are, sniffin' around that little sheep girl."

"Ease up on the boy, Johnny," Ralph said. "If he's got 'im a girl he likes, what's the harm?"

"What's the harm?" Johnny asked. "I'll tell you what's the harm. It's a matter of family. Somebody needs to tell him that cows and sheep don't mix, and if Pa won't tell him, I will."

"Who I see or do not see is none of your concern, Johnny Carlisle," Jesse said. "Now you and the others go on about your business and leave me be."

"Baaaa," Johnny said, imitating a sheep as they rode away. The others laughed.

Jesse dismounted in front of the store, tied off his horse, then went in. He walked over to the gents' furnishings table and started looking at denim trousers. Across the store he saw Hannah and her mother.

Hannah had seen Jesse come in to the store, and she started moving, slowly, toward him, examining items on the notion table. She picked a spool of thread, then looked in his direction. He moved from the gents' furnishings to the feed and seed part of the store; she moved from the notions' table to the ladies ready-to-wear. He moved to the hardware department, and she moved to the carpet department. Finally, they met.

"Good day to you, Miss Macgregor," Jesse said.

"Good day to you, Mr. Carlisle," Hannah replied.

"I heard of your father's accident," Jesse said. "I hope he is doing well."

"It wasn't an accident, Jesse," Hannah said.

Jesse nodded. "I know it," he said. "Hannah, I hope you don't think that I, or my father, had anything to do with that."

"I don't think you had anything, directly, to do with it."

"What do you mean, directly?"

"It's this whole cattle and sheep thing," Hannah said. "That's what's behind it . . . that's what caused my father to be hurt."

Jesse sighed. "Hannah, why does your father have to raise sheep? Why couldn't he raise cattle like everyone else?"

"Why does it matter?" Hannah said. "Shouldn't he have the right to raise anything he wants?"

"It's just that . . . this is cattle country," Jesse said.

"Before it was cattle country, it was silver mining country, and before that it belonged to the Indians and buffalo," Hannah replied. "It's a big country, Jesse, plenty big enough for cattle and sheep."

"Cattle . . . sheep," Jesse said. "That shouldn't have anything to do with us."

Hannah made a big show of making a critical examination of Jesse.

"What are you doing?"

"You're right," she said. "It doesn't have anything to do with us. Despite what my papa thinks, you don't have horns and a tail."

Jesse laughed.

"May I help the young lady and gentleman?" a store clerk asked. "Are you interested in buying a coffin?"

"What?" Jesse asked.

Looking around them, Jesse and Hannah saw that, in this large store, they had met in the coffin department. They both laughed out loud.

"Really," the indignant clerk said. "I see nothing humorous about coffins."

"Hannah, dear, would you come help me for a moment?" Cynthia called.

"I've got to go," Hannah said.

"I'll see you around," Jesse said.

Returning to the gents' furnishings section, Jesse fingered through items as if he was interested in them. In fact, the only thing he was interested in was Hannah, and he watched her until she and her mother left the store.

After Cynthia and Hannah were dropped off, Ian and Hawke made a couple stops of their own. Leaving the wagon parked at the livery, Hawke got the wheelchair out of the back of the wagon and helped Ian into it. Then he pushed Ian along the board sidewalk, stopping in the hardware store, where Ian bought more nails to replace the ones he and Hawke had used in repairing the roof. He also bought a pair of work gloves.

"What do you say we go into the saloon and have a couple of drinks while we're waiting on the ladies?" Ian suggested.

"Sounds good to me," Hawke said.

When Hawke pushed Ian through the bat-wing doors, nearly all conversation stopped as the patrons of the saloon looked toward them. It was obvious that many had never even seen a wheelchair before, and if they had, it was certainly not in a saloon. The piano player had been grinding out a song, but he stopped in mid-bar as Hawke and Ian entered. The saloon fell into silence and everyone stared.

"Well, I don't normally get that kind of a salute when I walk into a place, gentlemen, but I appreciate it," Ian said jovially, and several in the saloon laughed.

"Push me up to the bar, Hawke, and let me buy you a beer," he said.

Hawke complied, but because Ian was sitting in the chair, he was too low for the bar. Also, the chair couldn't get close enough.

"Ian," Chris Dumey called. "Come over here and join us."

Chris was sitting at a table with Mark Patterson, Allen Cummings, and Ed Wright.

"Roll me over there, Hawke," Ian said, and, obligingly, Hawke pushed Ian to the table.

One of the girls came over to get the order and smiled flirtatiously at Hawke. Ian ordered two beers, then teased Hawke.

"Too bad he's with us," he said. "I do think that young woman was taking a shine to him."

"Ian, have you been married so long that you can't remember?" Hawke responded. "Women who work in places like this take a shine to everyone."

The others at the table laughed.

"Mr. Hawke?"

Looking up, Hawke saw that the piano player had come over to the table.

"Yes?"

"My name is Dexter Manley, Mr. Hawke. I'm the piano player here." He extended his hand and Hawke took it.

"It's very nice to meet you," Hawke said.

"No, sir, it's my pleasure to meet you," Manley replied. "I've heard of you, Mr. Hawke. I know that you are a real pianist . . . not just a piano player."

"I may have been at one time," Hawke said self-deprecatingly. "But now I just play the piano like you and thousands of others."

Manley shook his head and snorted what may have been a laugh. "No sir, there is no way you are like thousands of others," he said. "I understand that you played it the other day when I was gone."

"Yes," Hawke said. "I apologize for such presumption."

"No, sir, I'm only sorry that I missed it," Manley said.

"And I was just wondering if you would do me the honor of playing it now?"

"Well, I'm with my friends here and—"

"Play it, Hawke," Ian said.

"Yes, play it," Ed Wright said.

Hawke nodded. "All right," he agreed.

"Ladies and gents," Manley called out.

"What are you talkin' about? There ain't no ladies in here. There's just a couple of whores is all," a big man at one of the tables shouted. There was a smattering of nervous laughter in the saloon.

"That's Johnny Carlisle," Ian said under his breath. "He's Rome Carlisle's son, and nearly as big a trouble-maker as Lonnie Creed."

"Ladies and gents," Manley said again. "I am honored to introduce to you Mr. Mason Hawke. Mr. Hawke is a wonderful pianist, and I have presumed upon him to play a number for us." Manley looked over at Hawke and held out his hand. "Mr. Hawke?" he said.

"Thank you," Hawke said.

There was absolute silence as Hawke walked over to the piano. Except for the bartender, there was not one person there who had heard him play before. A few, however, had heard about his piano playing, as well as hearing how he had disarmed Lonnie Creed.

Hawke stood beside the piano for a moment before he sat down.

"This piece is especially for the ladies," he said pointedly, looking at Johnny Carlisle.

Hawke sat at the piano for a moment, then began playing "Lorena."

Though nobody knew quite what to expect when he first sat down, this was a song that all of them recognized. Many of them remembered it as a haunting ballad from the Civil

War, and a few, recalling those dark and dangerous days, and perhaps where they were then, turned their heads away in embarrassment as they wiped away a tear or two. When the song ended, Hawke stood and shook Dexter Manley's hand again, then returned to the table.

"You know," Ian remarked, "all the time we served together, I never heard you play the piano."

"Yes, well, the war didn't exactly put me in a playing mood," Hawke said.

"I understand," Ian replied. He lifted his glass of beer and looked at the others around the table. "Boys, I know that some of us fought for the North and some for the South. But we are all united in our memories. I wonder if you would all join me in a toast to all our friends, those that are separated from us now by distance, and those who gave their last full measure of devotion."

"Hear! Hear!" Wright said. Ed Wright had been a sergeant in the Pennsylvania 9th.

"I'd be glad to," Hawke said, touching his glass to Ian's.

Everyone at the table touched their glasses, then took a drink.

"Bartender!" Johnny Carlisle shouted then, his voice booming out over everything. "Bartender. How about getting the smell of sheep shit out of the saloon?"

The several conversations halted again as everyone looked first toward the big man who had issued the challenge, then toward the table of sheep herders to see what they were going to do.

"Bartender, did you hear me?" the big man called again. "I asked you to get the smell of sheep shit out of the saloon."

"Johnny, why don't you just calm down and enjoy your drink?" the bartender replied.

"Enjoy my drink? Now you just tell me how'm I going to enjoy my drink with the smell of sheep shit in here?"

"Honey, don't go causin' any trouble in here now," one of the bar girls said, coming over to put her hand on his shoulder. "We're having a peaceful afternoon here."

"Hey, whore, when I want to hear from you, I'll ask you," Johnny said. "Bartender, this is the last time I'm going to ask you. Either you get the smell of sheep shit out of here or I'll do it myself."

"Excuse me for a moment," Hawke said, getting up from the table.

"Hawke, let it go," Ian said, reaching for him. "This isn't your fight."

"Oh? I thought it was. Isn't that why I came?"

"Perhaps it is, but you need to pick your fights. I mean, look at the size of that son of a bitch. You don't want to get into a fight with him now."

"I'll be right back," Hawke said, holding up a finger.

"Oh, now, look here, will you?" Johnny said as Hawke walked toward him. "Are you going to fight me, Nancy Boy? Or are you going to play me another tune?"

Although Dexter Manley had gone back to the piano, he hadn't begun to play yet, and now, like everyone else in the saloon, his attention was riveted to the drama that was unfolding.

"I heard someone call you Johnny," Hawke said. "Is that your name?"

"Yeah, that's my name. What's it to you?" the big man replied.

"I was just wondering, Johnny, if you would like to join us at our table," Hawke said, gesturing with his hand at the table he was sharing with the others. "We seem to have gotten off on a wrong track here. Let me buy you a drink."

Hawke's voice was smooth and patronizing, though Johnny didn't recognize it as such.

"Ha!" he said. "You expect me to come over there where the smell of sheep shit is the strongest?"

"I thought you might join us, yes," Hawke said. He looked back toward the table and at the anxious look in the faces of the men there.

"Well, you thought wrong, Nancy Boy," Johnny said. He stood up. "Now, are you going to get out of here or am I going to have to throw you out? You, and that crippled-up piece of sheep shit that you come in here with?"

"Well, now, just to make sure that I understand what's going on here, I'm going to ask you right out. Are you challenging me to a fight, Johnny?" Hawke said. The modulation in his voice had not changed from the moment he came over to talk to Johnny. It was still controlled and patronizing.

"You might say that, Nancy Boy," Johnny said. "Only it ain't goin' to be much of a fight." Smiling at everyone who was looking at him, Johnny made a fist, then drew his arm back.

Suddenly, and without warning, Hawke drew his pistol and brought it crashing down on the belligerent young man's head. Even before Johnny collapsed on the floor, falling like a sack of potatoes, Hawke had his pistol back in his holster. It all happened so quickly that even though everyone in the saloon was watching, anticipating a fight, more than half of them never even saw what happened. One moment Johnny Carlisle was standing there, loud and belligerent, and the next moment he was lying unconscious on the floor.

Hawk looked at the others who had been sharing Johnny's table. All three of them had shocked expressions on their faces, as if they were unable to believe what they had just seen with their own eyes.

"Your friend was right," Hawke said to the other cowboys at the table. "He didn't put up much of a fight."

"Mister, you . . ." one of the cowboys started, pointing at Johnny, who lay crumpled on the floor.

"I what?"

"You didn't fight fair," the cowboy said.

"No, I didn't, did I?" Hawke replied, totally unperturbed by the cowboy's accusation. "But then, I don't consider fighting a game," he added. "So, when you get right down to it, I don't figure there's any need to be 'fair.'"

Hawke walked over to the piano player. "Mr. Manley, I know what it is like when someone interrupts you while you are playing. Please, forgive me, and go back to playing."

"Yes," Manley said, as shocked as everyone else by what he had just seen. "Yes, thank you."

As the music started again, Hawke returned to the table. Ian laughed when Hawke sat down.

"You do get to the root of things fast," he said.

Chapter 12

"THIS IS GOOD FOOD," IAN AGREED AS THEY SAT at the table in the City Pig restaurant later that day. "But it isn't as good as your cooking."

"Oh, I think it is very good, especially because I *didn't* cook it," Cynthia replied.

They were all laughing as Sheriff Tilghman stepped up to their table. Courteously, he removed his hat before he spoke.

"Ma'am, miss," he said to Cynthia and Hannah. Then he handed a piece of paper to Ian, "Mr. Macgregor, I've been asked by Mr. Eckert, of the Bureau of Land Management, to serve you this injunction."

"Injunction? Injunction about what?"

"It is a court order, sir, saying that neither you, nor any other sheep herder, can allow your sheep to graze on the open range."

"What?" Ian said, taking the piece of paper. "Sheriff, this isn't right! This isn't right at all! Open range means open range!"

"It's only until a court hearing," Sheriff Tilghman said. "You'll be able to make your case then."

Ian looked at the document and shook his head. "Sheriff, I always figured you for a fair man," he said. "I never would have thought you would side with the cattlemen."

"Mr. Macgregor, please understand that I am not siding with anybody," Tilghman replied resolutely. "As sheriff, I am an officer of the court, bound by that court to carry out all court orders. This here," he pointed to the document Ian was holding, "is a court order."

Macgregor ran his hand through his hair. "I'm sorry, you're right," he said. "It's just that the whole thing seems so unfair."

"If you want my opinion, Mr. Macgregor, I believe it is unfair as well. And I think that a court hearing will overturn this. But until such time, this court order has all the authority of law. While this is in effect, you cannot allow your livestock to graze on the open range."

"When is the court hearing?"

"Next Wednesday in Mountain Home," the sheriff said. "I would suggest you be there to give your side. I know the judge who will be hearing the case, and I know him to be a fair man."

"Oh, we'll be there, all right," Ian said. "You can count on that."

"Mr. Macgregor, I also have court orders for all the other sheep ranchers. Now, I could ride out to each of the ranches and deliver them personally, but they might come easier from you, so I am going to make you a temporary deputy."

"You're right, they probably would come easier from

me. All right, give them to me," Ian said. "I'll take care of them."

"Thanks. Raise your right hand." After Tilghman swore in Macgregor, he reached into his inside jacket pocket and took out the other documents, then handed them to Ian. "I'm sorry," he said. "Oh, and, enjoy your meal."

"'Enjoy your meal,' he says," Ian grumbled as the sheriff left the restaurant. "Now how are we supposed to enjoy the meal after he gives us something like this?"

Shortly after the sheriff left, Johnny and Jesse Carlisle came into the restaurant, accompanied by three of their cowboys. They were laughing and talking loudly until they saw Hawke and the Macgregor family sitting at a table near the back of the café.

"Well, now, lookie here, lookie here," Johnny said. "Jesse, damn me if I don't think the piano player is trying to beat your time with that little ol' sheep girl."

"Let it go, Johnny," Jesse said, reaching out to take his brother's arm.

Johnny jerked away from him.

"Is that right, piano man?" Johnny asked. "Are you trying to beat my little brother's time with the sheep girl?"

"Johnny, let 'em alone. Come on, let's have our dinner," Jesse called.

"Now, how can we have our dinner when this whole place smells like sheep shit?" Johnny said. He walked over to the table and looked down at Hawke, who was still sitting.

"Johnny, come back here, please," Jesse implored.

"Johnny, if you know what's good for you, you'll do what your brother says," Hawke said.

"Nah, I don't want to do why my brother says." Johnny had a broad, evil smile on his face. "What I want to do is break you up a little for the way you snuck up on me this afternoon."

"He didn't sneak up on you," Ian said. "What are you talking about? He walked right up to you."

"Yeah, then he drew his gun and hit me on the head," Johnny said, rubbing the bump on his head. "Well I don't intend to let him draw his gun this time."

"It's too late," Hawke said.

"What? What do you mean it's too late?" Johnny demanded.

"I've already drawn my gun," Hawke said. "I'm holding it under the table, and right now it's pointed at your belly."

"Ha! You think I believe that? I know—"

Johnny's sentence was interrupted by the deadly sound of a double click from under the table.

"You were saying?" Hawke said.

Johnny stood there a moment, taking hard, angry breaths. He pointed his finger at Hawke.

"One of these days I'm going to catch you without your gun," he said. "And when I do, mister, I'm going to teach you a lesson you won't forget."

Jesse had by now walked to the table, and he stepped between his brother and Hawke, turning his back to Hawke as he began gently pushing Johnny away.

"Johnny, please," he said, more urgently than before. "Let's go somewhere else to have our dinner."

Reluctantly, Johnny started to leave the café, but just as he reached the front door he turned and pointed back toward Hawke.

"We ain't finished, piano man," he shouted back. "Do you hear me? We ain't finished!"

Jesse pushed Johnny through the front door, then came back to the Macgregor table, holding his hat in his hand.

"Mr. Macgregor, Mrs. Macgregor, and . . . sir," he said. "I apologize for my brother. He always has been hotheaded."

"With an attitude like that, your brother is going to get himself killed someday," Ian said. "And if you ask me, you'd be the better off for it."

Jesse shook his head. "No, sir," he said. "I wouldn't want my brother killed." He turned and started toward the door. "No, sir," he said, continuing to shake his head. He looked back at the table one more time. "I wouldn't want my brother killed," he said pointedly.

"Mr. Hawke, would you really have shot Johnny?" Hannah asked after Jesse left.

"It would have been hard to shoot him with this," Hawke said, putting his hands above the table. He was holding a fork in one hand, and he flipped a couple of tines with his thumb, duplicating the click he had made earlier . . . the click that sounded exactly like a gun being cocked.

Ian laughed out loud. "Well, now," he said. "If that's not the beatenist thing I've ever seen." He resumed eating even as he was chuckling.

"I see that you are eating again," Cynthia said.

"Yeah, well, watching a cattleman get made a fool is good for your appetite," he said.

"Papa, they aren't all like Johnny," Cynthia said. "Jesse isn't like Johnny."

"Honey, Jesse seems like a nice enough boy, but when you come right down to it, they are all alike."

"No, they aren't all alike."

"Jesse's not going to go against his family, now, you know he isn't."

"Well, no, he won't go against his family, but that doesn't mean . . ." She let the sentence hang.

"That doesn't mean what?" Ian asked. "If it comes right down to his family against your family—and believe me, darlin', it's going to come to that—where will Jesse be?"

"I just don't think he's like that," Cynthia said.

As they drove home that evening, Ian and Cynthia made plans to have a potluck dinner. They decided to invite all of the sheep ranchers to tell them about the court order banning them from grazing on the open range, and to make plans to go to Mountain Home next week to defend their rights in court.

"Mama, we could make apple pies," Hannah suggested.

"We could," Cynthia said. "Oh, no, wait. We don't have any cinnamon."

"I'd be glad to go back to town tomorrow and get some cinnamon for you," Hawke said.

"Oh, Mason, I can't ask you to do that," Cynthia said. "Go all the way into town just for cinnamon?"

"You're going to make an apple pie, aren't you?"

"Well, yes."

Hawke smiled. "Then it's worth it."

The next morning, Joshua Creed was waiting outside the door of Gilmore's office even before the lawyer showed up.

"My," Gilmore said, smiling broadly as he got out his key to open the door. "You are here early."

"A lot of good this injunction is doing us," Creed said, thumping the document with his fingers. "The hearing is going to be next Wednesday. What if the judge rules against us?"

"He's not going to rule one way or the other," Gilmore said.

"What do you mean he isn't going to rule?"

"As your lawyer, I can get an automatic sixty day stay, just by saying that I haven't had time to prepare the case. Then I can appeal for another sixty day extension for cause, and at the end of that sixty days appeal for another extension." Gilmore laughed. "I can put this hearing off for a full year."

"What happens then?"

"Well, if I were you, I would act while I had the law on my side. Surely a year will be enough time for you to . . . rid yourself of the problem."

Creed smiled. "Yeah," he said. "Yeah, I think a year will be enough."

When Creed stepped outside, he saw Lonnie and two of his hands.

"Pa, if you don't mind, Poke, Jules, and me are goin' to stay in town for a while today," Lonnie said.

"Stay if you want to," Creed said. "But before you come home, stop by the post office and pick up our mail."

"All right," Lonnie said. "Come on, boys, the saloon is open."

"Sounds good to me," Poke said as he followed the boss's son.

"Dan!" Lonnie called as he pushed through the bat-wing doors. "Dan, a bottle of whiskey and three glasses."

"Whiskey?" the bartender replied. "Lonnie, it's not even noon yet. Wouldn't you rather have beer?"

"Whiskey," Lonnie said. "And where are the women? This place looks as dead as a tomb!"

"The girls all work late, Lonnie, you know that," Dan said. "They don't even come down until afternoon."

Lonnie took thirty dollars from his billfold and put it on the bar. "See if this won't bring them down early," he said. "If I'm going to sit around drinking, I want something better to look at than these two ugly galoots."

Jules and Poke laughed.

Dan looked at the money and nodded. "Mr. Creed, I'm sure this will bring them down," he said.

"Drink up, boys, drink up," Lonnie said, pouring

whiskey for them while they waited for the girls to come down.

"Lonnie, can I ask you a question?" Jules asked.

"Yeah, sure."

"Why are you being so nice to Poke 'n' me?"

"What do you mean? You're both my friends, aren't you?"

Jules shook his head. "We work for you, but we ain't exactly your friends. We're on different sides of the corral, if you get my meanin'."

Lonny nodded. He pulled a piece of rawhide from his pocket and began chewing on it. "Yeah, I get your meaning," he said. "But is there any law that says that just because you work for me we can't be friends?"

Jules shook his head. "Ain't no law like that that I know about," he said. "How 'bout you, Poke? You know any law like that?"

Poke shook his head as well. "No, I don't know no law like that," he said.

"All right, we're your friends and we work for you," Jules said. "So now, tell me, why you bein' so nice to us?"

Lonnie took the rawhide from his mouth, tossed the rest of his drink down, wiped his mouth with the back of his hand, then smiled.

"I've got a proposition for you boys," he said.

"What kind of a proposition?" Jules asked.

"I happen to know that the cattlemen are plannin' on payin' a gunman fifteen hundred dollars to kill the piano player."

"The piano player? You mean they want someone to kill ol' Dexter?" Jules asked.

"No, not him. It's that Fancy Dan piano player."

"Oh, you're talkin' about the one that took your knife away from you, aren't you?" Poke asked.

"He didn't—" Lonnie started, then, with a sigh, he just acquiesced. "Yeah, that's the one I'm talking about."

"Well, what I want to know is, why?" Poke asked. "Why would they pay so much money to someone just to kill a piano player?"

"Turns out he's more than just a piano player," Lonnie said. "He's supposed to be a pretty good gunfighter."

"What does all this have to do with us?" Jules asked.

"Simple. I figure if we kill him, we can claim that money."

"You want one of us to go up against this gunfighter?" Jules asked.

"Not one of us. All of us," Lonnie said. "It will be three to one."

"Maybe so, but if he's really any good, he could get one of us while we're gettin' him," Poke said.

"Not if we don't give him a chance to draw," Lonnie replied.

"Fifteen hundred dollars?" Poke said.

"Yes. That's five hundred dollars each. You boys have any idea what you could do with five hundred dollars?"

"Five hundred dollars," Jules repeated. He nodded. "All right, I'm willin' to go along if you two are. What about you, Poke?"

"Hell yes, I'm game," Poke said. "For five hundred dollars I'd shoot my own brother."

By the time Poke and Jules had made up their mind to go along with Lonnie's plan, the three girls who worked at the saloon were fully dressed and downstairs. They joined Lonnie and the other two at the table.

Half an hour after later, someone stepped in through the swinging bat-wing doors. As soon as he came in, he moved to one side and, with his back to the wall, perused the saloon.

"Well now," Lonnie said under his breath. "I didn't think opportunity would come so fast, but look who just come through the door. Looks like payday, boys."

"Hello, Mr. Hawke," Dan the bartender said. "It's a pleasure to see you again. What brings you into town this morning?"

"Cinnamon," Hawke said.

"I beg your pardon?"

Hawke chuckled and walked toward the bar. "Mrs. Macgregor is going to bake an apple pie, but she needed cinnamon, so I just bought four sticks."

"Is that him?" Jules asked under his breath. "Is that the one you're talkin' about?"

"That's him," Lonnie said.

"Damn, he sure don't look like no gunfighter. Look at them fancy clothes he's wearin'," Poke said.

"Yeah, he's a Fancy Dan, all right," Lonnie said. He chuckled. "And it looks like he's goin' to make this just real easy for us."

"How are we goin' to handle it?"

"Just follow my lead," Lonnie said. "When the time comes, I'll give you the word."

"Would you like a beer, Mr. Hawke?" Dan asked.

"Yes," Hawke replied. He glanced toward the piano. "And if you don't mind, I'd like to play the piano for a moment or two."

"Mind? Why in the world should I mind?" Dan said. "I've heard you play before. Of course you are welcome to play."

Hawke went over to the piano, sat down and stared at the keys for a moment, then began playing Chopin's Polonaise Number One.

"Oh, listen to that," one of the girls said. "Isn't that just the most beautiful thing you've ever heard?"

The three girls got up from the table and moved to a table closer to the piano.

"Wait a minute, where you girls goin'?" Jules called.

"Let 'em go," Lonnie said after they had moved. "If they're pawin' over him, it'll just make it easier for us. Get ready." He smiled broadly. "We've got him now."

Following Lonnie's lead, Jules and Poke stood up and walked over to stand directly behind Hawke. One of the girls happened to look back toward them then, and saw the three men drawing their guns.

"Piano man! Look out!" she screamed.

Hawke threw himself to the right, off the piano bench, drawing his pistol even as he was diving to the floor. All three of his would-be assailants fired at the same time, their bullets crashing into the piano.

Hawke fired twice, hitting both Jules and Poke. But before he could fire a third time, Lonnie screamed and threw his pistol down.

"No!" he shouted. "No! I'm unarmed!" Turning, he ran toward the door. "I'm unarmed!" he screamed again.

A moment later, as the gun smoke drifted upward, they heard the sound of hoofbeats as Lonnie galloped out of town.

"Are you all right, mister?" one of the girls asked as Hawke stood up.

"Yes," he said. "Yes, I'm fine. Thanks for the warning."

"What about them two?" Dan asked, pointing to the two bodies on the floor.

"They're dead," Hawke said without looking any closer.

"How do you know they're dead?" the barkeep asked.

"Because I didn't have time not to kill them," Hawke replied.

Chapter 13

"I THINK YOU OUGHT TO KNOW," HAWKE SAID
when he got back to the ranch with the cinnamon, "that I
had to kill two men today."

"Not Jesse!" Hannah gasped. "Oh, Mr. Hawke, please
tell me you didn't kill Jesse!"

"It wasn't Jesse," Hawke said. "It was a couple of men
who rode for Creed. The sheriff said their names were Poke
and Jules."

Ian nodded. "I know both of them." Poke Tilly and Jules
Carr. They were as evil as they come. What happened?"

Hawke told the story.

"You said the sheriff told you their names," Cynthia
said. "Are you in any trouble with the sheriff?"

Hawke shook his head. "No. There were four eyewit-
nesses and they all told the sheriff exactly what happened."

"Thank God for that. I'd hate to think I was the cause of

you coming out here only to wind up in jail. Or worse yet, getting yourself killed."

Hawke smiled. "I don't plan to do either," he said. "On the other hand, I did bring back the cinnamon sticks you asked for, so I do plan to enjoy some of the apple pie."

"Oh!" Cynthia said. "Yes, the potluck. Come, Hannah, help me. We have a million things to do before they all come."

The next day, the sheep ranchers began arriving by mid-morning; families in wagons, buckboards, and on horse-back. As they arrived, the men greeted the men, the children ran to join the other children, and the women went into the house carrying their own contribution to the potluck dinner . . . fried chicken, sourdough bread, baked beans, corn pudding, and an assortment of pies and cakes.

There were twelve families in Camas Valley who raised sheep, and all twelve families came. By noon the Mac-gregor place was overrun with children as they played various games of tag, mumblety-peg, and red rover. The older children, and even some of the men, participated in a spirited game of baseball, which ended only when Cynthia rang a dinner bell.

A long table had been constructed by placing boards over sawhorses, then covering it with several tablecloths. Chairs, kegs, stools, boxes, and even hastily constructed benches provided a place for all to sit.

After the meal, as the women worked to wash the dishes and clean up, Ian asked the men to meet with him in the parlor. When Hawke hung back, Ian specifically requested that he come as well.

"What's this all about, Ian?" Clem Douglass asked as the men began to gather. "I mean it was a good meal and a good opportunity for all of us to get together, but you've been pretty mysterious the whole day."

"I'll get to that in a minute," Ian said. "Most of you have met Hawke today, but I want to take this opportunity to formally introduce him." He pointed to the back of the room, where Hawke had taken what he thought was the most inconspicuous chair available.

"This is my friend Captain Mason Hawke," Ian said. "Captain Hawke and I served together during the war, and I never knew a better officer. My wife asked him—that is, I asked him—to come spend some time with us, to help us in our . . . difficulties . . . with the cattlemen."

One of the ranchers put up his hand.

"We're not formal here, Patterson. If you want to say something, just say it," Ian said.

"Mr. Hawke, I heard you was involved in a shootin' in town, yesterday," Mark Patterson said. "Is that true?"

"It is," Hawke replied.

"They said it was three to one, but you come out on top."

"What are you getting at, Mark?" Ian asked.

"Is this man you brought out here, this Mason Hawke . . . a professional gunfighter? Because if he is, I don't want no part of it."

"Why don't you ask him yourself?" Ian asked. "He's right here in the room with us."

"All right, I will ask him," Patterson said. He looked at Hawke and was met with a steady, unblinking gaze. Patterson blinked a couple of times, then cleared his throat before he spoke.

"Are you a professional gunfighter, Mr. Hawke?"

"I'm a professional pianist," Hawke replied.

"A piano player? Is that what you said? That you are a professional piano player?"

"No, sir. I said pianist," Hawke said. "There is a difference."

"All right, if you are a professional piano play . . . uh . . . pianist, like you say, how is it you were able to handle all three of 'em?"

"Only two," Hawke said. "The third one, Lonnie Creed, threw down his gun and ran away. I could have killed him, but I didn't."

"You didn't answer my question, Mr. Hawke. How could you do that if you weren't a professional gunfighter?"

"Mark Patterson, will you for heaven's sake just shut up?" Ed Wright said. "He handled three cattlemen all by himself, and he is on our side. You wanted to know if he is a professional gunfighter, he said no, and I believe him. Now let it be. Mr. Hawke, welcome to King Hill."

"Thank you," Hawke said.

"All right, gentlemen," Ian said, "if you will, we'll get on with the meeting."

Emerson Booker nodded. "I was wondering when we were going to get around to that," he said. "I didn't figure you invited us all here just to meet Mr. Hawke."

"No, I didn't," Ian said. He paused for a moment. "You might say that I'm doing the work of the sheriff, but I figured it would be better coming from me than him."

"What?" Patterson asked. "What are you talking about?"

"The other day, as I was having dinner at a café in town, the sheriff stopped by our dinner table, swore me in as a temporary deputy, and presented me with a court order. He also had one for each of you, which I took from him, agreeing to deliver them."

"What is the court order about?" Douglass asked.

"It says we cannot use the open range to graze our sheep," Ian replied.

"I knew Creed was a powerful man in these parts," Douglass said, "but I didn't know he was so powerful that he could control the judges."

Several others voiced their opinions as well.

"This isn't fair."

"We've got to do something about this."

"This will be the end of us."

"I should've stayed in Tennessee."

"Wait a minute," Emerson said. He had been looking at the injunction handed to him. "You know, fellas, this could turn out to be a good thing."

"A good thing? How can you call it a good thing?" George Butrum asked.

"Because this isn't actually a court order," Emerson said. "This is merely an injunction."

"What's the difference?" Mitch Arnold wanted to know.

"A court order is a permanent cease and desist order. An injunction is in effect only until a court hearing," Emerson explained.

"Yes, Sheriff Tilghman said the hearing is next Wednesday," Ian said. "I agree that we need to go to court to give our side of it, but I don't know why you say that might be a good thing."

"Think about it," Emerson said. "If we go to court and establish our case, then we will not only have the law on our side, we will have court authority for the law to enforce our right to be there. The way it is now, we are sort of in limbo, us against the cattlemen, with the law staying out of it."

"By golly, I think Emerson is right," Douglass said, striking his open palm with a fist. "If we get a court order saying that we have the right to be there, the cattlemen will be in the wrong, and the sheriff will have to protect us."

"All right," Chris Dumey said. "Suppose you are right. What's our next move?"

"Our next move is simple," Emerson replied. "As Ian

said, we have to go to Mountain Home to plead our case before the judge."

"We will need a lawyer for that, won't we?" Douglass asked.

"I suppose so."

"That's what I was afraid of," Douglass said with a sigh. "That means we're out of luck. Gilmore is the only lawyer in town, and he is in Creed's pocket."

"Do you actually have to have a lawyer?" Ian asked. "I mean it isn't against the law for us to plead our own case, is it?"

"No, it isn't against the law," Emerson said. "But you are always better off if you have a lawyer."

"What if, instead of a lawyer, one of us pleads the case for all of us?" Ian asked. "Who would have a greater interest in our success than one of us?"

"All right, but who would that be?" Dumey asked.

Ian pointed to Emerson. "Booker is more educated than any of us," he said. "And he certainly has an interest in our succeeding. I suggest he be the one to represent us."

Emerson held up his hands. "Oh, no," he said. "I'm not qualified to be a lawyer."

"You said yourself that you don't have to be a lawyer."

"I also said you would be better off if you had a lawyer."

"What if we had Gilmore represent us?" Ian asked. "Do you think we would be better off with him?"

"Gilmore? No, I wouldn't think so," Emerson said. "Like Clem said, Gilmore is in Creed's pocket."

"So you would be better than Gilmore?"

"For our purposes, yes, I suppose so, but Gilmore isn't the only lawyer in the territory."

"Maybe he isn't," Ian said. "But how do we know whether to trust any of the other lawyers out here? This was cattle country before we brought sheep here. How do we know that any lawyer out here can be trusted to give our side? No, sir. You are an educated man, Emerson, and you are a smart man. I vote for you to represent us."

"Me too," Douglass said.

"Me too," Dumey added.

"Let me hear it from the rest of you," Ian said. "Is there anyone here who would not want Emerson to represent us?"

Nobody spoke up.

"Emerson, it's up to you, now," Ian said. "Will you do it?"

"You're putting quite a burden on my shoulders," Emerson said.

"I know we are. But all we are asking is that you do the best you can."

Emerson sighed, then nodded. "All right," he said. "I'll do what I can."

"Good man," Douglass said, being the first one to stick out his hand. Then everyone else came up to him to shake Emerson's hand and express their confidence in him. Emerson accepted their best wishes but said very little in return.

"Gentlemen," Cynthia called, coming into the parlor. "Tomas has put down a wooden floor outside, and some of our Basque shepherds have agreed to play music. We can have a dance."

"A dance, is it?" Ian said. He laughed. "Do I look like I can dance?"

"Sure you can dance, Ian," Butrum said. "Why, you just grab hold of Cynthia and I'll push you around myself."

The others laughed as everyone filed out of the parlor.

Hawke had been listening to the conversation, but added

nothing to it. He was still sitting in the same chair in the back of the parlor.

Emerson didn't leave with the others. Instead, he walked over to the window and stood there a moment, just staring outside.

"You'll do fine," Hawke said.

Emerson jerked around at the sound of his' voice.

"I . . . I didn't realize you were still in the room," he said.

Hawke stood up and walked over to stand by Emerson. He pulled a golden case from his jacket pocket, opened it, and offered Emerson a cheroot.

"Thank you," Emerson said, taking it.

Hawke extracted one for himself, then lit both of the little brown cigars.

"I don't know what they expect of me," Emerson said as he took a puff.

"They expect you to do the best you can," Hawke said. "And I know that you will."

"But I'm not a lawyer."

"Emerson, you have intelligence and a sense of justice," Hawke said. "It has been my experience that that makes you more qualified than half the lawyers in the country."

Emerson thought about it for a moment, then chuckled. "That's a pretty sweeping indictment of lawyers," he said. "Accurate, perhaps, but sweeping."

"Ian tells me that you were a schoolteacher," Hawke said.

"Yes. I taught grammar and elocution at Sikeston High School in Sikeston, Missouri."

"Why did you quit?"

"My wife died, and all of a sudden everything I saw reminded me of her. I felt like I needed to get out of Sikeston, and I'd always wanted to try something a bit more adventurous than teaching school, so I came out here and went into sheep ranching."

"Why sheep instead of cattle?"

"I didn't just stumble into it, I looked into it," Emerson said. "It is strictly a matter of business. I didn't have very much money, and sheep ranching gives you a lot higher return on your investment. Because of that, you don't need as many sheep, or as much land, to make it profitable."

"Makes sense, I suppose," Hawke said. He smiled. "And if you were looking for adventure, you are certainly getting your share."

"I must admit that, of late, it has been considerably more adventurous than I anticipated."

From outside they heard the music of an accordion, flute, and, guitar.

"Sounds like the dance has started," Hawke said.

"Let's join the fun," Emerson suggested.

When Hawke went outside, he saw Tomas on the accordion, Josu playing a *txistu*, which was a flute, and Felipe and Xabier playing the *txalaparta*, an instrument made up of one or more thick wooden boards. The two men, using short wooden sticks about ten inches long and an inch and a half in diameter, hit the boards following a set of rules for rhythm. Each player had his own space of time that become longer or shorter during a session of playing, and this respect for the other player's space established the rhythm.

"Señor Hawke, I know you can play the piano, but can you play the accordion?" Tomas asked, holding out the accordion.

Hawke smiled and took the accordion. The other musicians looked on with amusement until Hawke said, "Gentlemen, shall we play 'Harnon'?"

Amazed that he would know one of their folk songs, they smiled and nodded in agreement as the music started.

When the song was finished, everyone applauded, and Hawke handed the accordion back to Tomas.

"*Mila esker, eskerrik asko*," Hawke said.

"*Ez horregatik*," Tomas said, beaming brightly. "You speak Euskara?"

Hawke laughed. "You have just heard my entire vocabulary," he said. "But I've always thought that if you are only going to learn a few words in any language, you can't go wrong with thank you."

"We are honored that you chose to play with us," Tomas said.

"I was honored to be invited," Hawke replied as he walked away.

"Mr. Hawke, will you dance with me?" Hannah asked, catching up to him.

"Of course, I'd love to dance with you," Hawke said, taking her hand and leading her out onto the floor.

True to their promise, one of the other men was pushing Ian's chair around in an approximation of his dancing with Cynthia.

"Hawke!" Ian called out after that was over. "Come dance with Cynthia. She deserves a real dance, not something where she's trying to keep her toes from being run over by my wheelchair."

"Well now, Ian, you've hurt my feelings," Butrum teased. "And here I thought you and I were dancing very well with her."

The others laughed, then the music started and Cynthia came into Hawke's arms.

As they danced, a strange thing happened. It was as if time and space were suspended. To those watching, they were no different from any other couple on the dance floor, but to Hawke and Cynthia there was no one else there. The playing children disappeared, the onlookers faded, the swirling dancers went away, even the music went silent. And although the dance only lasted a few minutes, the years had rolled away . . . there had been no war, there were no cow towns and saloons, no long trails through winter's cold and summer's heat, and no disillusionment in between. There was just this dance, this moment, and the two of them.

When the dance was over, Hawke and Cynthia stayed together a moment longer than necessary, though not so long as to arouse anyone's attention.

That night, Hawke was awakened from his light sleep by a sound, the barely perceptible rustle of a piece of hay being dislodged as someone stepped silently into the barn. Reaching over in the dark, his hand curled around the handle of his Colt .44 and he pulled it quietly from its holster.

Then he smelled the perfume . . . a woody fragrance with notes of vanilla and sandalwood, as well as the fruity scents of fresh citrus.

He put his pistol back in his holster.

"Cynthia?" he called, softly.

"Yes."

"Cynthia, what are you doing out here?"

"I . . . I . . . God help me, Mason, I don't know what I'm doing here."

He heard her move again, then saw her when she stepped into the patch of moonlight that spilled in through an open window. She was wearing a white-silk nightgown that was iridescent in the silver spill of the moon.

Hawke moved to her.

She was trembling.

"Is something wrong?" Hawke asked.

"Yes . . . no," she said.

"Cynthia, what are you doing out here?"

"I don't know. I shouldn't have come."

Cynthia normally wore her hair bound up, but tonight it was hanging free and some of it fell across her face. She brushed it back, and Hawke, realizing that this was the way she wore her hair when she went to bed, felt a sense of intimacy with her.

"It's just that, today, when we danced, I could have almost believed that you were Gordon," Cynthia said.

"I know," Hawke replied. "I had the same feeling with you, only it was Tamara."

"Forgive me," Cynthia said, "but I need this." She leaned into him, and he felt every curve and rise of her body as she put her arms around his neck and pulled his lips down to hers.

The kiss grew deeper, and lasted longer than either of them expected. Finally, Cynthia found the strength to break it off and pulled away from him.

"No," she said, her word almost a cry. "We can't. We mustn't."

Hawke said nothing.

Cynthia walked back to the window and stood there, looking outside for a long moment, a softly gleaming pearl in the night.

"I'm sorry," she said. "I had no right to come out here . . . I had no right to kiss you like that. Please, if you can, forgive me, and forget that this ever happened."

"Cynthia, you weren't kissing me," Hawke said. "You were kissing Gordon."

"Yes," she said. "Yes, that is true, isn't it?"

"So, you see, there is nothing to forgive or to forget."

Cynthia was quiet for a long moment before she spoke again.

"Mason, there is something I have to tell you." Her

words were strained, and Hawke knew that whatever she was about to tell him would be painful for her.

"Don't be nervous, Cynthia," he said. "There is nothing you could ever say or do that would disturb me."

"Hannah is . . ." She paused for a long moment, then drew a deep breath before starting again. "Mason, Hannah is your niece."

"What?" Hawke said, shocked by the revelation. "Gordon was her father? I had no idea."

"Neither did Gordon," Cynthia replied. "I didn't learn that I was pregnant until after he was killed."

"What about Hannah? Does she know who her father is?"

"No," Cynthia said. "And Mason, please, I don't want you to tell her."

Hawke ran his hand through his hair. "Cynthia," he said, "you are asking a lot of me. You do realize, don't you, that this makes Hannah my only living relative?"

She nodded. "Yes, I know that. That's why I told you. I didn't want you to go on thinking that you were completely alone in the world."

"But you haven't told her, and you won't." It was a declaration, not a question.

"Please try to understand, Mason," Cynthia said. "Ian has been her father since birth. He has been a very good father, and he is the only father she has ever known."

"Does Ian know that Gordon is Hannah's father?"

"Yes, he has known from the beginning."

Hawke sighed. "All right," he said. "I'll keep your secret."

Cynthia nodded, then turned and started to walk away. Just before she reached the door, she looked back over her shoulder.

"Thank you, Mason."

Hawke watched her walk back up the path toward the house. He didn't know if Cynthia had thanked him for agreeing not to tell Hannah or for not allowing her nocturnal visit to get out of hand. For his part, he was just thankful that he had found the strength to turn away.

Chapter 14

WHEN CYNTHIA RETURNED TO HER OWN BED-room, Ian's deep and steady breathing told her that he was sound asleep. She adjusted the covers over him, then climbed into bed, but didn't go to sleep.

Did she love this man beside her? It was a question she had asked herself often during the first two or three years of their marriage. She didn't think she could ever love him, or anyone, with the wild, unbridled passion with which she had loved Gordon Hawke. But over time she came to real-ize that her appreciation of Ian's kindness, of his accep-tance of Hannah as his own daughter, and of the fact that he was as good and decent a man as she had ever known, was in itself a deep and abiding love.

She moved closer to him and put her head on his shoul-der. Without waking, he put his arm around her and pulled her closer to him.

She lay there in the darkness, recalling how Ian had come into her life.

By the end of the war her father's plantation, Cypress Hill, was a plantation in name only. Only two house servants remained, staying behind when the other slaves left only because they were too old to go anywhere else. There was no one left to work the land, and there had not been a crop planted in two years. Cynthia's mother and sister were dead, and her father, Langston Rathbone, was, as neighbors liked to put it when speaking politely, "not himself." Her brother, Edward, was the last hope of reviving the plantation, and he was still away at war.

A few months before the war ended, Gordon Hawke had managed a rare leave and visited. The two of them spoke of the cruelty of a war that had kept them apart for so long, and they shared the emptiness each felt without the other. They made plans for their future, and, in an unguarded moment, took advantage of their precious moments together to give in to the love that drove them both.

Then, shortly after he returned to his regiment, Major Gordon Hawke was killed. He never learned that Cynthia was carrying his baby.

Cynthia was torn with conflicting emotions about her condition. On the one hand she knew that the baby would be a permanent connection to the man she loved with all her heart. On the other, she knew that if she gave birth out of wedlock, it would just about be the end of her father.

She was contemplating these things on the afternoon that she saw a creaky old wagon rolling slowly around the great curving driveway at the front of the house. She recognized the driver as Ian Macgregor, the sergeant major of the same regiment to which both her brother and Gordon belonged.

Before the war, Cynthia knew who Ian Macgregor was, for though he had worked a very small farm with his father and they were in different social circles, the Macgregor farm was adjacent to Cypress Hill. But she knew very little about Ian other than having often heard her father say what a good man he was. And that he'd been selected sergeant major by the men of the regiment was indicative of the respect everyone had for him.

But what was he doing here now? she wondered.

Ian climbed down from the wagon, then had to grab hold of the wagon seat to keep from falling. That was when Cynthia saw that he was bleeding.

"Sergeant Major!" she called, hurrying down from the porch. "You are wounded!"

"Ma'am," Ian said, pulling himself up. "I have the sad duty of bringing your brother home to you."

"My brother?"

Ian reached into the back of the wagon and pulled away a canvas sheet, disclosing the blue-white face of her brother's body.

"Oh, Edward!" Cynthia cried. "Oh, no, not you too. Not you too. Sergeant Major, where—" she started, and turning toward him, saw that he was lying on the ground, passed out.

"Willie!" she called loudly. "Doney! Come out here, please! I need help!"

The two house servants, a black man in his sixties and his wife, only slightly younger, hurried outside.

"Lord have mercy, Miss Cynthia," Doney said. "What have we here?"

"It's the sergeant major of Edward's regiment," Cynthia said. "He's badly hurt. Help me get him inside."

It wasn't until later that she realized she had said nothing at all about Edward's body lying in back of the wagon.

A few days later, when his son Edward was buried, Langston Rathbone suffered a seizure and died. He himself was buried three days afterward, and Cynthia suddenly found herself the sole remaining heir to Cypress Hill.

But Ian Macgregor knew none of this. For two weeks he was in and out of consciousness as he fought infection and fever.

During that time, he became very important to Cynthia. She had lost everyone, and learned, after her father died, that she was losing everything as well. The taxes had not been paid on Cypress Hill, and there was no money to pay them, so she was given thirty days to vacate. In a strange and disconnected way, Ian Macgregor remained the last connection with what had been her life, and she fought hard to pull him through his illness, praying, daily, for him to recover.

Then, one day, she walked in and saw Ian sitting up on the side of the bed. He was wrapped in a blanket, but there was color in his cheeks and his eyes were bright. It was obvious that his fever had been broken.

"Ian!" she said excitedly. "Oh, Ian, you are well!"

"Yes, ma'am, I reckon I am," he replied, his face showing surprise that she had addressed him by his first name. He didn't know that she had been calling him Ian for several days now as she had bathed him, changed his bed covers, and fed him. "Miss Rathbone, I can't seem to find my uniform."

"That's because I burned it," Cynthia said. "It was filthy and crawling with lice. Believe me, you would not have wanted to put it on again."

"But that means I don't have anything to wear now."

"Of course you do. Edward had an entire closet of clothes," Cynthia said. "They are all yours."

Ian shook his head. "No, ma'am, I wouldn't feel right about wearing Captain Rathbone's clothes."

"Don't be silly, Ian," Cynthia said. "Edward won't be needing them."

Ian was quiet for a moment, then nodded. "No, ma'am, I don't reckon he will."

"Ian, I would like to talk to you about something," she said.

"All right."

"You knew my fiancé, Gordon Hawke?"

"Yes, ma'am, of course I did. Major Hawke was a fine officer and a good man," Ian said.

Cynthia ran her hand through her hair, then took a deep breath. "I am carrying his baby."

"Well, congrat—" Ian started, then stopped as he realized the implications. "Oh. Oh, I see. You and Major Hawke were not married, were you?"

"No. So I'm sure you can see my dilemma."

"Yes, ma'am, I reckon I do."

"I need a husband, Ian," she said.

Ian nodded. "Yes, ma'am, I suppose you're right."

"Ian, don't you see what I'm getting at?" Cynthia asked in exasperation.

Ian shook his head. "No, ma'am, not exactly," he said.

"I'm asking you to marry me."

Ian gasped. "I beg your pardon, ma'am?"

"Oh, for heaven's sake, quit calling me ma'am. I need a husband, Ian. I want you to marry me."

"But ma—" Ian started, then stopped in mid-sentence. "Miss Rathbone," he said. "You don't want to marry me. You and I aren't from the same social class. You're rich and high-toned, and I've never been anything but a dirt farmer."

"I'm not rich anymore," Cynthia said. "And only you

would call me high-toned. Look, if you don't want to marry me, I'll understand. I don't have that much to offer a man, and I'm carrying another man's baby."

"Oh, don't get me wrong," Ian said. "I'd marry you in a heartbeat if . . ."

"If what?"

"If I thought you were really serious."

"I'm very serious, Ian," Cynthia said.

"Then, yes ma—" Ian started, and again stopped in mid-sentence. "What's your first name?"

"Cynthia. Cynthia Diane."

Ian smiled broadly. "I'd be proud to marry you, Cynthia Diane."

Cynthia lost the plantation and moved onto the small farm with Ian and his father. Hannah was born there, and they stayed on the farm until after the elder Macgregor, a Scotsman who never lost his heavy brogue, died. It wasn't until then that Ian told Cynthia of his long held dream of going west. Cynthia had no more ties to Merriweather County, so she went along willingly.

Ian's background was in farming, so when they first moved west, he tried to make a go of a farm in Nebraska. A two-year drought made it impossible. They spent some time in Colorado Springs, where Ian worked as a wagon driver for a local mining company while spending his spare time prospecting. That didn't work out either.

Then he read an article in the *Colorado Springs Gazette* extolling the virtues of sheep ranching. Ian had always been a frugal man, and he took the money he had left from selling his farm in Georgia, what he got after selling his farm in Nebraska, and what savings he had managed to accumulate, and bought land and sheep in Alturas County, Idaho.

For the first time since leaving Georgia, he found a successful venture, and within two years had already earned back his entire investment. It wasn't until his run-in with the cattle ranchers that there had been any cloud on the horizon.

Just before she went to sleep, Cynthia offered a little prayer that the hearing in Mountain Grove would come out all right.

Chapter 15

WHEN THE TRAIN STOPPED IN MOUNTAIN HOME, Hawke and Emerson Booker maneuvered Ian and his wheelchair down from the car. Then, hiring a buckboard, they went directly to the courthouse for the scheduled hearing. Felix Gilmore and another man were already in the courtroom when they rolled Ian in.

"Good day to you, gentlemen," Gilmore said, greeting them effusively.

"Mr. Gilmore," Ian replied.

"Well, I take it you are here for the hearing?" Gilmore said.

"We are," Ian said. "Are you representing Creed?"

"No, actually I'm representing this gentleman. I believe you know Hodge Eckert," Gilmore replied.

"You're the land management officer for the U.S. government, aren't you?" Ian asked.

"I am," Eckert said.

"I thought government officials were supposed to remain impartial. Tell me, Mr. Eckert, how did you wind up in Joshua Creed's pocket?"

"Sir, I'll have you know that I am acting on behalf of the U.S. government in this matter."

"Are you now?" Ian replied. "You think the folks in Washington are concerned about whether or not sheep can graze in Alturas County, Idaho?"

Eckert chuckled patronizingly. "Well, to be sure, they aren't interested in your sheep in particular," he said. "But this case will establish precedence, and not just for the territory, but for the entire country."

"Good," Ian said. "That means that after we win, open range will be open range."

"Assuming that your lawyer can carry the case for you," Gilmore interjected. "By the way, who is your lawyer? Ken Stripland?"

"Ken Stripland? No. What makes you think Mr. Stripland would be our lawyer?"

"Because he is the only lawyer in Mountain Home," Gilmore said. "And I doubt that you would want to pay all the expenses of bringing a lawyer here from Boise City."

"Well, you are right that we aren't going to bring a lawyer from Boise City," Ian said. "But you are wrong about Stripland. Mr. Booker will be pleading our case."

"Booker? Booker? Odd, I thought I knew all the lawyers in the territory, but I don't recognize that name. Is he new?"

"I'm Emerson Booker," Emerson said, speaking for the first time.

"You? But you are one of the sheep men, aren't you?"

"I am."

"Are you a lawyer as well, Mr. Booker? Are you qualified before the bar in the territory of Idaho?"

"I am not," Emerson said. "But as I am one of the interested parties, it isn't necessary for me to be qualified before the bar."

"You do understand, don't you, that as you are not qualified before the bar, you will not be able to represent all the sheep ranchers?"

"It won't be necessary for me to represent all of them," Emerson said. "I will represent myself. But it amounts to the same thing. If I win, it will open the range for everyone."

"Oh, you looked that up, did you?"

"I did."

"I'll give you credit for that. But I hope you did a lot more research. I think you will find that pleading a case before a judge isn't going to be all that easy." He looked at Ian. "Mr. Macgregor, as a friend of the court, so to speak, I would strongly recommend that you separate your case from Mr. Booker's and hire a real lawyer."

"I appreciate your advice, Mr. Gilmore," Ian said. "But I think I will go with Mr. Booker. And all the other sheep men have made the same decision."

Gilmore clucked his tongue and shook his head. "You are making it so easy for me," he said. "Very well, good luck to you."

"*Oyez, oyez, oyez.* This honorable court, Judge J. Maynard Dollar presiding, is now in session! All rise!" the bailiff called.

From a door in the front of the courtroom, Judge Dollar entered. He was a very rotund man, and the black robe he wore made him look even larger. Dollar was bald headed but wore a full beard. He sat down, then looked out over the courtroom. Except for the judge and the bailiff, there were only four other people present: Felix Gilmore, a lawyer whom he knew, and three men he did not recognize.

"Be seated," he said. "Bailiff, publish the reason for this hearing."

The bailiff was as small as the judge was large. He had a protruding Adam's apple, a hook nose, and eyes that appeared enlarged by his thick glasses.

"Your Honor, there comes now before this honorable court the Bureau of Land Management of the United States of America, for the purpose of requesting a court order to ban the grazing of all sheep on public land," the bailiff said, reading from the docket.

"Is plaintiff in court?"

"I am, Your Honor. I am Hodge Eckert, field office manager for the Bureau of Land Management."

"And you are acting on behalf of the United States?"

"Yes, Your Honor."

"Very well. Who is attorney for the plaintiff?"

Gilmore stood. "I am, Your Honor."

"Very good, Mr. Gilmore," Judge Dollar said. He looked toward the defendant's table. "And there is someone in opposition, I take it?"

"That would be me, Your Honor," Emerson said, standing. "My name is Emerson Booker."

"And you represent the sheep men?"

"Yes, Your Honor. I mean, no, Your Honor."

"Well, which is it? Yes or no?"

"No, Your Honor. I am not a qualified attorney, therefore, I can only represent myself. But I am a sheep rancher, and it is my assumption that if my sheep are granted the right to graze on open range, then all other sheep ranchers will be granted that same right."

"Your assumption is correct, Mr. Booker. Very well, you may represent yourself in this case."

"Your Honor, if it please the court," Gilmore said.

"Go ahead, Mr. Gilmore."

"I would like a sixty day continuance, Your Honor."

"A sixty day continuance? But we just got here," Judge Dollar said. "For what reason would you need a sixty day continuance?"

"Your Honor, under Article fifteen, paragraph five, of the Statutes of the Territory of—"

"Don't quote the statutes to me, Counselor," the judge said irritably. "Do you think I don't know the statutes?"

"I'm sorry, Your Honor, I wasn't implying that you didn't know them," Gilmore said. "I was just using that statute as my justification. I'm entitled to a sixty day stay in order to prepare my case."

"Mr. Gilmore, Mr. Booker isn't even a lawyer, and I would venture to say that he is ready to proceed with this hearing. Am I correct, Mr. Booker?"

"Yes, Your Honor, I am prepared to proceed with this hearing."

"Why is it, Mr. Gilmore, that you, an attorney who is certified by the bar, representing the entire United States of America, are not ready, whereas Mr. Booker, a layman, who represents only himself, is ready?"

"Your Honor, I would submit that Mr. Booker is not aware of all the complexities involved with trying a case. In fact, I believe that he is doing himself, and his cause, a disservice by attempting to act as his own counsel, and I have told him so."

Judge Dollar looked over at Emerson. "Mr. Booker, the counselor has a valid point. Trying a case in a court of law isn't something that should be undertaken by anyone who does not have the education or temperament to do so. Are you an educated man, Mr. Booker?"

"I am, Your Honor. I have a bachelor's degree from Washington University in St. Louis."

"You have a bachelor's degree, but you are raising sheep?" the judge asked in surprise.

"Yes, Your Honor."

"Forgive me, I had no right to question you about that. Very well, Mr. Booker, I am prepared to allow you to plead your own case."

"Thank you, Your Honor."

"Your Honor," Gilmore said. "About my request? I am entitled to a sixty day continuance without cause. And I ask for it now."

"Very well, I—"

"And, Your Honor," Gilmore said, holding his finger up and interrupting the judge.

"And? And what?"

"And to stay in effect, the current injunction that bars the sheep from grazing."

"Very well, continuance is granted."

"Your Honor, I object!" Booker shouted.

"You cannot object, Mr. Booker. Not even I can object. Mr. Gilmore is entitled, by statute, the continuance he requested."

"I'm not objecting to that, Your Honor," Booker said. "I'm objecting to his request that the injunction stay in effect. Don't you see what he is doing, Your Honor? By putting off the hearing, he has won a de facto judgment already."

"Your Honor, in granting the sixty day continuance, you automatically keep everything in effect," Gilmore said.

"I disagree, Your Honor," Booker said. "All the sixty day continuance has done is say that we will wait until that time to make the final judgment as to the utilization of the open range. Whether or not the injunction should stay in effect is another question entirely, and I propose that we settle that issue here and now."

"And you have a proposal as to how this question should be settled?"

"I do, Your Honor. I request that you dissolve the injunction and allow the sheep to graze on open land until such time as the case can be adjudicated."

"Your Honor, since you did not issue the injunction, I suggest that you do not have the authority to dissolve it," Gilmore said.

"Who did issue the injunction?" Judge Dollar asked.

"His Honor, Jeremiah Briggs, issued the injunction."

Judge Dollar smiled. "I'm sure you don't know this, as it just happened yesterday, but Jeremiah Briggs has left the bench. His entire case load has been turned over to me. Therefore I do have the authority to dissolve this injunction if I see fit to do so."

"But, Your Honor, we can't argue this now," Gilmore said. "This comes under the umbrella of the sixty day continuance."

"No, Mr. Gilmore, in the case of the injunction, I do not believe it does," Judge Dollar said. "I will hear arguments."

"Your Honor, my argument to keep the injunction in effect would be the same argument I would use to have a court order issued to permanently bar the sheep from grazing there. What you are asking me to do is plead my case now."

"I do not agree," Judge Dollar said. "I will hear arguments as to why I should vacate this injunction. Mr. Booker, you may continue."

"Your Honor, the premise that the cattlemen used to get the injunction is that the sheep crop the grass so low that it will not grow back. Their argument is that by allowing sheep to graze on the open range, what is now grassland will be turned into desert. We know from the

Bible that they have been raising sheep in the Holy Land for over two thousand years without degrading the pastureland.

"On the contrary, many years of mixed-species grazing in Europe has proven to be very beneficial for pastureland. Cattle prefer grass over other types of plants and are less selective when grazing than sheep. Sheep are much more likely to eat broad leaf weeds. Therefore, grazing cattle and sheep together on a diverse pasture will result in all types of plants being eaten, thus controlling weeds and brush, while yielding more new grass growth per acre."

Emerson sat down and Judge Dollar looked over at Gilmore.

"Your rebuttal, Mr. Gilmore?"

"My rebuttal is that what Mr. Booker said simply isn't true," Gilmore said. "We've experienced the effects of sheep and cattle grazing on the same land and the result has been disastrous."

"Do you have any empirical proof of that, Mr. Gilmore?"

"Your Honor, gathering that specific evidence is what I intend to do during the sixty day continuance."

"Fine. You gather that evidence," Judge Dollar said. He turned to Emerson. "In the meantime, Mr. Booker, I believe that you have raised a valid point. Until such time as the plaintiff can prove their allegation that mixed breed grazing is harmful, I will dissolve the injunction and allow open range to be just that . . . open range."

"And, Your Honor, if it please the court," Emerson added. "Would you direct the sheriff to enforce our right to let the sheep graze on open range?"

"Your Honor, if I may?" Gilmore said, speaking quickly.

"Go ahead, Mr. Gilmore."

"If you dissolve the injunction, then the situation returns to status quo. To have the sheriff specifically enforce the right of the sheep to graze in the open range gives the false impression that sheep grazing is not only allowed, but is in fact encouraged by the law."

The judge stroked his beard for a moment. "Mr. Gilmore, that is a rather convoluted piece of logic," he said. "But, in a convoluted way, I can see the validity of it. I believe you may be right. Having the sheriff enforce the right of the sheep to graze may give the impression that the government is supporting the concept of sheep grazing on open land, perhaps even to the exclusion of all other livestock."

Smiling, Gilmore sat back down.

"This court will reconvene sixty days from today's date in order to hear the case as to whether or not the 'sheep may safely graze.' In the meantime, the injunction is dissolved. Court is adjourned."

As everyone was preparing to leave, the judge stepped over to the table where Emerson, Ian, and Hawke were getting their material together.

"Mr. Booker, my congratulations, sir, on the skillful handling of your case," the judge said.

"Thank you, Your Honor."

"And, Mr. Hawke, I hope you took notice of my little reference to Johann Sebastian Bach with the 'sheep may safely graze'. You *are* Mason Hawke, are you not?"

"Yes," Hawke said.

"I thought so. A couple of years ago I took a train out of Chicago. I believe you had been hired by the railroad to play the piano on that train, and I was very pleasantly surprised at how beautifully you played. That was you, wasn't it?"

"Yes, that was me."

"Are you still playing the piano?"

"Yes, I am."

"Good, good, you have a very rare talent, sir. Hold on to it. But I'm confused. What are you doing here, with these men? Are you now raising sheep?"

"No," Hawke said. "Mr. Macgregor here is an old friend of long standing. I'm visiting him."

"Yes, well, gentlemen, I will see you again in sixty days. Good luck to you."

"Thank you, Your Honor," Emerson said.

At the plaintiff's table, Gilmore was making haste to leave.

"We can't leave yet," Eckert said.

"Why not?"

"I haven't been officially served with the papers to dissolve the injunction."

"Exactly," Gilmore said.

"We need to wait for them."

"If we leave without them, what will happen?"

"They will be sent to me by registered mail."

"And if you don't pick up that mail?"

Eckert looked confused. "Why wouldn't I pick up the mail?" he asked.

"Think, Eckert. Why would it be sent to you by registered mail?"

"Because I will have to sign for it?"

"Because?" Gilmore continued.

"Because until I have signed for it, there is no proof that—" Eckert stopped in mid-sentence. "There is no proof that I received it."

"Precisely," Gilmore said. "And until there is proof that you received the order dissolving the injunction, the old injunction is still in effect."

"Ah, but that won't do any good," Eckert said. "If I don't sign for it, the judge will just send the papers to me by courier."

"Yes, but that's not going to happen tomorrow, is it?"

"No, I guess not," Eckert said.

"Right now, all we need is a little time."

Chapter 16

~

"I THOUGHT YOU SAID WE WOULD HAVE A SIXTY day delay," Creed said angrily. "We are worse off now than we were when you went to Mountain Home. At least then we had a court injunction saying they couldn't use the open range."

"You have nothing to worry about," Gilmore said.

"What do you mean I have nothing to worry about? Did the judge or did the judge not rescind the injunction?"

Gilmore smiled. "That's just it," he said.

"What's just it?"

"You don't know if the injunction was rescinded or not."

"You aren't making sense," Creed said. "Didn't you just tell me that it had been?"

"Yes, I told you," Gilmore said. "But I'm not the court."

"You're not the court? What is that supposed to mean?"

"The injunction was vacated by verbal decree only. We left before the order dissolving the injunction could be written and signed by the judge. As of right now, Eckert is still operating under the injunction that bars the sheep from grazing."

"When is he going to be served?"

"At least thirty days, perhaps longer," Gilmore said. "And even then, it won't have any immediate effect on you."

"Why not?"

"Because I also got the judge to agree that the sheriff will not enforce the sheep ranchers' right to graze in the open range. As far as you and the other cattlemen are concerned, you still have the right to graze your livestock on the open range, and, to the best of your knowledge, the sheep ranchers still cannot."

Creed smiled. "That's good to know," he said. "That's very good to know."

Hawke had just finished shaving and was tossing his shaving water out when Hannah came into the barn. At first she didn't see him, and he watched her as she began saddling her horse. Now that he knew she was Gordon's daughter, he could see some of his brother in her. He could see some of his mother as well. What a wonderful gift Cynthia had given him when she told that the girl was his niece.

"Good morning, Hannah," he said.

"Oh, Mr. Hawke," she replied, jumping at the sound of his voice. "You startled me."

"I'm sorry, I didn't mean to."

Hannah smiled. "Oh, it's my fault, I know you are staying out here. There is no reason why I should have been surprised."

"Can I help you saddle your horse?"

"Oh, I think Lancelot would be confused if anyone but I saddled him."

"Lancelot." Hawke chuckled. "That's a lot of name for a horse."

"Mr. Booker gave me a book about King Arthur and I had just finished reading it when Papa gave me this horse. Lancelot was barely more than a colt then."

"Well, he is a fine figure of a horse," Hawke said. "As is fitting for a beautiful young woman to ride."

Hannah smiled and blushed. "You are embarrassing me, Mr. Hawke."

"Never be embarrassed about the gifts God gave you," Hawke said.

"You mean, like the gift God gave you to play the piano?"

"I suppose my being able to play the piano is a gift," Hawke said. "But it can also be a curse."

"A curse? Oh, but how could that be? Surely you take as much joy from playing as others do from listening."

"It's a curse because it reminds me of—" Hawke started, then abruptly stopped. How could he explain to this beautiful, innocent young girl that he had lost his soul? He laughed self-consciously. "Never mind," he said. "However I may have squandered the gift is my own fault. Have a nice ride."

"Thank you," Hannah said as she mounted Lancelot.

Hawke watched her ride away before he went back into the tack room of the barn, where he was staying.

Meanwhile Hannah rode away from the main house and ranch compound toward a place she had discovered some six years ago, when she was ten. She called her secret hideaway Cypress Hill, after the stories she had heard her mother tell of the plantation where she was raised. It was actually a grassy glade at the extreme edge of the Macgregor ranch, a high escarpment that guarded the north end of the ranch.

In fact, Cypress Hill, as she called it, had no cypress trees, but it did have a mixture of pine and deciduous trees that offered green all year, while also providing a painter's palette of color in the spring when the dogwoods and redbud trees bloomed, and again in the fall when the leaves changed. In addition the meadow itself was blanketed with wildflowers of every hue and description. The tranquility and beauty of the place had been her primary attraction, but she also liked the idea of having a hideaway, some place she could go to when she wanted to be alone.

Hannah ground-staked Lancelot then walked over to sit on a large, flat rock. She had discovered the rock on the first day she came up here. It was worn smooth on top, as if people had been coming here for hundreds of years, and she imagined Indians of long ago stopping here to rest.

Of course, now there was another reason why she liked to come up to Cypress Hill. And when she heard the low, warbling whistle, she felt her heart leap in her chest.

"Jesse? Jesse, is that you?"

"'But, soft! What light through yonder window breaks?'" Jesse called. She could hear him, but not yet see him. "'It is the east, and Juliet is the sun. Arise, fair sun, and kill the envious moon, who is already sick and pale with grief.'"

"'Oh Romeo, Romeo!'" Hannah called back. "'Wherefore art thou Romeo? Deny thy father and refuse thy name;

or, if thou wilt not, be but sworn my love, And I'll no longer be a Capulet.'"

Jesse appeared at the top of the hill then, leading his horse. Hannah rushed to him and they kissed.

"I didn't think I was going to make it this morning," he said. "Mr. Creed has called a meeting for all the cattlemen, and Pa wanted Johnny and me to go as well."

"How did you get away?"

"I told him there were some calves loose in the west pasture and I was going to bring them back." Jesse sighed. "This business between the cattlemen and the sheep herders is getting worse every day."

"I don't think it will last much longer," Hannah said.

"Oh? Why? Is your pa going to sell his sheep and start raising cattle?"

Hannah laughed. "No, silly."

"Then what makes you think it's going to be over soon?"

"Yesterday, Pa and Mr. Hawke and Mr. Booker went to Mountain Home to go to court. The judge lifted the injunction, so the sheep can graze in the open range. And now that this has been settled by the court, I think it will all be over."

"So that's what he was talking about," Jesse said, stroking his chin.

"What?"

"Lonnie is the one who came to tell us about the meeting. He said there had been some new developments, but he didn't say what it was."

"I'm sure that's what it was," Hannah said. She smiled broadly. "So, don't you see? It's all over now."

Jesse shook his head. "No," he said. "No, it's not over. In fact, it might be worse."

"Why would you say that?"

"The cattlemen have hired Clay Morgan to protect our interests."

"Clay Morgan? Who is Clay Morgan?"

"I can't believe you have never heard of him," Jesse said. "Why, he is one of most famous gunfighters ever. They call him the Regulator."

"I don't understand. Why would the cattlemen hire a gunfighter?"

"Why, to go against the gunfighter your pa hired," Jesse said.

"What?" Hannah asked, her face registering her surprise. "Are you saying Pa hired a gunfighter? Who are you talking about?"

"Mason Hawke."

Hannah laughed.

"What are you laughing at?"

"You," she said. "Mr. Hawke isn't a gunfighter. He is a pianist. Wherever did you get such an idea?"

"He's not a gunfighter, huh? How else do you explain what happened in town the other day? He killed Poke Tilly and Jules Carr. Or haven't you heard about that?"

"Yes, I heard about it," Hannah said. "When he came back to the house, he told us what happened. But he said it was self-defense."

"Oh, it was self-defense, all right," Jesse said. "Lonnie, Poke, and Jules all three drew on him."

"Three? Three to one?" Hannah said. "Well, if even you admit that it was self-defense, then you can't blame him for killing them."

"I don't blame him," Jesse said. "But don't you see? The fact that all three drew against him but he still beat them proves my point. Your Mr. Hawke is almost as famous a gunfighter as Clay Morgan. According to Sheriff Tilghman, Hawke has killed over twenty men."

"What about Lonnie? You said Lonnie Creed drew on him as well, but he didn't kill Lonnie, did he?"

Jesse chuckled. "No. And from what I heard, Lonnie threw his gun down and ran. I don't mind telling you, I would like to have seen that. Lonnie is so full of himself, I would like to see him get his comeuppance."

"If Mr. Hawke really was a gunfighter, wouldn't he have killed Lonnie too?"

"I don't know," Jesse admitted. "Maybe. The point is, Hannah, ever since your pa hired Hawke, matters have gotten worse."

"Pa didn't hire Mr. Hawke. Mr. Hawke is an old friend of my mother and father. He grew up on a plantation next to my mother, and he and my father served together in the same regiment. He just came out here on a visit."

"It was a mighty convenient visit, wouldn't you say? To have a famous gunfighter show up at just this time?"

"So, you're chasin' down calves in the west pasture, are you?" a loud, chiding voice said.

Startled, Hannah and Jesse looked toward the sound and saw Jesse's brother, Johnny, coming toward them.

"Johnny! What are you doing here?" Jesse asked.

Johnny looked around the small glade. "So, this is your secret place, huh? I've been wonderin' where it was. What other secrets are you keepin'? Hah! No tellin' what I would have caught the two of you doin' if I had just been a little later."

"I asked you what you are doing here," Jesse repeated.

"Pa sent me after you," Johnny said. "I knew you wasn't goin' after calves, so I tracked you here."

"You tracked me here?"

"If you don't want to be tracked, don't ride a horse with a bar shoe," he said.

"What does Pa want with me?"

"He's your pa. What difference does it make why he wants you?"

"If it's to go to the meeting over at the Creed place, I'm not interested."

"Boy," Johnny said sternly. "I think it's about time you learned that you are a cattleman, not a sheep herder."

"I know that I'm a cattleman," Jesse replied.

"Do you? Or does this little girl have you counting sheep?" Johnny laughed. "Counting sheep," he said. "That's a good one."

"Yeah, it's hilarious," Jesse said sarcastically.

"Look, you're wastin' your time sniffin' around this little ol' girl anyway," his brother said. "You know you ain't goin' to marry no sheep herder's daughter. And as for anythin' else, why, the soiled doves at the Cattleman's Saloon are a lot easier to get to. You want my advice, you'll tell this girl good-bye now."

Jesse sighed, then took Hannah's hands in his. "I've got to go," he said.

"No," Hannah replied. "No, you don't have to go. You could stay with us. I know Pa would let you."

Jesse shook his head. "No," he said. "No, I can't do that. You are asking me to turn my back on my family, on who I am. I'm sorry. I can't do that. But," he said brightly, "you could come with me."

"And do what?"

"We could get married," Jesse suggested.

"Hah!" Johnny said, laughing out loud. "You're seventeen, and she's what, sixteen? I can see the two of you getting married." He laughed again.

"Johnny's right," Hannah said. "We can't get married. Not now, not yet. We're much too young."

"Then what is to become of us?" Jesse asked.

"I don't know," Hannah said as her eyes welled with tears. "God help me, I don't know."

Jesse started toward his horse but stopped and came back. Putting his arms around Hannah, he pulled her to him and kissed her full on the lips. She returned the kiss, feeling both the sweetness and the bitterness of this impossible situation.

"Will you be going into town for the Fourth of July celebration?" he asked her.

"Fourth of July? That's three weeks away."

"Will you be there for it?"

"Yes," Hannah said. "Yes, I'll be there."

Jesse smiled at her. "I will too," he said.

"Come on, let's go," his brother called impatiently.

Jesse stepped away from Hannah, gave her one long, heartrending look, then turned and went quickly to his horse. Hannah didn't weep out loud, but she did wipe away the tears as she saw them ride away.

"So, what does that mean, exactly?" Jared Wilson asked.

Wilson, Fenton, Rome Carlisle, and a handful of other ranchers had gathered yet again at Joshua Creed's house to discuss the latest events concerning their ongoing dispute with the sheep herders. Creed had just told them that the judge had set aside the injunction.

"Actually, it doesn't mean anything," Creed replied. "You haven't been told."

"What do you mean I haven't been told? You just told me," Wilson said.

"Do I work for the Bureau of Land Management?" Creed asked.

"No."

"Then until Hodge Eckert or another field manager of the Bureau of Land Management tells you otherwise, the injunction is still in effect, and we still have the authority to keep the sheep off the range."

"Are you sure about that, Creed?" Carlisle asked.

"Yeah, I'm sure. Eckert left Mountain Home before he could be served. And until such time as he is served and then informs us, the injunction is still in effect."

"How do you know that?"

"Gilmore told me."

"That's just what I'm afraid of," Carlisle said. "Have you ever thought that Gilmore might be telling us just what we want to hear because we are paying him?"

"Nah, I think he's right on this one," Creed said.

"But the sheep herders think the injunction has been lifted, don't they?" Carlisle asked.

"Yes."

"So that means they'll probably be putting their sheep out on the range again," Carlisle said.

"I'd say the chances are pretty good that they will," Creed said. "Probably as early as tonight."

At that moment Johnny and Jesse arrived.

"I'm glad you boys could join us," Creed said. "Find a seat somewhere."

Carlisle glared at Jesse, who looked away.

"So, if the sheep herders put their sheep out tonight, what are we going to do about it?" Fenton asked.

"We're going to run them off," Creed said. "We've got the law on our side."

"When does this gunfighter we hired get here?" Wilson asked.

Creed took out his watch and looked at it. "Clay Morgan is coming in on the noon train. I'm going to meet him."

"If we go out tonight, will he go with us?" Fenton asked.

"I doubt it, him just getting into town and all," Creed said.

"We don't need Clay Morgan anyway," Lonnie said. He stuck the little piece of rawhide in his mouth and chewed on it for a second or two before he spoke again. "Those of you who want to ride with me tonight, just show up over here before dark."

"All right, we won't have our gunfighter with us, but what if they have their gunfighter with them?" Fenton asked.

"You mean Fancy Dan?" Lonnie asked with a smirk. "Don't worry about him, I can handle him."

"Like you handled him in town the other day?" Fenton asked.

"I had the drop on him and I pulled the trigger but my pistol misfired," Lonnie said. "I didn't have any choice but to run."

"You had the drop on him, huh?"

"Yes," Lonnie said. "He pulled his gun against the three of us. Poke and Jules fired and missed, and he killed them. I would have killed him if my gun hadn't misfired."

"Why didn't he kill you?" Carlisle asked.

Lonnie shook his head. "I don't know," he said. "But not killin' me was the biggest mistake he ever made. 'Cause I guarantee you, I'm goin' to kill him."

"If Clay Morgan doesn't kill him first," Wilson said.

"Clay Morgan can help us with the sheep herders all he wants," Lonnie said. He pulled the little string of rawhide from his mouth and held it out for emphasis. "But when it comes to Fancy Dan, he's mine. He's all mine."

"Lonnie, I'll be here tonight," Johnny said. "What time do you want me?"

"We'll gather here just before dark," Lonnie said, putting the rawhide back in his pocket. "Anyone else comin'?"

"Jesse will be comin' too," Johnny said.

"What are you talkin' about?" Jesse asked. "I didn't say I was coming."

"I know you didn't," Johnny said. "I said you were comin'."

"Pa?" Jesse said.

"For God's sake, Jesse, it's time you became a man," Carlisle said.

Johnny laughed as the meeting broke up.

Chapter 17

JOSHUA CREED AND DALT FENTON MET CLAY Morgan at the depot in King Hill.

"Mr. Morgan, welcome to King Hill," Creed said, reaching for Morgan's grip. "I've got a room for you out at the ranch."

"I prefer to stay in town," Morgan said. "Get me a hotel room."

"In town? No, you don't want to stay in town. I assure you, you'll be much more comfortable out at the ranch."

Morgan took his suitcase away from Creed and started back toward the train.

"Wait a minute! What are you doing? Where are you going?" Creed called after him.

"I didn't come here to argue about where I am going to stay," Creed answered without looking around. "I'm going back."

"No! No, wait!" Creed called. "Of course, if you want to stay in a hotel room, you can. I was merely trying to look out for your comfort, that's all."

"I'll look out for my own comfort," Morgan replied.

"Of course, of course," Creed said. "Well, uh, shall we get you checked in to the hotel? Then maybe we could stop by the saloon and have a drink or two."

"All right," Morgan said. He handed his suitcase back to Creed.

Creed had been prepared to carry it to the buckboard, but he didn't like the idea of carrying it down the street to the hotel. He stood there for a moment, indecisive as to what to do next.

"Are you coming? Or are you just going to stand there?" Morgan asked.

Creed shrugged, then started up the street carrying the bag.

"We believe the sheep herders will be putting their sheep out on the range again, perhaps as early as tonight," Creed said, huffing now as he struggled to carry the suitcase. "So some of our people will be going out to, let's say, discourage them. I said that you were probably too tired to go out tonight because of your trip, but that you would probably go with them tomorrow night."

"Not tonight, not tomorrow night, not any night, will I go out with a bunch of ranchers," Morgan said.

Creed stopped in the middle of the street and looked at Morgan.

"I beg your pardon?"

"You heard me. I'm not going out on any night rides with anyone," Morgan said.

"Mr. Morgan, you will excuse me, sir, but just what in the hell am I hiring you for?"

"I believe you said it was to keep the sheep herders

from running their sheep on the open range," Morgan said.

"Yes. But if you aren't going to ride with any of us, to . . . lead us . . . then how do you expect to do that?"

"I don't lead anyone. I work alone."

"But there are at least twenty to thirty sheep herders, counting the hands that work for them."

"I work alone," Morgan said again. "If you have any trouble with that, I'll just take the deposit and leave."

"The deposit?"

"One thousand dollars," Morgan said.

"You . . . you want a thousand dollars for doing nothing?"

"That's my price," Morgan said. "Now, either you let me work my way, or pay me the deposit and I'll leave."

"No," Creed said. "No, you don't have to leave. Very well, Mr. Morgan. You can work in any way you wish."

"I thought you might see it my way."

After Clay Morgan checked into the hotel, he, Creed, and Fenton walked two doors down to the Cattlemen's Saloon. The piano was grinding away in the back, sounding more off-key than before, because the bullets of the shooting incident of a few days ago had severed some of the strings. The saloon was quite busy, with several men standing at the bar, while many others were at the tables. The various conversations, interspersed with outbreaks of laughter, were almost louder than the piano.

"It seems a little more crowded than usual," Creed said. "We'll be lucky if we can get a table."

"We'll take that table," Morgan said, pointing to a table close to a side wall. There were two cowboys sitting at it.

Creed was about to point out the obvious, that there were two men sitting at the table, but even though he had only just met Morgan, he knew better than to say anything about it. Instead he walked over to the table ahead of Morgan and Fenton.

"Boys," he said. "Here's ten dollars apiece if you'll give us your table."

Although neither of the cowboys worked for Creed, both knew him.

"Ten dollars each?" one of them said with a broad smile. "Yes, sir! You can have it!"

The two cowboys got up and walked away.

"Move the table over there, against the wall," Morgan said, pointing to where he wanted it to go.

Both Creed and Fenton were successful cattlemen, more used to giving orders than accepting them. But, as if they were no more than hired hands, the two men grabbed the table and started to reposition it.

"Here, you men!" the bartender called. "What are you doing with that table?"

"It's all right, Dan," Creed called back to him. "This is Mr. Morgan. Mr. Clay Morgan. He wants the table up against the wall."

"It's the Regulator," someone said, and the name was repeated several times over the next few seconds. All conversation stopped as everyone looked toward the men moving the table.

"Bartender, is your name Dan?" Morgan asked.

"Yes, sir," Dan answered nervously.

"Well, Dan, as long as I am in town, I intend to make your saloon my headquarters. So I'd appreciate it if you would keep this table over here, and keep it reserved."

"Well, I, uh—" Dan started, but was interrupted by Morgan himself, who addressed his remarks to all the saloon patrons.

"If I come in here and see anyone sitting at this table, I'm going to be very upset. I know none of you folks in here would be dumb enough to sit at my table. But you might pass it on to some of your friends who aren't here now. I'm sure they would appreciate that information."

A few nodded, but nobody made a verbal response.

"And now, Dan, would you bring us a bottle and three glasses? My friends and I have some business to discuss."

"Yes, sir, Mr. Morgan," Dan said. "Right away."

Morgan sat down at the table with his back against the wall. This position allowed him to keep his eye on the entire room, from the bat wings front door to the stairs that climbed up to the second story at the back of the saloon.

"Now, gentlemen, we have something to talk about," Morgan said.

"Yes, the rest of your money," Creed said. "As we agreed, you will get the final five hundred dollars when the job is completed."

"The final one thousand," Morgan said.

"One thousand?" Creed gasped. "Mr. Morgan, we agreed upon fifteen hundred dollars, and I've already given you a thousand."

"Yes, but that was before I knew," Morgan said.

"Before you knew what?"

"That Mason Hawke was on the side of the sheep herders."

"Mason Hawke?" Creed said. He barked a cynical laugh. "You are afraid of Mason Hawke?"

"You aren't?" Morgan asked.

"No, of course not."

"Then you are a fool," Morgan said. "Mason Hawke is not a man you want to have as an enemy. And, it would appear, you already have him as an enemy."

"He's a piano player, for crying out loud," Creed said.

"Nevertheless, my price has gone up. One thousand dollars when this is over."

Creed sat and fumed for a long moment as he drummed his fingers on the tabletop.

"All right," he said. "I have no choice. Otherwise you'll leave and I will have lost the first one thousand dollars."

"Josh, you only have a commitment from the others for five hundred dollars more," Fenton said.

"I know that, Dalt, but what else am I going to do? You heard him, same as I did."

"I guess you can try and get another five hundred out of 'em," Fenton said. "I know I'll put in my part."

"Thanks," Creed said, and looked at Morgan. "All right. We've got a deal."

Morgan had taken out a deck of cards and was dealing himself a game of solitaire. If he heard Creed, he made no acknowledgment.

"Did you hear me? I said we have a deal," Creed repeated."

"Of course we have a deal," Morgan said as he played a red seven on a black eight. "The issue was never in doubt."

"I have to ask the question, though," Creed said. "Are you better than Mason Hawke?"

"Yeah," Morgan said. "I'm better."

George Butrum and Mitch Arnold were in King Hill, having come into town to buy some supplies at the hardware store.

"Come on," Arnold said as they dropped their supplies in the back of the wagon. "Ian has called another meeting today."

"It's not another potluck is it? 'Cause if it is, I don't think Anna knew anything about it. Leastwise, she wasn't cookin' nothin' when I left."

"No, I think it's just to tell us what happened in court,

and probably to talk about takin' our sheep out into the open range again," Arnold said.

"Yeah, I think I would like to hear about it. I mean, I've already heard that the judge took away the injunction, but I'd like to hear all the particulars. What time is the meeting?" Butrum asked.

"It's at four o'clock this afternoon," Arnold answered.

"Ah, well, then we've got plenty of time for a couple of drinks. What do you say we stop in down at the Cattlemen's Saloon?"

"I don't know," Butrum said. "It looks like there are a lot of horses down there. I expect it might be pretty full, and this time of day I doubt that there will be any of our people there."

"You don't think it'll be so full that we get turned away, do you?"

"No, I don't reckon that's the case. But . . ."

"But what?"

"There is a reason they call it the Cattlemen's Saloon. We're going to be outnumbered while we are in there."

Butrum laughed. "Then we probably shouldn't start any fistfights, should we?"

Arnold laughed with him. "I guess you're right," he said. "What trouble can we get into just by going in to have a drink or two? Come on, let's go."

Nobody noticed Butrum or Arnold when they first entered the saloon except for the bartender, Dan. As he passed the damp cloth over the bar in front of them, he spoke quietly.

"This is not a very good time for you boys to be in here," he said.

"Why not?" Butrum asked.

"You see the man at the table in the back? The one with the moustache and the scar on his face?"

Butrum started to look around, but Dan hissed, "No! Don't turn around. Just look for him in the mirror."

"All right, I see him. What about him?"

"They call him the Regulator," Dan said. "The cattlemen have hired him."

"Hired him to do what?"

"I don't know," Dan answered. "But it can't be good."

Across the room, Joshua Creed said, "There are a couple of sheep herders now, standing over there at the bar," and pointed them out to Butrum and Arnold.

Morgan heard him as well and nodded. Then he got up and walked over to the bar. He stepped in beside Butrum, crowding in so close that Butrum was forced to move.

"Mister, there's room enough for both of us," Butrum said, his voice showing his irritation. "You don't have to crowd in."

Morgan turned toward him and stared at him with cold, dead eyes. He ran his finger along his scar, then preened his moustache.

"Sheep herder, are you telling me you don't like my company?" Morgan asked

"No, I'm not saying that," Butrum replied. Seeing who it was, his irritation was replaced by intimidation.

"Then what are you saying?" Morgan asked.

"I . . . I'm not saying anything," Butrum said. "I just . . ."

"You just what?"

Butrum cleared his throat. "Uh, Mitch, didn't you say we had to be somewhere soon?"

"Yes, and we're already late. We'd better be going."

"You didn't drink your beer," Morgan said.

"That's all right."

"No, really, I hate to see good beer go to waste," Morgan said. "Here, why don't you take it with you?"

All conversation in the saloon had stopped as everyone watched the drama playing out before them. They saw Morgan reach up and take Butrum's hat off his head. After pouring the beer into the crown, Morgan put the hat back on Butrum's head. The beer ran down across Butrum's face and onto his shirt. Some of it splashed onto Morgan's shirt.

The saloon patrons laughed nervously.

"You spilled beer on me, sheep herder!" Morgan said angrily.

"I'm sorry."

"Get a towel and wipe it off!"

"Dan, d-d-do you have a towel?" Butrum asked, stuttering in his fear.

"D-d-d-do you have a towel?" Morgan mocked.

Dan gave Butrum a towel, and Butrum wiped at the spot of beer on Morgan's shirt.

"That's not going to do it," Morgan said. "Bartender, you got a Chinaman in town who does laundry?"

"Yes, sir, Lin Cho does laundry."

"How much does he charge to clean a shirt?"

"Fifteen cents."

Morgan held his hand out, palm up. "You owe me fifteen cents, sheep herder."

"What? What about *his* shirt?" Arnold asked in quick anger, pointing to Butrum's beer-soaked shirt. "You poured beer all over his shirt."

"His shirt is his problem," Morgan said. He chuckled. "And as it turns out, my shirt is also his problem. I want fifteen cents, sheep herder."

Butrum took out a dime and a nickel and dropped the coins into Morgan's outstretched hand.

"Very good," Morgan said. "Now, didn't the two of you say you had somewhere to go?"

"Y-Y-Yes," Butrum replied.

Morgan turned his hand over, then made a dismissive motion. "Then go," he said.

Butrum and Arnold hurried out of the saloon, their exit followed by the laughter of all the cattlemen who were there.

Chapter 18

"YOU SHOULD HAVE SEEN HIM," IAN SAID, TALK-ing to the other sheep ranchers who had again gathered at his house. He was extolling the brilliance of Emerson Booker in his role as an advocate for their cause.

Ian pointed to Emerson. "I'm telling you, you've never heard a more golden tongue. He had Gilmore hacking and wheezing like a man who'd just taken a bite out of a sour persimmon."

"So, we can graze our sheep on the open range?" Clem Douglass asked.

"Absolutely. We have full authority to do so," Ian said.

"Well, I'm glad of that. No more acreage than I have, my sheep were beginning to find the pickings pretty slim," Douglass said.

"Yes, it's the same over at my place," Mark Patterson said.

"All right, why don't all of you send your sheep out this evening," Ian suggested. "We'll join our flocks again, and I'll send mine out with Tomas."

"I'll go out as well," Hawke said.

"Sure, if you want to," Ian said. "But since Judge Dollar set aside the injunction, I don't think there will be any trouble."

"Ian," Emerson said, "if you recall, there was no injunction against us the last time we went out, but that didn't stop Creed and his boys from attacking us and killing many of our sheep."

"Emerson is right," Douglass said. "We had as much right then as we do now, but that didn't make any difference to them."

"All right, all right," Ian said. "I really don't think there will be any trouble, but if there is, I'm sure that Hawke can handle it."

"Sorry we're late," Arnold said as he and Butrum came into the room.

"That's all right," Ian said. "We were talking about the court case and planning on sending our sheep out."

"I don't know if we should be so quick to do that," Butrum said.

"What?" Ian replied. "Why not? We have the legal right to do it."

"The cattlemen have brought someone in," Butrum said.

"What do you mean, they've 'brought someone in?'" Ian asked.

"He's a big fella, with a scar on his face," Butrum said, drawing his finger down his cheek to indicate the scar."

"Who is he?" Ian asked.

"His name is Clay Morgan," Hannah said, and Ian

looked around, surprised that Hannah had come into the parlor.

"Yeah, Clay Morgan. That's what the bartender said the big man's name was."

"Hannah, how in the world would you know that?" Ian asked.

"Jesse told me that the cattlemen had hired him," Hannah said. She looked over at Hawke, who so far had said nothing about Clay Morgan. "Jesse said they hired him because of you, Mr. Hawke."

"Because of Hawke? Why because of Hawke?" Douglass asked.

"Maybe they felt as if they needed a gunfighter to deal with our gunfighter," Patterson said.

"What are you talking about, Mark?" Ian asked. "Hawke isn't a gunfighter."

"Then how would you explain this?" Patterson asked. He took a piece of paper from his jacket pocket, the clipping of a newspaper article. After unfolding it, he passed it around for the others to read.

A story of violence and heroics has reached us from the town of Bellefonte, Kansas. There, according to our sources, two of the most evil men who ever breathed the sweet air of God's own earth precipitated the events that follow in this narrative, doing so in as foul and despicable a manner as can be imagined.

There, the two men, Joseph Tangeleno and Sal Vizzini, took control of an entire town, placing every citizen in the church and holding them as their prisoners. In order to establish their dominance, they killed the pastor of the church, Timothy Gadbury, who by all accounts was a good and reverent man.

Not content with that, they threatened to begin killing children if a certain woman who had witnessed a murder they had committed in New Orleans did not surrender herself to them. One can understand the dilemma the woman found herself in when one realizes that Tangeleno and Vizzini wanted her to surrender to them so that they might kill her.

What the desperadoes did not count on was the presence of Mason Hawke, who for all intent and purposes is little more than a meek piano player. However, he is much more than a piano player, and perhaps never has a person been more misjudged, with greater peril to the one making the hasty judgment than on this occasion.

Tangeleno and Vizzini, taking a hostage with them, left the church and went into the main street of the town. Armed with shotguns, the two ordered Hawke to show himself and surrender his pistol, the order being enforced by means of Vizzini holding a shotgun to the head of his hostage, a young woman. Complying with the request, Hawke removed his pistol with his thumb and forefinger and dropped it in a watering trough.

During the conversation that ensued, Hawke said something to Vizzini that so enraged him that he pushed the young woman aside and brought his shotgun to bear on Hawke. This was exactly the purpose of Mr. Hawke's intemperate remarks, and seeing that the hostage was no longer in danger, Mr. Hawke acted precipitously to take advantage of the opportunity thus presented. Using a knife he had secreted on his person, he threw it, causing it to embed in Vizzini's forehead, said action bringing about the instant demise of the evil Vizzini.

Having killed Vizzini, Hawke quickly retrieved the shotgun Vizzini was carrying. Realizing that he was no longer in control of the situation, Tangeleno fired his own shotgun. Some of the pellets thus discharged struck the calf of Hawke's leg, having the effect of wounding him slightly. Tangeleno was unable to pull the second trigger because Hawke fired both barrels at the same time. This double charge, fired at such close range, had the effect of blowing half of Tangeleno's head away.

By his brave action, Mr. Hawke earned the gratitude of every citizen of the town. This would be noteworthy if it had only happened one time, but one need only delve into Mr. Hawke's past to find several other examples of him standing toe to toe with the most ferocious of adversaries and besting them at their own game.

"Mr. Hawke," Patterson said, "I asked you before if you were a professional gunfighter and you said you were a pianist. Now, given what happened in town the other day, and given this story that ran in the *Atchison Gazette*, I ask you again. Are you a professional gunfighter?"

"No."

"Are you or are you not the man in this story? Is this story true?"

Hawke nodded. "Yes, the story is true, and yes, I am the man in the story."

"Then how can you stand there and tell me you are not a professional killer?"

"Mark, didn't you read this story?" Douglass asked. "For God's sake, what Hawke did was a good thing. Those two men had already killed, and were threatening to kill children."

"According to this story, you killed two men," Patterson said. "You also killed two men in town just a few days ago. Just how many men have you killed, Mr. Hawke?"

"I don't know."

Patterson gasped. "You don't know? You mean you have killed so many men that you don't even know how many you have killed? God in heaven, Mr. Hawke, what sort of man are you?"

"I killed men during the war, Mr. Patterson. I don't know how many men I killed, but I killed many. And, as far as I know, they were good men; they were fathers and sons and brothers. They were farmers and merchants and mechanics, and their only crime was that the color of the uniform they wore was different from my own.

"If I could kill good men during the war, then I have no problem killing evil men now, if my life is danger, or if I perceive that the life of an innocent man, woman, or child is in danger."

"So you are a professional gunfighter," Patterson said.

"Mr. Patterson, what is your definition of a professional gunfighter?" Hawke asked.

"That is an easy question to answer," Patterson said. "A professional gunfighter is someone who sells his ability as a gunfighter to whoever is in need of such services."

"I have never been paid for the use of my guns," Hawke said. "On the other hand, I have been paid to play the piano."

"Let it go, Patterson," Emerson said. "Let's just be thankful we have a man like Hawke on our side."

"Hear, hear," the others said.

"Hawke, what about this man, Morgan?" Dumey asked. "Have you ever heard of him?"

"Yes," Hawke said. "I've heard of him."

"Is he good?"

"Yes."

"Are you as fast as he is?" Douglass asked.

"That's not a valid question," Hawke replied.

"What do you mean it's not a valid question? Are you as fast as he is or not?"

"You don't understand what it takes to be a good gunfighter. Fast has nothing to do with it. Morgan isn't good because he is fast or accurate. He is good because he can kill a man without giving it a second thought."

"What do you mean?" Douglass asked.

"If you looked down right now and saw a roach, could you step on it?"

"Of course I could. I do it all the time."

"What do you think about, when you step on it?"

"What do I think about?" Douglass asked, confused by the question. "Why, I don't think about anything."

"Do you think you could kill a man as easily as you can kill a roach?"

"Well, I . . ." Douglass started, then paused. "I suppose I could . . . if I had to," he concluded.

Hawke shook his head. "It's too late, you're already dead," he said.

"What do you mean, I'm already dead?"

"You stopped to think about it. If you had been in a gunfight just now, you would be dead."

"Yes, but you were just asking a question. If it had been real, why, I'm sure I could do it," Douglass said.

"As I said, if it had been real, you would be dead," Hawke repeated. "Taking a man's life isn't like killing a roach. It's an awesome thing, and at that last moment, just before it's time to pull the trigger, most men will hesitate, just as you did when I asked you the question."

"Yeah, well, everyone would," Douglass insisted.

"No, not everyone," Hawke disputed. "Morgan would

not hesitate. I guarantee you, Clay Morgan can kill a man as easily as you can step on a cockroach."

"Can you do that, Mr. Hawke?" Patterson asked. "Can you kill a man as easily as you can step on a cockroach?"

"Yes," Hawke answered.

Hawke's simple and unemotional answer so stunned the others that they were quiet for a long moment. They stared at him as if he were some dangerous animal on display in a zoo somewhere.

"You know a lot about this sordid business, don't you?" Patterson asked.

"Yes, I do."

"Mr. Hawke, do you mind if I ask you a question?" Patterson continued.

"No, Mr. Patterson, I don't mind at all," Hawke replied, his response disarming in that it contained not the least bit of animus, even though Patterson seemed to be going out of his way to challenge him.

"How does one get to such a point?" Patterson asked. "How in the world could someone ever reach the point that he can kill a man without thinking about it?"

"It's simple," Hawke said. "All you have to do is be a man without a soul."

"Everyone has a soul, Mr. Hawke," Douglass said.

Hawke shook his head. "I don't," he insisted. "I lost my soul at a place called Devil's Den."

"Gentlemen, gentlemen, that's enough now," Ian said. "If we are going to turn our sheep out to pasture open range, we need to start getting ready."

Agreeing with him, the others left to start making preparations. Hawke walked back out to his room in the barn, and Hannah stood at the door watching him. When she turned back she saw that Ian was still in the room with her.

"Is that right, Papa?" Hannah asked. "Has Mr. Hawke really lost his soul?"

Ian shook his head. "No, darlin'," he said. "Mason Hawke is one of the finest men I have ever known and he has soul as big as all outdoors. But he has been through so much in his life that his soul is hidden behind a big ball of pain that he carries in his heart."

Out in his room in the barn, Hawke lay on his bedroll with his hands laced behind his head. He stared up at unpainted wide boards that made up the hayloft just over his head.

He tried to keep from thinking about the old . . . painful memories of the war, but sometimes the memories took on a life of their own, intruding into his senses, like the memory of Gettysburg and Devil's Den that troubled him now.

Realizing that he could not shake the memory, Hawke knew that there was nothing he could do but close his eyes and let the memory play out.

The angry buzz of bullets could be heard even above the rattle of musketry, the heavy thump of cannon fire, and the explosive burst of artillery rounds. Men were screaming, some in defiance, some in fear, and many in agony.

By now the blood was pooling in the rocks and boulders of Devil's Den, but still the fighting continued. Mason Hawke had taken shelter in those rocks, and from his position was engaged in long distance shooting, killing Yankee soldiers from five hundred to one thousand yards away. He shot until the hexagon barrel of his Sharps breechloader was so hot that he could no longer touch it, so he took off his shirt to use as a pad to allow him to hold the rifle and continue his killing. Hawke lost count of how many men he had killed, but he knew that one of his victims was a brigadier general.

Around him, sixty-five of his fellow soldiers had already fallen victim to the Yankee sharpshooters under the command of Colonel Hiram Berdan.

"This ain't never going to stop!" a private next to him shouted in horror. "We're just goin' to keep on a-killin' each other till ever' last one of us is dead."

Hawke turned to answer him, to assure him that this battle, like all the others they had been in, would end. But before he could say a word, a minié ball slammed into the private's head. The man's blood, brains, and tiny fragments of bone splinters sprayed into Hawke's face.

Hawke didn't even bother to wipe off the detritus as he selected his next target.

"Señor Hawke," Tomas called. Hawke sat up. He didn't know if he had been jerked out of the memory or if the memory had been jerked out of him. Either way, the memory was gone, and he was glad to be back in the present.

"Yes, Tomas, I'm in here," Hawke replied.

"I have a horse saddled for you, señor, if you are going with us."

"Yes, I'm going," Hawke said. He came out of the barn and swung into the saddle. "Where are the others, Josu and Felipe?"

"They have already started," Tomas said. "They are taking the sheep to pasture."

"All right, let's go," Hawke said.

As Hawke and Tomas rode off at a trot, Hawke saw that not only Ian, but Cynthia and Hannah as well, were out on the front porch. The expressions differed on each of their faces, and almost as if he were blessed with what his grandmother used to call "the gift," he could read what they were thinking as easily as reading a book.

Ian was frustrated because he could not go with them.

Cynthia was worried that Hawke might be hurt or killed if anything happened.

Hannah was thinking about Jesse, wondering if there was any chance that he and Jesse would have some sort of encounter tonight.

On the porch, Ian said, "I should be with them."

"Don't be ridiculous," Cynthia replied. "You can't even ride with your legs in a cast. And I'm worrying enough about Hawke now, I couldn't bear it if I had you to worry about as well."

"Oh, please God, if Jesse is out there, don't let him be hurt," Hannah said.

Chapter 19

JESSE HAD TO RIDE HARD TO KEEP UP WITH THE others as they galloped through the night. The thunder of drumming hooves was interspersed with the squeak of leather and the jangle of bridal and tack. The churning hooves brought up the aroma of crushed grass, the same grass that was the center of all the trouble.

With every ounce of his being, Jesse wanted to turn away from the others, to leave them to whatever foul deed they had planned for the night. In fact, he wished he could leave the entire territory. He fantasized about going someplace else, like Texas or California. He would take Hannah with him, and they would start a new life, away from the war between the cattlemen and the sheep men.

Of course, he was only seventeen and she was but sixteen, so they would have a hard time getting started. And some would think they were foolish for even trying. But he didn't think she was too young to know what she wanted, and he was sure he wasn't too young to make a life for the two of them.

Lonnie Creed, who was leading the riders, held up his hand to stop them. The riders called out to their horses, and the hoof beats slowed, then stopped. The dust floated in the air around them. In the distance they heard the call of a coyote.

Closer in, an owl hooted.

"What are we doing out here?" Jesse asked.

"You know damn well what we are doing out here," his brother Johnny answered. "We are going to teach those sheep herders a lesson they'll never forget. After tonight, no more sheep on the open range."

"Keep quiet, you two," Lonnie hissed. "Stay in close and be ready to go when I give the word."

There were at least twenty men with Lonnie, and except for Jesse and Johnny Carlisle, they were all cowboys who rode for one or more of the ranches. With the horses walking quietly now, Lonnie led them up to the top of Squaw Ridge. There, in the valley below, their white wool coats shining brightly in the moonlight, were well over one thousand sheep.

Down in the valley, the sheep herders were waiting with their combined flock of sheep.

"Maybe nobody will come tonight," Mark Patterson suggested.

"They'll be here," Hawke said.

Patterson, Dumey, Douglass, Cummings, Emerson Booker, Andoni Larranaga, and Mikel Mendiolea, as well as Ian, Josu, and Felipe, the Basque who worked for Emerson, were lying behind a low rising ridge line. In addition to these ten men, there were four more men out tending the grazing sheep.

Hawke had deployed the ten between the sheep and the most likely approach of any cattlemen who would come to challenge them. He was walking back and forth behind this improvised skirmish line, checking each of their positions while at the same time keeping an eye open for approaching cattlemen.

He had a sense of déjà vu in what he was doing, because it was a deployment he had often utilized during the war.

"Hawke, if they come, what do we do?" Allen Cummings asked.

"Let me ask you this, Cummings," Hawke replied. "What do you think would be the purpose of their coming?"

"I imagine it would be to kill sheep," Cummings said.

"Or us," Emerson added.

"And why are we here?" Hawke asked.

"To keep them from doing that," Cummings replied.

"That's right," Hawke said.

"But you still haven't answered my question," Cummings said. "What do we do if they do come?"

"We do whatever it takes to stop them."

"You're . . . you're talking about shooting them, aren't you?"

"Yes, I am talking about shooting them. That's why you are lying there with a rifle in your hand."

"I don't know," Cummings said. "I've never shot anyone before. I've never even shot *at* anyone before."

"Allen, a few years ago we had a great war in this country," Emerson said. "You may have heard of it."

"The War Between the States," Cummings said. "Of course I heard of it. Who hasn't heard of it?"

"During that war, we had hundreds of thousands of young men who had never shot at another man. And yet, when the chips were down, they did just fine. I have no doubt but that you will as well."

"Yeah," Cummings said. "Yeah, I haven't thought of it like that before. But I guess you're right. This is sort of like a war, isn't it?"

On the crest of Squaw Ridge, Lonnie Creed stood in his stirrups for a second, not to get a better look, but to restore circulation to his legs. Then, sitting back in his saddle, he snaked his Winchester from its sheath. "All right, boys," he said. "Same as before. Let's kill us some sheep."

"What if the sheep herders are there?" one of the cowboys asked.

Lonnie took the string of rawhide from his pocket and stuck the end of it in his mouth. He smiled. "Well hell, boys, then we'll have us some fun. We'll kill them too."

"No," Jesse said, holding back. "I'm not going down there."

"Oh yes you will," Johnny said. "I'll see to it that you will." Johnny started toward him but stopped when he heard the deadly click of a pistol being cocked.

"I said I'm not going," Jesse said defiantly, pointing his cocked pistol toward his brother. The barrel gleamed dimly in the moonlight.

"Let him be, Johnny," Lonnie said. "We don't have time for him now."

"All right, you stay here," Johnny said angrily, pointing his finger at his younger brother. "But don't think I won't take care of you when I get back."

"Let's go," Lonnie said, and following his lead, the others started down the long slope of Squaw Ridge, heading toward the gathered sheep in the valley below.

The hoofbeats of the galloping horses spread like thunder over the valley. From their position behind the low ridge, the sheep men watched in morbid fascination as the cowboys galloped toward them.

"They're not stopping!" Cummings said.

"Then we'll stop them," Hawke said, firing the first shot.

The cowboys, surprised that the sheep herders were putting up a fight, returned fire. Bullets whistled back and forth in the dark, then one of the Mexican shepherds cried out.

"Tomas!" Felipe shouted in pain. "I am hit!"

"Felipe has been wounded!" Tomas said, going to the Basque shepherd.

Although the others were lying down, Hawke was still standing behind them, firing a rifle, shooting as quickly as he could jack round after round into the chamber. The night was lit up with the light of muzzle flashes, and the sound of gunshots was redoubled by the echoes that rolled back from the hills.

"They're running!" Dumey shouted. "They're running away!"

"Keep shooting!" Hawke called. "Let's hurry them along!"

The sheep herders kept up the shooting until, finally, Hawke called for a cease fire.

A cloud of gun smoke hung over the field, illuminated by the bright moon above. The smell of the spent gunpowder irritated their nostrils and burned their eyes.

"Tomas, how is Felipe?" Hawke asked.

"Felipe, zer moduz?" Tomas asked, speaking in Euskara.

"It is not bad," Felipe said, answering in English. "I was hit in the arm."

"Hawke, I see some people lying out there," Dumey said.

"Let's go see if we can do anything for them," Hawke answered. "But keep your guns handy."

He led the others out to check on the men who were lying on the ground.

"This one's dead," Dumey called.

"Who is it?" Emerson asked.

"I don't know, he must be one of the hands. I don't recognize him."

"I recognize this one," Cummings said. "His name is Ralph Day. He rides for Rome Carlisle."

"Dead?" Emerson asked.

"Yeah."

"So's this one," Douglass said. "But I don't have any idea who he is."

"Uh-oh," Patterson said. "This isn't going to be good."

"What?" Hawke asked.

"This one isn't just some cowboy."

"Who is it?"

"Maybe you'd better come over and look for yourself."

Jesse was still on Squaw Ridge when Lonnie and the riders came back at a gallop. Without even counting, he could tell there were fewer than had gone out.

"What happened?" he asked. He didn't see his brother. "Where's Johnny?"

Lonnie pulled up beside him, stopping so quickly that his horse twisted around with him and he had to bring it under control.

"You want to know where Johnny is?" he asked.

"Yes."

Lonnie pointed behind him. "He's lying on the ground back there. Dead."

"Dead?"

"Yes, thanks to you," Lonnie said.

"Lonnie, you got no call to say that to the boy," Asa Crawford said.

"Yeah, I do," Lonnie replied, scowling at Jesse. "Johnny was a good man. And our boy Jesse here is a traitor. I figure Johnny is dead because Jesse told the sheep herders we were comin'."

"I did not!" Jesse insisted.

"Really? Everyone knows you are sweet on Macgregor's daughter."

"That doesn't mean I would tell them anything like this," Jesse said.

"Come on, let's go," Lonnie said. He looked over at Jesse. "Can you keep up with us? Or do you need a sugar tit to suck on?"

"Are we just going to leave Johnny out there?" Jesse asked.

"He's in good company," Lonnie said. "There are three more out there with him."

Jesse shook his head. "It's not right to just leave them out there."

"If you want to go out there and get him, go ahead," Lonnie said.

"Boy, now's not a good time," Asa put in. "Anyone goin' out there now is likely to be shot. He'll be all right till mornin'. We'll get 'em all, come mornin'."

By breakfast the next day everyone in King Hill knew of the fight between the cattlemen and the sheep herders. Oddly, there was no boisterous talk from those who had taken part in the fight. Most of the talk came from those who had not participated at all.

Three of the cowboys who had been in the fracas decided they were leaving the valley.

"I'll tell you what I was thinkin' the whole time I

was out there," one of them said as he rolled his few belongings into a blanket. "I was thinkin' about the baby Jesus."

"What?" one of the other cowboys asked.

"I was thinkin' about the baby Jesus," the first cowboy repeated. "You know, how there was shepherds in the fields and angels come to tell 'em about Jesus bein' born in a manger an' all? I was thinkin', what if a bunch of cowboys had come ridin' in on 'em, shootin' 'em up that night and killin' their sheep like we done? I don't think the baby Jesus woulda liked that."

"Yeah, well, the baby Jesus ain't lyin' in a manger in King Hill," one of the other cowboys said.

"Maybe not, but there's shepherds here, just like in the Bible, and it don't seem right to be killin' off their sheep."

The cowboy who had been thinking about the baby Jesus, and the other two, left the valley that very day. The rest of the riders, whether acting under some pact of secrecy or out of shame, didn't come into town, or if they did, kept their involvement quiet.

By mid-morning a wagon came rolling into town, driven by Rome Carlisle. Jesse was riding on the seat with his father, and in the back there were four canvas-covered lumps. These were the four cowboys who had been killed in the fight, and even before the wagon reached Prufrock's Mortuary, everyone in town knew what was under the canvas.

Abner Prufrock came out on the front porch to meet the wagon. "I heard about your boy, Mr. Carlisle," he said, before Carlisle even spoke. "You have my deepest condolences."

"Thank you," Carlisle replied, his voice low and filled with sadness.

Prufrock stepped to the rear of the wagon and pulled

back the canvas. "I recognize Johnny, of course. And this one is Pete Lowery, he rides for Mr. Fenton, I believe. But I don't know the other two."

"That's Ralph Day, he was one of my riders," Carlisle said. "And that's Gene Bailey. He was one of Jared Wilson's riders."

"Mr. Fenton and Mr. Wilson will be paying for the funeral costs?"

Carlisle shook his head. "There won't be a funeral for them," he said. "Not for Ralph either. Ralph was from Texas, Pete was from Colorado, and Gene was from Kansas," he explained. "All we want you to do to them is embalm them and put them in a crate that we can ship on the train. Mr. Fenton, Mr. Wilson, and I will take care of the shipping arrangements."

"Yes, sir," Prufrock said. "And your boy?"

"I want a good coffin. Your best."

"Of course you do," Prufrock said. "Come down with me to the Farmers and Ranchers Supply. I have an arrangement with Mr. Dunnigan, and he keeps my coffins on display there."

"What about my boy?" Carlisle asked, pointing at the body.

"He will be all right here until we get back," Prufrock assured him.

Carlisle and Jesse followed Prufrock to the Farmers and Ranchers Supply. Everyone in town knew of Carlisle's loss, and they tipped their hat or nodded as they passed him, Jesse, and Prufrock on the boardwalk.

Inside, Prufrock led Carlisle back to the display of coffins. Jesse couldn't help but recall, just a few weeks ago, when he and Hannah had stood on this very spot and were approached by one of the salesmen.

Prufrock showed Carlisle a black coffin, its ebony finish

shining brightly in the kerosene lamps of the store. It was richly decorated in silver.

"This is our very finest," he said. "It is called 'Heavenly Dream.'" The undertaker ran his hand over the ebony finish. "You can feel the quality for yourself. And it's guaranteed for one hundred years."

"Guaranteed for a hundred years?" Carlisle asked.

"Absolutely."

Carlisle snorted. "That's the dumbest damn thing I've ever heard. Who the hell is going to dig it up in a hundred years to check on it?"

"Well, uh, nobody of course," Prufrock sputtered. "It's just a way of explaining the quality of the workmanship. Run you hand over the finish and you'll see what I mean."

Carlisle did as Prufrock suggested.

"And, as you can see," Prufrock said, demonstrating, "the top half comes off, so the decedent can be exhibited."

"He's not a decedent, he's my boy," Carlisle said angrily.

"Of course he is, Rome," Prufrock replied condescendingly. He was experienced in handling angry grief. "Please understand that I meant no disrespect."

"I do like that you can take the top off, though," Carlisle said. "I'm going to buy him a fine suit, and I want you to keep the top off the coffin until just before he's buried. I want the town to see what those murderin' sheep herders did to my boy."

"Very well," Prufrock said. "I'll take care of everything, Mr. Carlisle. And again, you have my sympathy for your loss."

"Come along, Jesse," Carlisle said. "We have to go pick out a suit for your brother."

"Yes, sir," Jesse said, speaking for the first time since they arrived in town.

Chapter 20

"THEY WAS GOOD BOYS, ALL OF THEM," FENTON said. He, Wilson, and Carlisle were in the Cattleman's Saloon. "It broke my heart to have to send a note back with Pete's body, expressin' my sorrow to his folks."

"Yeah, me too," Wilson said.

"But neither one of us had to go through what you did, Rome, losin' your boy like that," Fenton said. "They didn't come no better'n Johnny. You must have been just real proud of him."

"I was proud of him," Carlisle said.

Sheriff Tilghman was in the saloon as well, and he was sitting at a nearby table, drinking a cup of coffee. Carlisle turned to him.

"If you were any kind of a sheriff, you would go out there right now and arrest the ones who were responsible for killing my son and the other three boys," Carlisle said.

"And just who would I arrest?" the sheriff asked. "I understand that it was dark. Can anyone say, for sure, who was shooting?"

"If it was up to me, I'd say arrest the lot of 'em," Carlisle said. "Or at least Mason Hawke. Hell, you know those lily livered sheep men couldn't have done this by themselves. He had to be the one behind it. He's the one that led them onto our land, then set up an ambush."

"As I understand it, everything took place on open range," Sheriff Tilghman said.

"So?"

"So that means it isn't exactly your land."

"Sheriff, you've seen that judge's injunction, same as all the rest of us. You know that the open range has been closed to the sheep herders. They had no business bein' out there."

"The last word I had was that the range wasn't closed," the sheriff said.

"Oh, yeah? Did you see that in writing?" Carlisle asked.

"No."

"Then, according to Mr. Gilmore, until we see it in writing, it ain't happened yet."

"I also understand that the reason the cattlemen were out there last night was to shoot sheep," the sheriff said. "Is that true? Did those men go out there to shoot sheep?"

"Maybe so, but shootin' sheep ain't the same as shootin' people," Carlisle said.

"Perhaps not. But a person has the right to protect his property. So if your men went out there to start shooting sheep, then the sheep herders had every legal right to shoot back."

The heated conversation between Sheriff Tilghman and the cattlemen was interrupted by a low, evil chuckle. Looking toward the sound of the laughter, the men saw Clay Morgan sitting at his table, playing solitaire.

"You think this is funny, do you, Mr. Morgan?" Carlisle asked.

"Yeah," Morgan replied, his voice low and sibilant. "I think it's funny."

"Four men were killed, Mr. Morgan, including my son," Carlisle said angrily. "What makes you think something like that is funny?"

"Amateurs," Morgan said.

"I beg your pardon?"

"Amateurs," Morgan repeated. "Amateurs always make me laugh."

"I see."

Morgan looked up from his card game. "You hired me to take care of the situation for you, didn't you?"

"Creed hired you, I didn't."

The smile left Morgan's lips. "Oh? Well, that's too bad."

"What do you mean, it's too bad?"

"When I come into a place to do a job, I divide the people into two groups. Those who hired me, and everyone else. Those who hired me have nothing to fear from me."

"Meaning the rest of us do?" Carlisle challenged.

"Rome, back off," Wilson cautioned, putting his hand on Carlisle's shoulder.

"I would listen to your friend, if I were you," Morgan said.

"Don't pay him no never mind, Mr. Morgan," Wilson said. "He lost his boy last night. He's upset."

Morgan stared at Carlisle for a long moment, then, without saying another word, he went back to his game of solitaire.

In the parlor of his house, Ian was sitting in his wheelchair, poking a long stick down inside his leg casts.

"Oh, this blessed itch!" he said. "That bothers me more than the break did." He poked the stick in again and began jabbing it back and forth.

"The doctor said your casts can come off tomorrow," Cynthia said.

"Get me a knife," Ian said.

"A knife? What for?"

"If they can come off tomorrow, they can come off today," he said. "I don't think I can stand another blessed minute of it."

"All right," Cynthia said. "But be careful."

She got the knife, as requested, and Ian cut the casts off. For the first few moments he scratched his legs, sighing in contentment.

"Papa, I need to ask you something," Hannah said.

Ian looked up.

"I want to go to Johnny Carlisle's funeral."

Ian shook his head. "I don't think that would be a good idea, child."

"Papa, please."

"Why would you want to go to the funeral anyway? You know what kind of a person Johnny was. He was no good."

"I know he was no good," Hannah said. "But I'm not doing it for him, Papa. He was Jesse's brother, and I'm doing it for Jesse."

"I still don't think it's a very good idea. I can't go with you. And I don't want you to go by yourself."

"What if Mr. Hawke takes me?"

"I'm sure that the last thing Hawke wants to do is take you to Johnny Carlisle's funeral," Ian said.

"If he says he'll take me, is it all right? Papa, please, this is very important to me."

Ian sighed, then he chuckled and shook his head. "I swear, darlin', you could talk a rabbit out of his hole. All right, I'll ask Hawke to take you."

Hannah smiled broadly, then threw her arms around Ian's neck and kissed him. "Thank you, Papa, thank you," she said.

"Give me those two canes," Ian told Cynthia. "This is as good a time to try them as any. I'll go ask him."

As Hannah watched her father's laborious walk, aided by his canes, Cynthia came up behind her and put her hands on Hannah's shoulders.

"Sweetheart, I hope you know what you are doing," she said.

"Mama, I feel like I must go," Hannah replied. "Jesse needs to see me there."

"I just don't want to see you hurt, is all."

The churchyard was filled with saddled horses, wagons pulled by oxen, buckboards by mules, buggies by a single horse, and surreys pulled by matching teams. The church itself was too crowded for Hannah and Hawke to go inside, so they stayed on the buckboard, parked just outside. When the funeral service ended, the doors were opened and several people filed out. Most of the mourners were cowboys, not only from the Carlisle ranch, but from all the other ranches as well.

Finally, Hannah saw Jesse coming out of the church,

walking beside his mother. Callie Carlisle was dressed all in black, including a long black veil. Jesse's father was at his wife's side, and, despite what she knew about Johnny, Hannah couldn't help but feel a sense of pity for the mother's loss.

Jesse happened to look toward Hannah, and for a moment his face almost registered his joy at seeing her. Then, seeing who was with her, his expression changed to anger.

"Oh," Hannah said quietly. "Oh, he hates me now."

"No he doesn't, Hannah," Hawke said. "He hates me."

"Oh, I . . . I should have realized," she said. "It was a mistake to come, wasn't it?"

"No," Hawke said. "You did what your heart told you to do. It is never a mistake to follow your heart."

A glass-sided hearse was backed up to the front door of the church, and the six pall bearers, which included Lonnie Creed, bore the coffin out. Lonnie was dressed in a new black suit, complete with a vest and tie, and, as per Carlisle's instructions, the top half of the coffin was left open so everyone could see the body.

Prufrock stood by giving directions as the coffin was placed in the hearse. He had put a wedge on the floor of the hearse so the upper part of the coffin was slightly elevated. This gave the people who lined the route between the church and the cemetery an opportunity to view the body.

A sign on the hearse read:

JOHN BARTLETT CARLISLE
A WONDERFUL SON AND A GOOD BROTHER
SHAMELESSLY MURDERED BY
NIGHT RIDING SHEEP HERDERS

A team of matched black horses, wearing black bunting and black plumage, pulled the hearse smartly away from the church. Hawke waited until the last conveyance had passed before he pulled in behind to follow the cortege south on Pitchfork Road, then west on Meridian Road until they reached the cemetery. There, again, the horses and conveyances were left as the occupants moved to the open grave where Johnny would be interred.

"I'm going to the graveside," Hannah said.

"Are you sure you want to do that?" Hawke asked.

"Yes."

"I'll go with you." Setting the brake and wrapping the reins around the brake handle, Hawke started to climb down from the buckboard.

"No, please, Mr. Hawke, don't," Hannah said, reaching out to put her hand on his. "I think it would be better if I go alone."

Hawke nodded. "All right, if you say so," he said. He sat back down. "I'll wait here for you."

"Thanks."

Hannah picked her way unobtrusively through the crowd until she was standing no more than ten feet from where Jesse and his parents were sitting on folding chairs beside the grave.

Using ropes, the pall bearers lowered the coffin, which now had the top in place and was closed, into the grave. After the ropes were withdrawn, the Reverend E. D. Geers signaled Jesse, who stepped up to the edge of the grave. He picked up a handful of dirt and held it, as the Reverend Geers began the interment prayer.

"'For as much at it hath pleased Almighty God, in His wise providence, to take out of this world the soul of our deceased brother, Johnny, we therefore commit his body to the ground; earth to earth.'"

The Reverend Geers nodded at Jesse, and Jesse dropped the dirt into the grave. Hannah heard it thump on the coffin below.

The preacher continued. "'Ashes to ashes, dust to dust; looking for the general Resurrection in the last day, and the life of the world to come, through our Lord Jesus Christ.'"

When the graveside services were over and everyone started to leave, Hannah stayed in place until Jesse and his family left the graveside.

"Jesse?" Hannah called.

He looked toward her, then away.

"Jesse, please!" Hannah called.

Jesse said something to his parents, then came over to talk to Hannah.

"You shouldn't have come," he said.

"I had to come. He was your brother. I knew how hurt you would be."

"And so you thought that coming to the funeral with the very man who killed my brother would make me feel better?" Jesse asked bitterly.

"What do you mean, the man who killed Johnny?" Hannah asked. "It was dark, everyone was shooting, including your brother."

"Hawke had two run-ins with my brother," Jesse said. "And consider this. Hawke is a known gunfighter. The other men there were nothing but sheep herders. Now, do you really think he didn't kill Johnny?"

"I don't know," Hannah admitted.

"Jesse," Carlisle called.

"I have to go," Jesse said.

"Jesse, when can we meet at our spot again?"

Jesse shook his head. "I don't think we should see each other anymore, Hannah," he said. "Too much has happened."

"Jesse, no," Hannah said.

"Jesse, come on," Carlisle called. "It is time to take your mother home."

"Good-bye, Hannah," Jesse said.

With tears streaming down her face, Hannah watched as Jesse helped his mother into the surrey. She stood there as they drove away, hoping that Jesse would look back at her, but he did not.

When Hannah turned around, she was surprised to see Hawke standing right behind her.

"Oh, Mr. Hawke," she said, her voice breaking. "He doesn't want to see me anymore. He hates me."

Hannah went to Hawke, and he found himself in the unfamiliar position of providing comfort for a young girl. He wrapped his arms around her and let her cry against his chest. He couldn't help but appreciate the fact that he was comforting his niece, a young woman who was, by birth, a part of him. It touched him more deeply than he would have thought.

"I don't think he hates you, Hannah," Hawke said. "He is just a young man who is overwhelmed by events. Have you ever heard the term 'star-crossed'?"

"'Some consequence yet hanging in the stars,'" Hannah said.

"What?"

"That's a quote from *Romeo and Juliet*. Mr. Booker said it refers to the fact that Romeo and Juliet were star-crossed."

"Then you do understand."

"Yes."

Hawke walked Hannah back to the buckboard and

helped her up. As they drove back through town, they passed in front of the Cattlemen's Saloon. A big man dressed in black pants, black shirt, and wearing a black hat, was leaning against one of the pillars that supported the porch roof. There was a purple scar on his face that started just under his left eye and ended in his moustache. He was wearing a badge on his shirt and an ivory-handled pistol in a holster that was low and tied down on his right leg.

Staring, unblinking, at Hawke, he stuck a cheroot in his mouth, scratched a match on the porch pillar, then lit it. Hawke did not give him the satisfaction of staring back.

"That was him, wasn't it?" Hannah said. "That was the gunfighter they sent for."

"Clay Morgan, yes," Hawke said.

"Do you know him?"

"Not really. But I have heard of him."

"Do you think he knows who you are?"

"Until just now, I would have said no," Hawke said. "But from the way he was looking at me?" Hawke nodded. "Yes, I'd say that he knows all about me."

"He may be the single most frightening person I have ever seen," Hannah said.

"You are right to be frightened of him," Hawke said, without making any attempt to calm her uneasiness about the man.

"Mr. Hawke?"

"Yes?"

"Did you kill Johnny?"

Hawke hesitated but a half beat before he responded.

"Probably," he admitted.

"Thank you for not lying to me."

"I've learned that if you lie to try and spare someone's

feelings, you only wind up hurting them more," Hawke said.

"Oh, how did this ever get this far?" Hannah asked. "Why can't we just live here in peace?"

Hawke didn't respond to her question, because he had no answer for her.

"You are right not to see her anymore," Carlisle said.

Jesse was driving the surrey. His father was by his side and his mother was in the back seat, weeping quietly.

"It wasn't her fault," Jesse said. "She didn't have anything to do with killing Johnny."

"Sure she did."

Jesse looked at his father in surprise. "What do you mean, sure she did?"

"It's like a war," Rome said. "In the war, there were many in the South who had nothing to do with killing us. But they were part and parcel of what caused the war in the first place, so everyone who lived in the South was our enemy. Well, we are in another war. Only this war is between the ranchers and the sheep herders. And every sheep herder, whether they were out there with guns the other night or not, is our enemy. It would be the same thing if you had been around during the war as having a girlfriend who lived in the South."

"I . . . I guess if you put it that way," Jesse said.

Carlisle looked sternly at his son. "And if you have anything to do with that girl, Jesse, you are our enemy too."

Jesse didn't answer his father. Instead, he stared straight ahead as the team continued to pull the surrey, their hoofbeats the only sound for a long moment.

"I know that's harsh, Jesse. But that's the way it is."

Jesse wiped a tear from his eye, and Rome reached over to put his hand on his son's shoulder.

"You do see that, don't you, Jesse? You are the only son I have left now. I don't want to lose you, especially like this."

"I understand," Jesse said in a choked voice. "It's hard, but I understand."

"You're a good boy," Rome Carlisle said.

Chapter 21

❧

"WHAT I WANT TO KNOW IS, WHEN IS THE SON of a bitch going to earn his pay?" Fenton asked angrily.

Once again the cattlemen were meeting in Joshua Creed's parlor.

"Because as far as I can tell, all he's done from the first moment he got here is sit on his ass in the saloon, drinking beer and playing solitaire," Fenton continued.

"Yeah," Wilson said. "Maybe if he had gone out with our boys the other night, we wouldn't have gotten four of them killed."

"He said he didn't want to go out," Creed said. "He said he would handle it his way."

"Well, when does 'his' way get started?"

"I'll talk to him," Creed promised.

"Get out of my light," Morgan said as he played a red jack on a black queen.

"I beg your pardon?" Creed replied.

"I said, get out of my light," Morgan repeated. "I can't see the cards."

"Oh, uh, I'm sorry," Creed said, moving, and watching his shadow clear the table.

"What do you want, Creed?"

"Well, I was wondering . . . that is, some of the other ranchers were wondering . . ." Creed let the sentence hang.

"Wondering what?"

"When . . ." Creed cleared his throat nervously. "When, uh, you are going to get started."

"You were wondering that, were you?"

"Yes," Creed said. "After all, Mr. Morgan, we have paid you a great deal of money. I'm sure that even you would agree to that. But so far you haven't actually done anything."

"Are the amateurs finished?"

"I beg your pardon?"

Morgan played a black nine on a red ten. "The amateurs," he said. "Do they plan any more of their nighttime raids? Are they going to go out and get themselves shot up again?"

"No," Creed said. "I do not intend to send them out again."

"Then I'll get to work," Morgan said.

"Good," Creed said. "I'm sure that we will all appreciate that."

"Are you squeamish?"

"Squeamish?"

"Are you going to change your mind once I get started?"

"Well, I don't know," Creed said. "What, exactly, are you going to do?"

"I'm going to run the sheep herders off. That's what you want, isn't it?"

"Well, yes, but how are you going to do it?"

"How I do it is of no concern of yours," Morgan said.

"No, I . . . I suppose not," Creed said. "And to answer your question, no, I'm not squeamish. I saw all the posters on the wall in your office back in Boise City. I know that people who cross you wind up getting killed. As far as I'm concerned, that's one of the reasons I hired you."

Morgan collected his deck of cards, stuck them in his pocket, then squared his hat on his head.

"I'm glad we see things eye to eye," he said.

She did not know what awakened her in the middle of the night, but when twelve-year-old Lucy Wright opened her eyes, she saw that the walls of her bedroom were glowing orange.

She lay in bed for a long moment, just staring at her walls, trying to figure out what was causing this unusual sight. Not only were the walls glowing, they seemed to be waving.

Then she heard a horse, not the ordinary whinny they sometimes made in the night. This was a high-pitched scream of terror.

Suddenly, Lucy knew what was happening, and she jumped out of bed and looked out of her window. The barn was on fire!

"Mama! Papa!" she shouted. "The barn is burning! The barn is on fire!"

Lucy heard her father bolt out of his bedroom. He was still wearing his sleeping gown as he ran by.

"Turn out!" Ed shouted. "Janet, Lucy, Cindy! Turn out! We've got to save the horses!"

By the time they reached the front porch, the barn was totally enveloped in flames, and the high-pitched scream of the horses was louder than the roar of the fire. Wright started toward the barn.

"Ed, no!" Janet called to him.

"I've got to save the horses!" her husband called back.

"Ed, no, you can't!" Janet said. "You can't get in there!"

Just as Wright reached the barn, the front half of it collapsed, sending up a shower of sparks. Wright threw his arms across his face and backed away to keep other pieces of flaming debris from falling on him. It wasn't until then that he realized that the horses weren't screaming anymore.

On top of a hill, about a quarter of a mile away from Wright's house, a lone rider, dressed in black, sat on his horse and watched as the barn continued to burn, folding in on itself as the fire consumed more and more of the structure. Then, rubbing the scar on his cheek, he turned his horse and rode away.

Chris Dumey was the first one to arrive at the Wright ranch the next morning. When he came out for his early toilet, he saw a wisp of smoke curling up from the Wright place, and he woke his family and took them over to see what they could do. Chris sent his fifteen-year-old son Andy around to the other sheep ranches to spread the word, and by noon nearly everyone had arrived, all bringing food.

"I know damn well the fire was set," Wright said as he and the others picked through the smoldering remains, which included the charred bodies of four horses.

"Did you see anyone, Ed?" Emerson Booker asked.

Wright shook his head. "No, I didn't see anyone. And I got no proof that I can go to the sheriff with, but I know damn well it was set."

"The sheriff," Allen Cummings said, making a spitting sound. "A lot of good he would do."

"I think the sheriff is a good man," Ian said. "He's just got more than he can handle right now."

"Which means it's all up to us," Dumey said.

"Yes, we'll have to fight this ourselves."

"I'm not fighting," Wright said. "If I can interest any of you in buying my sheep, I'm going to take the money and buy a team of mules, and we're going back to Kansas."

"Ed, I wish you wouldn't do that," Ian said. "Don't you see? That is exactly what Creed wants you to do."

"Well, then Creed ought to be happy," Wright replied.

"Look, I've got a couple of extra horses I can let you have until you get back on your feet," Ian said.

"And I've got some lumber," Mark Patterson put in.

"I have some too," Emerson said. "And some shingles."

"I've got the nails," Ian said. "We could get your barn rebuilt for you?"

"What do you mean 'we,' Ian?" Dumey teased. "We'll rebuild his barn for him, but what are you going to do? You just got your casts off . . . you can barely walk."

"I'll have you know that I put a roof on my barn, with these broken legs," Ian said. "And that's when I was still wearing casts."

"How in the Sam Hill did you do that?" Emerson asked.

Ian laughed. "Well, it wasn't all that easy." He went on to explain how Hawke was able to pull him up to the top, using the hay bale hoist.

"You men would do that for me?" Wright asked.

"You're damn right we will," George Butrum said.

Wright looked back at Janet, who was standing with several of the other women.

"Janet, what do you think?" he asked.

She wiped the tears from her eyes. "I think it is the most wonderful thing I have ever heard," she said.

"Yeehah!" Wright said, jabbing his hand into the air. "All right, boys, when do you want to get started?"

"I'll be over here first thing in the morning with a wagonload of lumber," Patterson said.

"As will I," Emerson said.

The others made their own commitments as well, then after a shared lunch and half a day of commiserating with the Wrights over the loss of their horses, they started back to their own homes.

"Ian," Cynthia said as they rode back home in the buckboard. "Do you think Ed was right? Do you think someone set the fire?"

"There's no doubt in my mind," Ian answered.

"But who? Who could do such a thing?"

"Is there any doubt?" Ian replied. "You know it was Joshua Creed."

"That's frightening," Cynthia said. "Why, if he burned Ed's barn, he could burn someone else's barn as well. He might even burn their house."

"That's a possibility," Ian said. "We're just going to have to keep a closer watch on things, that's all."

The next morning, true to their promises, everyone showed up ready to work. Ian brought two horses, plus a keg of nails and hammers, saws, a plumb, and a carpenter's square. Other wagons arrived with lumber, shingles, and other supplies so that everything necessary for building a new barn was there.

The first thing they had to do was clear away all the debris from the barn that had burned. While doing so, Mitch Arnold found a can marked KEROSENE.

"Well, here's the cause of your fire," he said, holding up the can.

"What's that?" Wright asked.

"You were keeping a can of kerosene out here," Arnold said. "It probably fell over, maybe a horse's hoof kicked up a spark and—"

"That's not my kerosene," Wright said.

"What do you mean? I found it here."

"I only have one can of kerosene, and it's in the house." ""I can go get it right now and show it to you."

"Then where did this—" Arnold said as he held out the can, then he stopped in mid-sentence. "I'll be damn," he went on. "You're right. Somebody used it to start the fire."

"Not somebody. Joshua Creed," Wright said bitterly.

"I doubt that Creed did it himself," Ian said. "But I have no doubt but that he paid someone to do it."

"Well, we knew what we were getting into when we decided to take him on," Emerson said. "Come on, boys, standing around and talking isn't getting the barn built."

The barn was up before dark, and a tired but exhilarated group headed back to their homes that night, chased by the heartfelt thanks of the Wrights.

Chapter 22

THREE DAYS AFTER THE BARN RAISING AT ED Wright's place, Hawke was having his morning shave when he saw two wagons approaching. Both were laden with furniture and personal belongings. George Butrum was in the first wagon, his wife Anna and his twelve-year-old son Marvin riding on the seat with him. Mitch Arnold was driving the second wagon, with his wife Susan and fifteen-year-old daughter Ellie Mae.

Hawke wiped off the remaining lather, then walked over to the main house and stepped into the kitchen where Cynthia and Hannah were busy making breakfast.

"Good morning, Mason," Cynthia said brightly, pouring him a cup of coffee. "I trust you slept well."

"I did, thanks," Hawke said, taking the coffee. "Is Ian awake yet?"

"Yes, I think so."

"Maybe he had better come outside."

"Why?" Cynthia asked, a puzzled expression on her face. "What is it?"

"Butrum and Arnold are coming."

"Oh?"

"They are both driving wagons," Hawke said. "The wagons are full, and they have their entire families with them."

"Hannah," Cynthia said. "Go get your father."

Hannah hurried toward the back of the house.

"Oh, dear, I hope I have enough eggs gathered to feed them breakfast," Cynthia said. "I wish they had given me some warning."

"I don't believe this is a social call," Hawke said.

Ian came into the kitchen then. "They're pulling out, aren't they?" he said.

"Yes, I believe they are," Hawke replied.

By the time Hawke and Ian were outside, the two wagons were just rolling in. The drivers called to their teams, then set the brakes.

"George, Mitch," Ian said. He was leaning on the two canes. "Good morning to you."

"Morning, Ian, Hawke," Butrum said. When Cynthia came out onto the porch, Butrum touched the brim of his hat. "Good morning to you, Mrs. Macgregor."

"Mr. Butrum," Cynthia replied.

"Mama, can I tell Hannah good-bye?" Ellie Mae asked. At fifteen, Ellie Mae and Hannah were the closest in age of all the sheep ranchers' daughters.

"Yes, dear," Susan Arnold replied. "But be ready to leave when Papa calls."

"I will," Ellie Mae said as she climbed down from the wagon.

"George, Mitch, what's this all about?" Ian asked.

"Me 'n' Mitch have talked it over," Butrum said. "We've, uh, we've . . ." Butrum paused, unable to complete his thought.

"We've sold our places to Creed," Mitch said.

Ian pinched the bridge of his nose and shook his head. "How many pieces of silver did he give you?" he asked.

"Ian!" Cynthia scolded.

"I'm sorry," Ian said. "Cynthia's right. I have no business questioning what you do."

"We got two hundred dollars apiece," Butrum said.

"Two hundred dollars?" Ian said in surprise. "Why, your places are worth five times that."

"To who? Would you pay us a thousand dollars? For that matter, would you pay us two hundred dollars?"

Ian shook his head. "I don't have the money," he said.

"No, and neither does anyone else, except for Creed."

"What happened?" Ian asked. "Just the other day, when we all got together to build Ed's barn, you two were as anxious as the rest of us to get him to stay. Now you are hell-bent on leaving. Why?"

"When we got home from Ed's place the other night we found every window in our house broken out, and both doors smashed in," Butrum said. "Tar was poured all over the floors and over most of our furniture." He nodded toward the wagon. "We salvaged what we could, but there's scarcely enough left to set up housekeeping at our next place."

"I'm sorry, George," Ian said. "But we could've helped you get back on your feet, same as we did with Ed."

"What good would that have done? They'd just do it again."

"What about you, Mitch?"

"Just like George said," Arnold replied. "Windows and doors smashed, tar over everything."

Ian was quiet for a long time. "So, you went to see Creed?"

Butrum shook his head. "We didn't have to. Lonnie come around to the house to make us an offer, sittin' up on his horse, suckin' on that little piece of rawhide he's always got in his mouth. 'Course, he acted all surprised about our house bein' messed up like it was, said he didn't know nothin' about it. He said his pa was just wantin' to make a friendly offer to buy the place."

"And you took his offer?"

"He didn't come right out and say it, Ian, but it was pretty clear that if we didn't take the offer, somethin' even worse would happen next time. I've got a wife and kid, I didn't want to see anything happen to them."

"He came to see you too?" Ian asked Arnold.

Mitch Arnold nodded. "Yeah, probably within an hour after he was over at George's."

Ian sighed. "Well, I don't suppose I can really say that I blame you. But we are going to miss you."

"Ellie Mae is my only friend," Hannah said.

"I know, darlin'," Susan Arnold said. "And believe me, she is going to miss you." Susan looked at her daughter, who was weeping quietly.

"George, we need to get going," Arnold said.

"Yeah," Butrum answered. He started to climb back on his wagon, then turned and looked back toward Ian. "Oh, Ian, me 'n' Mitch turned our sheep out. We figure they'll probably join your flock, since you're the closest to us. If you sell 'em an' get 'nything for 'em, we'd appreciate it if—"

"Just let me know where to send the money," Ian said. "I'll see that you get it."

Butrum nodded but didn't say anything. He climbed back onto the wagon seat, then clucked at his team. His wagon, and Arnold's behind it, pulled away slowly.

"It's not fair," Hannah said, choking back a sob. "It just isn't fair."

"No, darlin', it isn't," Cynthia said. "But it is life."

"Mama?" Hannah said later that same afternoon.

"Yes, dear?"

"Someone's coming."

"This *has* been our day for visitors, hasn't it?" she said, drying her hands on a towel. She walked over to look through the same window as Hannah, and saw three riders approaching the house. "Oh," she said. "Oh, my. I believe that is Mr. Creed."

"And Lonnie and Clay Morgan," Hannah said.

"Clay Morgan?"

"He's the gunman that the cattlemen hired."

"How do you know that's Clay Morgan?"

"I saw him when I went into town with Mr. Hawke," Hannah said. "I think we should tell Papa."

"No need," Cynthia said, pointing toward the barn. "Ian has seen them too."

Ian was walking out to the front of his house. He wasn't using canes.

"Oh, my!" Cynthia said, gasping.

"What is it?"

"Ian is carrying his rifle. Oh, please God, don't let Ian start anything."

Joshua Creed, Lonnie, and Morgan rode into the front yard. None of the three dismounted, but they stopped their horses about twenty feet away from Ian. Lonnie was chewing on his ever present string of rawhide, the end of it dangling down.

Cynthia went out into the front yard quickly, then came up behind Ian and put her hand on his shoulder. Hannah realized then that her mother was putting herself in a position to prevent Ian from doing anything rash. She went out to join them. Then she saw Hawke walking toward the house from the barn. She noticed, also, that though he didn't always wear his gun around the ranch, he was wearing it now.

Hawke stopped at the edge of the house and leaned back against the front porch with his arms folded across his chest.

"Mr. Macgregor, Mr. Hawke, good afternoon to you," Creed said.

"Afternoon," Ian replied.

Hawke said nothing, but maintained his same casual pose against the front of the house. Hannah knew that his casual look was deceptive. She had learned a lot about him since he arrived, and knew that despite his outward appearances, he was as poised for action as a cat.

"What do you want, Creed?" Ian asked.

"You know my son," Creed began. "And this gentleman has recently come to work for me. His name is Clay Morgan."

"I know who they are," Ian said.

"Yes, well, I wonder if you might invite us inside so we could talk a little business?"

"No need to invite you in. I can't imagine any business you and I might have to talk about," Ian replied. "And anything else you have to say, you can say it out here."

"Oh, I think when you hear my offer, you might change your mind," Creed said.

"What offer?"

"My offer to buy this place," Creed said. "I am prepared to be very generous. I'll buy your spread, your house . . . I'll even buy your sheep."

"Ha!" Ian said. "Are you telling me you want to go into the sheep business?"

Creed laughed. "That is a good one. No, the first thing I would do would be to take your sheep down to the railhead and ship them to market. Like I've been saying all along, this is cattle country."

During the conversation, Hannah began feeling uneasy, then realized why. Lonnie Creed had taken the rawhide string from his mouth and was now staring at her with eyes that were very deep and disturbing. She could almost believe there were tiny red dots way at the bottom.

"Mr. Creed, I'm not in the least interested in selling my place to you," Ian said.

"Oh, don't make up your mind so quickly," Creed said. "As I said, I'm prepared to make you a very generous offer."

"A generous offer? Like what you paid George Butrum and Mitch Arnold for their places?"

"Butrum and Arnold were small men with no courage, no influence, and of little importance," Creed replied. "They got what they were worth. You, however, are different. You have proven yourself to be a man of courage and influence." Creed smiled. "In fact, you have much more influence than I care to admit. You've been making things very difficult for me, Mr. Macgregor. Or should I say, Sergeant Major Macgregor. I can see, now, why we had such a difficult time defeating the South, if they had many men like you."

Ian supposed it was meant to be a compliment, but he let it slide by with absolutely no recognition.

Meanwhile, as Creed and Ian were talking, Hannah noticed that Hawke and Morgan continued to look at each other with steady, unblinking, stares. Then Morgan got down from his horse, dismounting so slowly as to almost make it a ballet, never taking his eyes off Hawke in the process. The gunfighter walked over to a nearby rosebush, cut off a bloom, then brought it to Hannah and held it out toward her.

Hannah's heart almost stopped beating. If Satan himself had suddenly appeared before her, she did not believe she would be confronted with any more evil than what was standing before her now. She glanced toward Hawke, who had not taken his eyes off Morgan. With her eyes, she asked him what she should do.

Hawke gave a barely perceptible nod, and Hannah, holding her breath in fear, reached out to take the rose bloom from Morgan.

Morgan returned to his horse and remounted in a repeat of his dismounting, a slow, graceful, balletlike movement without once taking his eyes off Hawke.

"I am prepared to offer you one thousand dollars for your spread," Creed said, "and another thousand dollars for your sheep."

"Creed, you couldn't buy me out with ten thousand dollars," Ian said.

Creed sighed audibly. "Mr. Macgregor, I thought you were an intelligent man," he said. "I had hoped you would be reasonable. Your sheep are going to die of starvation because you can't feed them. You must know I have a court injunction preventing you and your friends from having access to the open range."

"No, you don't," Ian said. "That injunction has been set aside, pending the hearing."

Creed smiled, but it wasn't a smile of mirth. "Maybe if you had hired a real lawyer instead of a schoolteacher, he would have told you that until Mr. Eckert has been served with papers that rescind that injunction, it is still in effect."

"No," Ian said. "That isn't true. I heard the judge lift the injunction with my own ears. We are going to run our sheep on the open range."

"As I said, the law is on my side of this question," Creed said. He nodded toward Morgan. "And Mr. Morgan here, as a private detective, is duly authorized to enforce the injunction. I have hired him to do just that, and believe me, he will, with the utmost efficiency."

"You have no right to do that. You can't enforce that order," Ian insisted.

"Oh, but I do have the right to enforce it, and I will," Creed said. "Mr. Macgregor, I'm sorry we were unable to come to any kind of an accommodation. Regretfully, I must tell you now that any future meetings between us will be much less cordial." He touched the brim of his hat. "Good day to you, sir."

Creed and Lonnie turned their horses to ride off, but Morgan backed his horse up for several feet, all the while staring at Hawke. Finally, he turned his horse as well, then urged it into a gallop to catch up with the others.

"Oh, Ian, what are we going to do?" Cynthia said.

"Do? We're going to do the same thing we've been doing," Ian replied. "We are going to continue to run our ranch."

"But Mr. Creed and that awful man with him. . . . I'm afraid we are going to lose the ranch."

"Don't be afraid, Cynthia," Hawke said. "You aren't going to lose this ranch."

Those were the first words Hawke had spoken since Creed had arrived.

"Cynthia, do you have any coffee left?" Ian asked.

"Yes."

"Good, good. I think I would like to have a cup."

"I just might join you," Cynthia said.

Hannah watched her mother and father go into the house. She watched, also, as Hawke walked casually back toward his room in the barn. She went after him.

"Mr. Hawke?" she called to him.

He turned and looked back at her. The hard, almost frightening expression she had noticed in his face while he was staring at Morgan changed now to a warm and inviting smile.

"Yes?" he said. "What can I do for you?"

"Were you scared?" she asked.

"Yes, a little. Were you?"

"I was terrified," Hannah said. "But you? You were scared? I didn't think you were ever afraid of anything."

"Oh, yes," Hawke said. "A man would be a fool never to be afraid of anything. Fear is one of the tools of survival that God gives us."

"So, when you were in that gunfight a couple of weeks ago, when you killed Poke and Jules, you were afraid?"

"Yes."

"Then I guess I shouldn't be ashamed for being afraid a while ago."

"Not in the least."

"Did you mean it when you told Mama that we weren't going to lose our ranch?"

"Yes, I meant it."

"But how?"

"How, what?"

"How can you be so sure that Papa won't lose his ranch?"

"Because your father is one of the best men I have ever known," Hawke said. "And in the end, good always triumphs over evil."

"I hope—" Hannah started, but Hawke interrupted her by putting his hand on her shoulder.

"I want you to believe me," he said softly. "Your mother and father are not going to lose this ranch."

Looking at him, Hannah thought she had never seen anyone more handsome, or brave, or reassuring. She wondered if she would ever be able to find someone like him.

Then, almost as quickly as she had the thought, she put it away, feeling that it was a negative comment on Jesse.

"I believe you," she said.

"Hannah?"

"Yes."

"I want you to understand that it might be necessary for me to do some things . . . some harsh things, things that might be hard for you to accept."

"You mean you might have to kill Clay Morgan."

"I'm afraid it won't be just Clay Morgan."

"I know," Hannah said.

"I don't want to lose your . . . respect," Hawke said, looking for the word.

"Mr. Hawke, I don't believe there is anything you could ever do that would cause me to lose my respect for you," Hannah replied.

Chapter 23

SOMEWHERE IN THE DARKNESS A LAMB BAWLED anxiously and its mother answered. In the distance a coyote sent up its long, lonesome wail, while out in the pond, frogs thrummed their night song. The moon was a thin sliver of silver, but the night was alive with stars . . . from the very bright, shining lights, all the way down to those stars that weren't visible as individual bodies at all, but whose glow added to the luminous powder that dusted the velvet-black sky. Beside the milling shapes of shadows that made up the small flock, Andoni Larranaga and Mikel Mendiolea, two young Basque men, were sitting, their shepherd's hooks on the ground beside them.

The two were engaged in conversation, speaking in their native Euskera language.

"I can't believe you don't know the Eskal national anthem," Larranaga said.

"We can't have a national anthem," Mendiolea replied. "The Basque don't even have a nation."

"Sure we have a nation," Larranaga insisted.

"Really? Where is it? What does our flag look like? Who is the president of Eskal?"

"You don't need borders and flags and presidents and governors to be a nation. All you need are people. And we have people, back in the Pyrenees of Spain and France, in Canada, in Mexico, and here in Idaho. The Basque people make up the nation of Eskal."

"All right, what is the national anthem?"

"It is called 'Gernikako Arbola,'" Larranaga said.

"Ha!" Mendiolea replied. "I know that song. It's a folk song, not a national anthem."

"It's a song about our folk," Larranaga said. "That makes it our anthem." He began to sing, and Mendiolea, to show that he also knew the song, began to sing with him.

> *"The tree of Gernika is a blessed symbol*
> *loved by all the Basque people with deep love.*
> *Give to all the world your fruit;*
> *we adore you sacred tree."*

The lamb called again for its mother. And this time the mother's answer sounded anxious.

"Sounds like one of 'em's wandered off," Larranaga said. "Maybe I'd better go find it."

"Why bother? It'll find its way back," Mendiolea said.

Larranaga stood up and brushed the grass away from his trousers. "Mikel, for thousands of years the Basque people have been helping lambs find their way back to their mothers," he said. "Should I stop now just because you ask me to?

Mendiolea chuckled. "You know your problem, Andoni?

You think you have to carry the history of all the Basque people on your shoulders. Go, find the little lost lamb."

"I will," Larranaga said as he disappeared into the darkness.

"Do you want me to come with you?" Mendiolea called after him.

Not getting an answer, Mendiolea stood and brushed off his trousers as well. "Andoni, do you want me to come with you?" he called again.

"Mikel!"

The scream that came from the darkness was filled with such terror that Mendiolea felt his blood run cold.

"Andoni! What is it?" Mendiolea shouted, running into the darkness toward where he'd heard the sound.

The sheep, so docile moments earlier, now began to run, and it was all Mendiolea could do to keep his feet as they rushed passed him.

"Andoni!" he called again.

Suddenly, a gunshot erupted in the night, and at nearly the same moment that he heard it, Mendiolea felt a heavy blow to his chest, as if someone had hit him with a hammer. He put his hand to his chest and pulled it away, looking at the blood in his palm as if unable to understand where it came from.

Then the pain subsided and Mendiolea felt himself growing light-headed. He fell.

What followed was the frightened shuffle of the sheep and the moan of a ceaseless wind.

No more than twenty yards from the two men he had just killed, Clay Morgan sat on his horse, his hat pulled low over his head. He took out a cheroot, struck a match on his saddle horn, lit it, then rode off enjoying the smoke.

It had been a good night's work.

* * *

The town of King Hill was temporarily taken over for the funerals of Andoni Larranaga and Mikel Mendiolea, both of whom had worked for Emerson Booker. Not only did all the sheep ranchers come to the funeral, but so too did all the Basque shepherds and their families. In addition to the Basque who lived and worked in the Camas Valley, many others came by train, so there were as many Basque in town as there were citizens of the town.

The tolling of the church bell announced the beginning of the funeral. Larranaga and Mendiolea's coffins were draped with the red, white, and green colors of the Basque and were borne on the shoulders of their fellow Basques along a corridor of onlookers down Main Street to the church.

The religious service began amidst expressions of grief and muted conversations. At its conclusion, the strains of "Gernikako Arbola," the Tree of Gernika, came from the church organ.

As Larranaga and Mendiolea's bodies, once more flanked by mourners, began their journey toward the graveyard, musicians preceded the coffins, leading the way to the music of the *txistu* and the *txalapata*, the flute and wooden rhythm percussion instrument. Behind the coffins, Larranaga's wife, Enara, and Mendiolea's wife, Usea, walked with relatives and close friends.

After the coffins had been lowered, family members dropped flowers and handfuls of earth into the grave as Josu played "Gernikako Arbola" on his flute. This time, all the Basques who were present joined in and sang.

After the funeral there was a traffic jam of horses and wagons as people hurried to leave the cemetery. Everyone was heading to the meeting that had been called at Emerson Booker's house, and because he wasn't married, Cynthia and some of the other wives had arranged to bring food.

As Hawke, Ian, Cynthia, and Hannah returned to their buckboard, they talked in quiet tones about the funeral. Ian stopped and looked toward the edge of the cemetery.

"What's he doing here?" he asked, nodding at a clump of trees on the periphery.

"It's Jesse," Hannah said. She looked at Ian. "Papa, can I go talk to him?"

"Why in heaven's name would you want to?" he asked. "You know what all has happened."

"Yes, and it's all bad," Hannah agreed. "I just don't believe that Jesse had anything to do with it."

Ian held his hand out and motioned dismissively. "All right," he said. "Go talk to him."

Hannah brightened. "Thank you, Papa," she said, kissing him on the cheek before she hurried over to see Jesse Carlisle.

"Thanks," Jesse said when she came up to him. He looked back toward the cemetery. "I didn't think you'd want to see me. Not after what I said the last time we spoke."

"What are you doing here?" Hannah asked.

Jesse was holding a single red rose, and he looked down at it as he answered. "I, uh, came to visit my brother's grave." He pointed with the rose. "It's right over there, if you remember."

"Yes, I remember."

Jesse sighed and shook his head. "No, that's not right," he said. "I didn't come to see Johnny. I came to see you." He handed the rose to Hannah.

"To see me?"

Jesse nodded. "Yes. I knew you would be here for the funeral."

"It was awful, those two men getting killed," she said. "Enara—that's Mr. Larranaga's wife—is pregnant. Now her baby will come into the world without a father."

"I'm so sorry they were killed," Jesse said. "And I'm sorry for their families. But, Hannah, I hope you don't think I had anything to do with this."

"Oh, Jesse, I know you wouldn't have anything to do with it. Not personally. But don't you see? It's all part of this crazy war that's going on between my people and your people."

"It doesn't have to be my people or your people," Jesse said. "As far as you and I are concerned, it could just be us."

"How?"

"It's simple," Jesse said. "Marry me and we'll go our own way."

"Marry you? Jesse, I'm only sixteen years old!"

"Some women get married when they're sixteen. Pa told me that lots of girls down South get married when they are only sixteen, and sometimes even younger. And you're from the South, aren't you?"

"Well yes, but—"

"Hannah, if we don't get married now, while we have a chance, I don't know what's going to happen to us. This . . . this business between the cattlemen and the sheep herders is never going to end."

"I can't, Jesse," Hannah said, her voice pained. "Please try to understand. I can't leave my mother and my father now, not while all this is going on."

"Then this is it," Jesse said sadly. "I'm sorry it had to turn out this way."

"What are you going to do?" Hannah asked.

"What can I do?" Jesse replied. "You called it. You said my people and your people. I'm going to stay with my people."

"Hannah!" Ian called.

"Your pa is calling."

"Yes, I know. We're all going to Mr. Booker's house. He's the one that Mr. Larranaga and Mr. Mendiolea worked for."

"You'd better hurry, then," Jesse said.

Hannah stood there a moment longer, then reached out and touched his hands.

"Hannah?" Jesse said.

Hannah said nothing, but continued to look into his eyes.

"I have to do this," Jesse said. He pulled her to him and kissed her.

At first Hannah struggled against him. This was no place for such a thing, in a cemetery with mourners still present, and in the presence of her parents. But the harder she struggled, the more determined he was to hold her, until finally she abandoned the struggle and let herself go limp in his arms. The rose slipped from her hand and fell to the ground, there to lie just beneath the foot she lifted as she leaned into him.

Not until she abandoned the struggle and returned the kiss did Jesse break, leaving Hannah standing there as limp as a rag doll.

"Good-bye," he said, turning and walking away from her. She noticed then that his horse was tied to a tree just a few feet away. She watched him until he mounted. He glanced back at her one last time but said nothing as he turned his horse and rode away.

Chapter 24

"I FEEL GUILTY," EMERSON TOLD THE PEOPLE WHO had gathered at his house after the funeral. "Andoni and Mikel said they wanted to take the sheep out into the open range, and I told them to go ahead. I should have held them back until there were more who wanted to go."

"It's not your fault, Emerson," Ian said. "What happened with Ed's barn and with George and Mitch proves that Creed is going to make trouble, no matter where you are."

"Yes, but this is more than trouble," Ian said. "Two of the finest young men you would ever want to meet were murdered in cold blood."

"What I don't understand is why the sheriff hasn't taken a hand in this," Dumey said.

"Or at least a U.S. Marshal," Patterson added.

"Yes," Cummings said. "Eckert knows that we have a

right to be in the open range. It seems to me like he would
get the U.S. Marshal to help him enforce it."

"I've been thinking that same thing," Emerson said.
"And tomorrow I think I'll just go into town and have a talk
with Mr. Eckert."

A banner spread across Main Street read:

105 YEARS OLD! HAPPY BIRTHDAY, AMERICA

All of the posts and porch pillars in town were wrapped
in red, white, and blue bunting, and another big sign read:

FOURTH OF JULY GALA, NEXT MONDAY,
DOWNTOWN KING HILL

The Bureau of Land Management occupied an office on
Park Street. Emerson Booker knew the office well, because
it was here that he had filed his land claim when he first
arrived in Idaho. The office consisted of two rooms—the
front room, in which the entrance was separated from the
reception area by a counter that ran from wall to wall, and
the back room, which was the private office of the field
manager.

The walls of the entrance and reception area were covered with maps of Alturas County showing land that was
owned and land designated as open range. Emerson saw his
own ranch marked out on the map, as well as the ranches that
belonged to the other sheep herders. The cattle ranches were
marked out as well, and he thought it interesting that just one
cattle ranch was larger than all the sheep ranches combined.

"You've got all the land in the world," he said under his
breath. "Why are you trying to run us out?"

"Good afternoon, Mr. Booker, may I help you?"

Turning away from the wall map, Emerson saw Emile Horner, Eckert's clerk.

"Yes, I'm here to see Mr. Eckert," Emerson said.

"Just a moment, please, I'll tell him you are here," Horner said, stepping through the door that led into Eckert's office. He returned a moment later.

"I'm sorry," Horner said. "But Mr. Eckert said it would not be convenient for him to see you today."

"Not convenient?" Emerson replied angrily. "Not convenient?"

"Yes, sir. He is meeting with Mr. Creed at the moment."

"Well, fine," Emerson said. "This effects Creed as well. I'll just see both of them at the same time."

Emerson opened the little gate and walked through.

"No, Mr. Booker, you can't—" Horner said, but Emerson waved him off as he opened the door and stepped into Eckert's office.

"Show a little gumption, man," Creed was saying angrily.

"But you don't understand, I—" Eckert started to say, his reply interrupted by an angry announcement from Emerson.

"Eckert, I need to talk to you, now."

Both Eckert and Creed looked around at Emerson, their expressions revealing surprise and annoyance at his intrusion.

"I'm sorry, Mr. Booker," Eckert said. "But as you can see, I'm busy with Mr. Creed at the moment."

"Well, good, because this effects Creed as well," Emerson said.

"I—" Eckert started.

"That's all right, Eckert, let him speak his piece," Creed said.

"Very well, Mr. Booker," Eckert said. "What is it?"

"I'm sure you heard that two of my men were murdered the other night."

"I, uh, did hear that two men were killed," Eckert said. "I didn't hear who they worked for, nor did I hear any of the details."

"Then I'll give you the details," Emerson said. "They were tending my sheep when someone murdered them."

"Where were your sheep?" Creed asked.

"My sheep were on the open range," Emerson said.

"Oh, well, I'm sorry your men were killed, but they were violating the law. I'm sure you are aware of the injunction against any sheep grazing on open range."

"Creed, you know damn well that injunction has been lifted. You were there when the judge lifted it. Yet you and the other cattlemen are acting as if it is still in effect," Emerson said. "Why is that?"

"You are the official government spokesman here, Mr. Eckert," Creed said. "Perhaps you should tell him."

"Mr. Booker, they are acting as if the injunction is still in effect because technically it has not yet been dissolved," Eckert said.

"What? What do you mean it hasn't been dissolved?" Emerson demanded. "You know damn well it has been dissolved. We were both there when Judge Dollar dissolved it."

Eckert shook his head. "Yes, you and I both heard him say that he was going to dissolve it. But until he actually signs the court order doing so, it is still in effect."

"Are you telling me he hasn't signed a court order?"

"I don't know if he has or not."

"How can you not know?"

"Look, Mr. Booker, I am a field manager for the United States government. I strive to remain absolutely neutral on all disputes. And that means I cannot interpret. I am very strictly bound by the laws of the United States, and the law says that until such time as I have a written order rescinding a previous written order, the previous order remains in effect."

"Well, when are you going to get that order?"

"I don't know."

"You don't know?"

"No. And until the order is actually placed in my hand, I'm powerless to do anything to change the status quo."

"How much is Creed paying you to do this?"

"I haven't paid him one cent!" Creed said angrily.

"Mr. Booker," Eckert said. "You are coming dangerously close to slandering a U.S. government official. I caution you, sir, that, that is a federal offense."

Emerson stroked his chin, then nodded. "You have to have it placed in your hand, you say?"

"That is correct."

"Very well, Eckert. I will go to Mountain Home myself. I am going to see the judge, and I am going to get two copies of his order. One, I will give to you, and the other I will give to the United States Marshal."

"The U.S. Marshal?" Eckert said.

"I believe he has an office in Mountain Home."

"Really, Mr. Booker, that isn't necessary," Eckert said.

"Oh, I think it is very necessary," Emerson replied. "I'm taking the afternoon train. I'll be back tomorrow with the judge's order."

Turning, Emerson left the office without saying goodbye.

"Oh, dear," Eckert said after Emerson left. "Oh dear, that is very troubling."

"It's nothing you have to worry about," Creed said.

"Oh, but it is. Don't you understand? It is a very serious

crime for a public official to take a bribe. Why, if he goes to the U.S. Marshal and that gets out . . . I could lose my position. I . . . I could even go to prison."

"I'll take care of it. He's not going to see the U.S. Marshal," Creed said. "He won't even see the judge."

"How will you take care of it?"

"That's none of your concern," Creed said. "But as I was telling you before he came in here, you have to show a little more gumption. I want you to enforce the injunction."

"How am I going to do that if I can't use the sheriff?"

"You have as much authority as the sheriff," Creed said. "Use it, man, use it!" Creed took an envelope from his inside pocket and put it on the desk in front of Eckert, who looked inside the envelope and saw that it was filled with greenbacks.

"Yes," he said. "Now that you bring it up, I do have as much authority as the sheriff." He slipped the envelope into his own jacket pocket.

Emerson Booker stood on the street outside the land office for a moment, breathing deeply to try and calm down. He got a big whiff of a fresh pile of horse droppings, deposited in the street just in front of the office, and laughed. That would teach him better than to take a big breath downtown. Over a period of time the streets had been completely paved with horse, mule, and oxen dung. It was bad enough on a clear day, but on days when it rained, the streets became a shimmering pool of liquid ooze, and then it became almost unbearable.

Mounting his horse, he rode down to the depot and bought a round-trip ticket to Mountain Home.

"The train leaves today, Tuesday, June twenty-eighth at two-fifteen and arrives in Mountain Home at four forty-five this afternoon," the clerk said. "Your return train leaves tomorrow, Wednesday, June twenty-ninth, at ten o'clock in the morning and will arrive here at twelve-thirty in the afternoon."

"Thank you," Emerson said.

"That will put you back in town in time for the big Fourth of July celebration next Monday," the clerk said as he pulled the tickets from a book, then stamped them and handed them to Emerson. "You won't want to miss that."

"Thanks, I plan to be here for it," Emerson said, pocketing the tickets.

Emerson then took his horse to the livery and made arrangements to leave it overnight. Before he turned the horse over, though, he reached down into his saddlebag and pulled out his holster and pistol.

"I don't want to leave this here," he said to the stable man.

The stable man chuckled. "No, sir, that might not be such a good idea."

Emerson strapped on his pistol, then decided to go to the saloon and wait until train time.

When he stepped into the saloon, he saw Mark Patterson standing at the bar, drinking a beer. There were several others in the saloon as well, a few townspeople he knew, some he didn't, and several cowboys he did not know by name but had seen in there before.

Seeing Emerson Booker come in, Patterson smiled and waved at him, inviting him over to the bar.

"Hello, Mark."

"Emerson," Patterson replied. "I am glad to see you in here. Seeing as I'm the only sheep man in here, I was beginning to feel like the hen in the fox den," he said, chuckling at his reversal of the cliché.

"Yes, sir, Mr. Booker, what can I get for you?" the bartender asked.

"Hello, Dan. I'll have a beer, please."

"With or without a head?"

"With."

"Very well," Dan answered, leaving to draw the beer.

"So, Mark, what are you doing in here in the middle of the day?" Emerson asked.

"I came to have a new wheel put on my wagon," Patterson said. "What about you?"

Emerson sighed. "I came to talk to Eckert," he said. "I wanted to find out why he isn't enforcing the judge's order to let us use the open range."

Dan put the beer, with a foaming head, in front of Emerson and picked up the nickel from the bar. "You plan to be here for the big Fourth of July celebration?" he asked. "The volunteer Fire Brigade Band is going to perform. I play the tuba, you know."

"Well, then, I shall have to be here," Emerson said.

"Oomp-pah, oomp-pah, oomp-pah," Dan mimicked, pretending to hold a tuba as he walked back down the bar. Emerson and Patterson laughing at his antics.

"What did Eckert say?" Patterson asked.

Emerson took a swallow of his beer. "Ha! He said that the injunction has not been dissolved."

"What? But it has, hasn't it? I mean you and Ian and Hawke were all three there when the judge dissolved it."

"Oh, it's been dissolved, all right," Emerson said, wiping the foam from his lips with the back of his hand. "But Eckert says that until the written order is in his hand, the injunction remains in effect."

"Damn, that doesn't seem right."

Emerson chuckled. "I know, but don't worry. He'll have it in his hands tomorrow, because I'm catching the two-fifteen to Mountain Home and I plan to personally put the order in his hand. And I'm also going to put the order in the hands of the U.S. Marshal in Mountain Home."

"Good idea," Patterson said. "That ought to end this mess once and for all."

"Hey you, schoolteacher!" a raspy voice called.

Looking in that direction, Emerson saw Clay Morgan standing beside his table, and sitting at the table, an evil smile on his face, was Josh Creed.

"I don't believe we've met," Emerson said, though he knew who the gunfighter was.

"I hear you are about to take a trip," Morgan said, not responding directly to Emerson's remark.

"I am," Emerson replied. "I don't know that it is any of your business, though."

"Well, here's the thing," Morgan said. "If you leave town, that's going to give me the idea that you don't like my company. Is that it?"

"What? No, of course not."

"Then I wish you would stay," Morgan said.

"What are you talking about?" Emerson asked. "That's a dumb comment."

"Oh," Morgan said. "So, now you are telling me that you're going to leave town because you don't like my company, and you're telling me that I'm dumb." Morgan's raspy voice was cold and challenging.

Emerson suddenly realized that Morgan was baiting him. Everyone else in the saloon knew as well, because all conversation halted.

"I said no such thing," Emerson said in as quiet and un-challenging way as he could.

"So, now I am a liar, am I?"

"What? No! You're crazy!" As soon as he spoke, Emerson gasped. He realized, too late, that calling Morgan crazy was playing right into the gunman's hands.

"You are really beginning to make me mad, school-teacher. First you say you are leaving town because you don't like my company. Then you call me dumb, then you call me a liar, and now you say I'm crazy. Just how many insults can a man take and still be a man? I'm calling you out."

"No!" Emerson shouted, holding his hands out in front of him, as if by that action he could stop everything from happening. "What are you talking about?"

"Everyone in this saloon has heard you insult me."

"Mr. Morgan, let's be reasonable here," Patterson said. "If you think my friend insulted you, I'm sure he will apologize."

Morgan shook his head. "It's too late for an apology. There's only one way to settle this now. Draw your gun whenever you are ready, schoolteacher."

"No," Emerson said, shaking his head. "I'm not going to draw on you. If you kill me, you will have to do it in cold blood, in front of all these witnesses."

Abruptly, Morgan drew his gun and fired, the shot explosively loud in the confines of the room. Mark Patterson let out a shout of pain, then collapsed to the floor, holding his bleeding knee. Morgan put his pistol back in his holster.

"You'll draw on me, or I'll shoot his other leg," Morgan said.

"My God," Emerson said. It wasn't a curse, he was actually calling on God. "You really are crazy."

Emerson made a desperate grab for his pistol. Morgan smiled at him, and watched as Emerson actually cleared his holster and brought his pistol to bear. Then—just as Morgan knew he would—Emerson hesitated.

Morgan pulled his pistol, fired, then returned his pistol to his holster. He smiled as Emerson was slammed back against the bar by the bullet he'd fired. Emerson fell, his head but inches away from Patterson, who was still lying on the floor, clutching his knee.

After the sound of the gunshot receded, the saloon remained in dead silence for several seconds, with everyone too stunned by what they had just witnessed to talk.

"Dan," Creed finally called to the bartender.

"Yes, sir?" Dan replied, staring wide-eyed at the two men on the floor.

"I think this unpleasantness has been a shock to us all. I'm sure everyone could use a drink. Set them up, I'll pay."

"Yes, sir," Dan answered.

Chapter 25

～～～

EMERSON BOOKER WAS BURIED ON SUNDAY, THE third of July. After the funeral, the sheep ranchers had yet another meeting.

"It is now obvious to me that if we don't leave, Creed is going to kill every one of us," Dumey said.

"He isn't going to kill every one of us," Patterson said. "Not if we don't give him cause."

"What cause did Emerson give him?" Cummings asked. "You said yourself that Clay Morgan egged him into drawing."

"Emerson was going to Mountain Home to get the court order lifting the injunction, directly from the judge," Patterson said. "He was going to leave one copy with the U.S. Marshal, and he made no bones about what he was going to do. Yes, Morgan egged him into a fight, but that was the real reason."

"I still think we should leave," Dumey said.

"You can leave if you want to," Patterson said. "I'm not going to."

"Mark, I would think with you getting shot like that, you'd be the first one to leave," Dumey said.

"That's exactly why I'm not going to leave," Patterson replied. "I've got too much invested in this now."

"Look," Ian said. "Don't be so hasty. Monday is the Fourth of July, let's all go in and have a good time. Afterward we can meet again and decide what to do."

"All right," Cummings said. "If Mark is going to stick around, I guess I can too. Chris, you stay too. At least until after the Fourth."

Dumey sighed. "All right, I guess I can stay a little longer."

On the morning of the fourth all thought of the war going on between the cattlemen and the sheep ranchers was put aside. Like all western towns, the Fourth of July was a major holiday, not only because it was a celebration of the nation's birthday, but also because it enabled the small, isolated towns to feel a kinship with the rest of the country on that day.

The town of King Hill planned a parade, a band concert, a demonstration by the firemen, fireworks, and a dance.

There was a picnic as well, and a very long table had been laid out along Main Street to receive the food brought by all the visitors. There were several hams, dozens of fried chickens, beef roasts, and legs of lamb. There were vegetables too, selected from the local gardens. And, of course, cakes, pies, puddings, and cobblers.

A large wooden floor had been put down in the park and various bands provided music for dancing.

"Hannah, may I have this dance?"

Looking around, Hannah saw Jesse. She smiled at him. "I thought we had said good-bye," she said.

"Yes, well, I can't seem to get that job done," Jesse replied. He held out his hand. "Shall we?"

With a glance toward her father, who nodded his approval, Hannah went out on the dance floor with Jesse.

"My pa is going to talk to your pa today," Jesse said.

"What about?"

"A truce."

"A truce?"

"Pa heard about what happened to Mr. Booker," Jesse said. "He said that was wrong and this has all gone too far."

"Oh, Jesse, does he mean that?" Hannah asked.

"Yes."

"Oh, wouldn't it be wonderful if this whole thing between the cattlemen and the sheep men would end?"

"It's not going to end," Jesse said.

Hannah looked at him with a curious expression on his face. "But you said—"

"I said, as far as my pa is concerned, it's going to end. And I think he will be able to convince most of the other ranchers as well. But that's not going to stop Creed."

"At least your family and mine won't be enemies anymore," Hannah said happily.

By the time Jesse took Hannah back, Rome Carlisle was already talking to Ian, and from the expressions on their faces, the talk was going well.

"I have to ride in the race," Jesse said to Hannah. "Don't forget to come watch me and cheer for me."

"I'll be there," she promised.

Shortly after he left to get ready for his race, Hannah wandered over to the table to get a glass of fruit punch.

"I saw you dancin' real close to Jesse boy," a voice said.

"Now, why don't you see what it's like to dance with a real man?"

Hannah turned around to see Lonnie Creed standing right behind her. He was chewing on a string of rawhide and wearing the same leering expression he had on the day he, his father, and Clay Morgan had come out to her father's house. And, again, she could almost see the red lights in the depths of his eyes.

"I wouldn't dance with you, Lonnie Creed, if you were the last man on earth," she said.

Jesse won the race, which was no surprise. Everyone knew what a good horseman he was, and many had bet on him. He came back to the congratulations and accolades of everyone, and then, after arranging to meet Hannah during the fireworks display, left to take care of his horse.

For the children, the fireworks was the favorite event of the day, and Hannah had agreed to watch over all the children of the sheep ranchers, as well as those of the Basque workers. The fireworks show was to take place down on the bank of the Snake River, and Tomas and Felipe had built benches especially for the children down at the end of Pitchfork Road.

Shortly after it got dark, firecrackers began going off, though these weren't part of the official display. For the most part they were lit by people who were getting into the spirit of the Fourth.

When Jesse had finished ministering to his horse and looking for Hannah, someone threw a firecracker at his feet as he approached Ian, Cynthia, and Hawke. It popped, he jumped, and everyone, including Jesse, laughed.

"Let me congratulate you again on the fine race you rode," Ian said.

"Thank you, sir," Jesse replied, then asked, "Can you

tell me, Mr. Macgregor, where Hannah is? I thought she was going to be down at the end of Pitchfork Road with the children to watch the fireworks display."

"You didn't see her?" Ian replied. "She went down there half an hour ago."

Jesse shook his head. "No sir, I've been there and didn't see her."

"Well, that's odd," Ian said. "I wonder where she is?"

"You don't think anything has happened to her, do you?" Cynthia asked her husband.

"I'll go look for her," Hawke said.

"Someone needs to be with the children," Jesse said. "I'll go back. Maybe she's there by now."

Hawke walked around the picnic area, looking for Hannah, then widened his search to the far end of town, away from the picnic tables, the dance floor, and the fireworks. There were no people at that end of town, but sensing something in a nearby alley, he stopped.

Not wanting whoever it might be to realize he'd seen them, he took off his hat and casually wiped the sweat from his forehead. He wasn't surprised when two men suddenly stepped out of the alley to confront him. One had a yellow snaggletooth hanging in a gap of missing teeth. The other had a pockmarked face.

"Hey, piano man," Pockmark said. "We got a message for you from Lonnie."

Both men were holding pistols, and they were pointed at him.

"Oh?" Hawke replied. He kept his hat at his waist. "And what would that message be?"

"He says he wants you on the next train out of here. There's one that leaves at nine tonight."

"Is the train going east or west?"

"East or west?" The two men laughed. "What difference does that make?"

"If it's going the wrong way, I may not want to be on it."

"Yeah? Well, it don't make no difference which way it's goin', you're goin' to be on it. That is, if you don't want nothin' to happen to that little ol' sheep girl."

"Does Lonnie have Hannah?" Hawke asked.

"Yeah. He's got her," Snaggletooth said.

"How do I know he does? He might just know that I'm looking for her and he's running a bluff."

"It ain't no bluff, piano man. He has her, 'cause we snatched her and took her to him," Snaggletooth said.

"You snatched her?"

"Yeah."

"Is she all right?"

"Yeah, she's all right for now," Snaggletooth said. "But Lonnie says if you ain't on that train at nine o'clock tonight . . . well, let me just say this." Snaggletooth rubbed his crotch. "I hope you ain't on that train. 'Cause if you ain't, well, Lonnie has done tol' us we could have our turn."

"I see," Hawke said.

"Is that all you got to say?"

"Yes."

"So, what do you want us to tell Lonnie?" Pockmark asked.

"Oh, you won't be telling Lonnie anything," Hawke said. He eased his pistol out of his holster, the action hidden by his hat.

"What do you mean we won't tell him anything?" Pockmark asked.

"Because you aren't going to live long enough to tell him anything," Hawke replied.

The two cowboys laughed again.

"Mister, maybe you ain't noticed, but we're both holdin' pistols," Snaggletooth said.

"So am I," Hawke said, pulling his hat away.

"What the hell?" Snaggletooth shouted.

All three pistols fired at the same time. Hawke fired twice.

Snaggletooth and Pockface missed.

Hawke didn't.

Because of the fireworks, nobody even noticed the gunshots.

Hawke put away his gun and continued down the dark street, looking for Lonnie and Hannah.

"Mr. Hawke," a voice called from the darkness of one of the alleys.

Quickly, Hawke drew his gun and spun toward the sound.

"No, don't shoot," the frightened voice called from the darkness. "I don't want no trouble." The man came out in the open with his hands up in the air. "My name is Asa Crawford," he said. "I ride for Crown Ranch. That is, I used to. I don't no more, and I want to help."

"Help, how?"

"I think I know where Lonnie has the girl."

"Where?"

"The Creeds keep 'em a downtown apartment over the feed store. If I was a bettin' man, I'd say that's where he has her."

"Thanks," Hawke said.

"Mr. Hawke. I want you to know, I killed some sheep, but I didn't have nothin' to do with burnin' that fella's barn, and I didn't have nothin' to do with killin' them sheep herders. I'm leavin'. I've had enough of this."

Hawke looked at him for a moment, then nodded, and Crawford, with a sigh of relief, turned and walked away.

* * *

In the apartment, Lonnie Creed's attention was focused on Hannah, who was tied up on the bed. She was also gagged so she couldn't call out.

"I'm goin' to get double duty out you, did you know that?" Lonnie said around the little string of rawhide hanging from his mouth.

Hannah stared at him through large, frightened eyes.

Lonnie ran his finger across her cheek. "Yes, ma'am," he said. "A couple of my boys are tellin' that Fancy Dan piano player right now that if he doesn't want to see you hurt, he'll get on a train and get out of town."

He let his finger drop down to the hollow of her neck.

"He'll do it too, 'cause he won't want to see anything happen to you."

Lonnie's hand dropped down the top of her dress and jerked the camisole down, exposing her breasts.

"Whooee, you got some pretty titties there, you know that?" he asked lecherously. "Has ol' Jesse boy ever seen them titties?" He rubbed himself. "You know what? I just believe he has seen 'em," he said. "I'll just bet you and Jesse boy have had a roll in the hay more than once."

Lonnie reached out and touched each nipple. Hannah's eyes welled with tears.

"But him bein' no more'n a boy, he probably didn't know what he was doing. Tell you what, girlie. Soon as I take care of the Fancy Dan piano player, maybe I'll just show you what it's like with a real man."

At that moment, Hawke crashed through the window. Startled by the sound of breaking glass, Lonnie turned toward him.

Hawke reached for his pistol—only to discover that it was gone. He looked around in surprise. His gun had fallen out of his holster as he climbed onto the porch overhang to get to the second floor apartment.

Seeing that Hawke didn't have his pistol, Lonnie's panic suddenly turned to jubilation.

"Ha!" he said. "What are you going to do now, Mr. Fancy Dan?"

Lonnie raised his own pistol to shoot, but even as he did, Hawke's arm flashed in front of him. Hawke held a large shard of glass from the broken window, and for an instant there was nothing more than a thin, red line across Lonnie's neck. Then the line grew darker as blood began to gush from Lonnie's severed carotid artery. He dropped his pistol and grabbed his neck even as the blood spurted through his fingers, then fell to the floor. After a couple of spastic convulsions, he lay still and the string of rawhide fell from his lips.

Hawke took his jacket off and put it around Hannah, removed her gag and began untying her.

"I'm going to take you home," he said.

Chapter 26

JOSHUA CREED BURIED HIS SON AND THE TWO cowboys who had worked for him in his private cemetery at Crown Ranch. Most of the other ranchers came to the funeral, though Rome Carlisle and his son Jesse were conspicuous by their absence.

Creed pointed toward the private graveyard. "There's five good men lyin' out there dead," he said. "Four men who rode for me, and my son. Dalt, you 'n' Jared have each lost a rider, 'n' Carlisle's lost a rider and a son. It's time we ended this war once and for all," Creed said. "Tonight, I want to raid Macgregor's ranch. If we get rid of him, all of them will leave."

Dalt Fenton and the other ranchers looked at each other, but nobody spoke.

"What is it?" Creed asked. "What's going on?"

Fenton cleared his throat. "Josh, me 'n' the other ranchers have been talking," he said. "We think you're right, this war has gone on long enough. Only we don't plan to raid the Macgregor ranch tonight, or any other night. The truth is, we think it's time we started gettin' along with the sheep herders."

"Are you turning against me now? Like Carlisle?"

"We ain't turnin' against you, Josh," Jared Wilson said. "You're still our neighbor. But the sheep men, why, they are our neighbors too. If they'll let bygones be bygones, I'm for callin' this war off before anyone else gets killed."

"Get off my ranch," Creed ordered, his face turning red with rage. He pointed toward the arched gate at the end of his drive. "Ever' damn one of you, just get out now," he said. "I'll take care of this by myself."

Cynthia and Hanna were sitting on the front porch shelling peas when Cynthia looked up and saw four riders coming across Clover Creek.

"Honey, where's your papa and Mason?" Cynthia asked.

"They are out back, working on the windmill," Hannah said.

"You'd better go get them."

Hannah put her bowl down, wiped her hands on her apron, and hurried around to get them. Ian and Hawke reached the front of the house just as the four riders came around the garden.

"Neither one of us are armed," Ian said under his breath.

"Neither are they," Hawke replied. "Do you know them?"

"They're all cattle ranchers," Ian said. "That's Dalt Fenton, that's Jared Wilson, that's Ben Percy. I don't know the other one."

The four riders pulled up in front of the house, and while

three of them remained mounted, Dalt Fenton dismounted. Taking his hat off, he approached the front porch.

"Ma'am," he said to Cynthia. "Miss." He nodded toward Hannah. "Mr. Macgregor, I . . . that is we," he raised his arm to include the other three riders, "are here to tell you that the war between us is over. Rome Carlisle was right. Josh Creed is wrong."

"That's very decent of you," Ian said. "I appreciate your coming over to tell me that."

"As far as we're concerned, you folks can graze your sheep on open range anytime you want."

"Dalt," Jared said from the saddle.

"Oh, yeah," Fenton said. "But we have to tell you that Creed hasn't come around yet. He may still try to give you trouble, but I promise you, there won't none of it come from us."

"I'll tell the others," Ian said. "They will be glad to hear it."

Fenton nodded, then remounted. "I wish you all the best, Mr. Macgregor," he said as he left.

Joshua Creed and Clay Morgan were waiting for the train to arrive at the depot in King Hill the next day. After it pulled in, four men, all dressed in black, with badges identical to the one worn by Clay Morgan and wearing pistols, stepped down from the train. Seeing Clay, they came toward him.

"Hello, Bull, Marty, Sam, Trace," Clay said. "Are you boys ready to go to work?"

"We're ready," Bull said. "Where do we start?"

"We start at the sheriff's office," Clay replied.

Sheriff Tilghman was sitting at his desk reading the newspaper when Creed, Morgan, and Morgan's four deputies came in.

"Hello, Creed," he said. Then, seeing the five men with him, he became uneasy. "What is this?" he asked. "What's going on?"

"We're giving the town a new sheriff," Morgan said matter-of-factly.

He drew his gun and killed Tilghman before Tilghman could reply.

"All right, Mr. Creed, it's your money that's paying for this," Morgan said as he put his smoking gun away. "What do we do next?"

Creed was momentarily stunned by what had just occurred. Then he said, "We let the town know we are in charge."

Creed, accompanied by Morgan and the other gunmen, went down to the newspaper office, where Joe Blanton, the editor and publisher of the *King Hill Gazette,* was setting type for the next edition.

At a nod from Morgan, Bull walked over and picked up the page Blanton had just set.

"Here, what are you doing?" Blanton asked in alarm.

Bull dumped the type on the floor.

"Do you know how long it took me to set that?"

"I have a new story for you," Creed said. "I want you to set it in the biggest, boldest type you have, and I want you to get out an extra. I want a copy of your paper in the hands of everyone in town before dark."

"Not everyone in town subscribes to the paper," Blanton replied.

"They are all going to get a copy today," Creed said.

"What am I supposed to say?"

"Say exactly what I tell you," Creed said.

Ian looked at the newspaper Dexter Manley showed him.

**JOSHUA CREED APPOINTED
MAYOR OF KING HILL
CLAY MORGAN IS NEW SHERIFF
ALL ORDERS WILL BE PROMPTLY OBEYED**

"What is this?" Ian asked.

"It's hell is what it is," Dexter said. "Clay Morgan brought four more gunfighters in, just like him. Creed and them have taken over the entire town. Nobody can do anything without their permission."

"When did this happen?" Hawke asked.

"Two days ago," Dexter answered. "They killed Sheriff Tilghman right off. Then, yesterday, they killed Dan and took over the saloon. They've drunk up most of the whiskey and they've kept the girls busy ever since they got here. Uh, no offense meant, ma'am," he said to Cynthia.

"I knew Creed was an evil man, but I never knew he would do anything like this," Ian said. "I wonder what in the world got into him?"

"It's Mr. Hawke," Manley said.

"I beg your pardon?" Ian replied.

Manley nodded toward Hawke. "He said you killed his boy, and he's not going to leave town until he settles with you. He sent me out to get you."

"Ha! You say there are five gunmen in town, and he thinks all he has to do is send for Hawke?" Ian said.

"He said if Hawke doesn't come in, he'll kill the girls at the saloon."

"He's bluffing," Ian said. "You said yourself that they were keeping the girls busy."

"He's not bluffing," Hawke replied solemnly.

"Well, what if he is not? You are just one man," Ian said. "You can't go against all of them."

"Somebody has to," Hawke said, starting toward the barn.

"Hawke, no!" Ian called, but Hawke kept walking.

Ian watched him for a moment, then turned to his wife. "Cynthia, go stop him," he said.

"What makes you think I can stop him?"

"Because I know how the two of you feel about each other," Ian said, measuring his words carefully.

"Ian, I would never—" she started, but Ian held up his hand.

"Do you think I don't know that, Cynthia? Now, please, try and stop him."

Cynthia nodded, then hurried out to the barn where Hawke was saddling his horse.

"Mason, please," she said. "Don't go."

"I have to," Hawke said.

"Mason, no. I . . . I don't know what I would do if anything happened to you now." Impulsively, she put her arms around him and, leaning into him, kissed him.

Gently, Hawke disengaged himself.

"Mason, if you won't go I'll do anything. I'll even—"

Hawke held up his hand to stop her. "Cynthia, don't say something you don't mean," he said.

Cynthia realized then there was someone else in the barn. Turning, she saw Hannah standing there, looking at them with eyes open wide in hurt and confusion.

"I have to go," Hawke said. "I'm flattered that you would pretend there is something between us, just to keep me. But I have to go."

The hurt and confusion left Hannah's face. She could understand that her mother might use deception to keep Hawke there.

"All right," Cynthia said. "Go if you must."

* * *

When Hawke reached King Hill, he kept to the middle of the street. He had barely gotten into town when the first shot was fired, coming from the loft of the livery stable. He spurred his horse into a gallop and, throwing his leg over the saddle, so only his left foot was in the stirrup, used the horse as cover as he galloped by the livery. The shooter in the loft showed himself then, and that was a mistake.

Hawke snapped off a shot and the shooter dropped his gun, grabbed his stomach, then tumbled forward out of the loft, turning half over and landing on his back in the dirt below.

The second shooter was behind the false front on the roof of the apothecary. He fired at Hawke, who got off two quick shots as he leaped from his horse and scooted behind a water trough.

"Bull!" the shooter on the roof shouted. "Bull, do you see him?"

Nobody answered.

"Trace, Marty, do you see him?"

"I seen him go behind the watering trough," another voice answered.

The shooter on the roof started firing, the bullets thumping into the trough, splashing into the water, and hitting the porch behind Hawke, who returned fire, shooting two more times. Then the shooter on the roof got careless and presented a bigger target.

Hawke took advantage, hitting him in the neck. The shooter fell, then slid off the roof.

Realizing he was out of ammunition, Hawke punched out all the empty cartridges in order to reload. He had just put one bullet in when he glanced up into the front window of the apothecary and saw the reflection of someone running across the street. It was the third of Morgan's depu-

ties. Clearly, the deputy had counted the shots and knew
that he was empty.

Though he had only reloaded one bullet, Hawke stood
up to confront his adversary. He pulled the trigger, but it
fell on an empty chamber, the bullet not yet having worked
itself up.

"Ha!" the gunman shouted. "I knowe'd you was out
of shells." He raised his pistol to take careful aim. Hawke
pulled the trigger again . . . and again there was a click as
the hammer fell on an empty chamber. He pulled the trigger still again, and this time the bullet had worked its way
up under the firing pin. The gunman went down with a bullet in his heart.

Hawke ran across the street to the open area between the
apothecary and a dress store. Working quickly, he reloaded
his gun. Then, looking up, he saw a man standing in a back
doorway, a bystander to the gunplay. The man had a terrified look on his face.

Hawke pointed, silently asking if one of the gunmen
was there. Almost imperceptibly, the man nodded, then
carefully and surreptitiously pointed toward the door that
was swung open to his right. Hawke made a motion for him
to leap to his left.

The man stared at Hawke, either not understanding or
too frightened to react. Hawke motioned again, and this
time the man did react. Hawke fired three quick shots
through the door. There was a thump, and Morgan's fourth
deputy fell back into the room where he'd been hiding.

Now there was only Clay Morgan.

"Morgan!" Hawke called as he reloaded his pistol.
"Morgan, there are just the two of us now! You want to
settle this?"

"I'm coming out," Hawke heard him say, his voice coming from the far end of the street.

Looking that way, Hawke saw Morgan step out of the sheriff's office.

From closed windows and through the cracks of doors, the citizens of the town watched the two men walk toward each other.

They stopped when they were no more than fifty feet apart.

Both men had their guns in their holsters.

"Ever since I heard of you, I've wondered which one of us was the best," Morgan said. "I'm sure you've wondered the same."

Hawke shook his head. "Not really," he answered. "Until I got here, I'd never heard of you."

In fact, Hawke had heard of Morgan, but he knew that saying he hadn't would anger him, and the expression in Morgan's face revealed that he was right.

"How are we going to play this?" Morgan asked.

"Just draw your gun when you're feeling lucky," Hawke replied.

The two men stared at each other for a long moment, then, abruptly, Morgan drew his pistol and fired.

Morgan was fast, perhaps the fastest Hawke had ever gone against. In fact, he actually beat Hawke, getting his own shot off first. But Morgan's bullet took off Hawke's hat, while Hawke's bullet, fired a split second later, crashed into Morgan's chest.

Morgan fired a second time, but now he was gravely wounded and this bullet missed as well.

Hawke fired again, and Morgan went down.

With his gun still drawn and ready, Hawke ran to him and looked down.

"Anyone you want me to say hello to in hell?" Morgan asked, trying to laugh. The laugh turned into a cough, and flecks of blood came from his lips.

"I doubt you'll be doing much socializing there," Hawke said.

"I thought I could beat you," Morgan said. "I really thought I could do it." There was one last rattle of breath, then he died.

Now, another shot was fired, catching Hawke unawares. He spun around in alarm and saw Joshua Creed pitching forward, a rifle in his hand. Behind him, holding a smoking pistol, he saw Jesse Carlisle.

"He was about to shoot you," Jesse said.

Hawke nodded. "Thanks," he said. "It looks like maybe Hannah has good taste after all."

Jesse smiled.

One week later, Ian, Cynthia, Hannah, and Jesse were at the railroad station to see Hawke off.

"I can't tell you how thankful I am that Cynthia asked you to come here," Ian said. "You saved our hides."

"Ahh, you would've gotten along without me," Hawke replied. "Look at what's going on between you and the cattlemen now."

Ian chuckled. "Yeah, who would have believed that we are going to be grazing sheep and cattle on the same land at the same time? We worked it out with Carlisle, Fenton, and Wilson, and the others came along. We'll see if what Emerson said about grazing sheep and cattle together as being beneficial to both is right or not."

"Emerson Booker was a smart man," Hawke said. "Maybe one of the smartest men I ever knew. I expect if he said so, it's true."

"Did I tell you? The town's voted to name the school after him," Ian said.

"I can't think of an honor Emerson would like more," Hawke said.

"Board!" the conductor called.

The engineer rang the bell.

"Well, I'd better get on board," Hawke said.

"Will you write to me, Uncle Mason?" Hannah asked.

Surprised, Hawke looked over at Cynthia as he said to Hannah, "What did you call me?"

"I called you Uncle Mason," Hannah said with a broad smile.

"We told her," Ian said. "I think she deserves to know that she has an uncle. Especially an uncle like you."

Hawke nodded, then embraced Hannah, and then Cynthia. Then he shook hands with Ian and Jesse and climbed onto the train.

As the train pulled out of the station, Hawke leaned back in his seat and closed his eyes. All this time, he had thought he was totally alone in the world.

It was nice to know that he wasn't.

BILL BROOKS

BRINGS THE WILD
AMERICAN WEST ALIVE

DAKOTA LAWMAN:
LAST STAND AT SWEET SORROW

0-06-073718-2/$5.99 US/$7.99 Can

When skilled Union surgeon Jake Horn is pursued for a crime he didn't commit, he must abandon his home, his name, and his true calling and instead pick up a gun if he wants to stay alive. On his way to Canada he runs into trouble and finds refuge as a city marshal in a small town in the Dakota Territories.

DAKOTA LAWMAN:
KILLING MR. SUNDAY

0-06-073719-0/$5.99 US/$7.99 Can

Billy Sunday, a feared gun artist with a price on his head, is suffering from a fatal illness. But he is determined to reconcile with his daughter before he dies. Lawman Jake Horn may find himself faced with a suicidal duty: to stand side-by-side with a dead man who has nothing left to lose.

DAKOTA LAWMAN:
THE BIG GUNDOWN

0-06-073722-0/$5.99 US/$7.99 Can

Lawman Jake Horn recognizes a murdered body when he sees one. But asking too many questions of the wrong people is asking for trouble, and suddenly expert killers are gathering with their sights on him.
